One

Freya Greengrass liked the girl who came to play in her bedroom at night. The girl wore pink pyjamas, rather like Freya's own, and she had a smile that lit up her pale face and showed the gap where her front tooth was missing. The girl said her name was Anna.

Freya was glad she hadn't seen Jack, who sometimes appeared in her brother Tom's room and stood by the wardrobe saying nothing and looking sad. Each time Jack appeared Tom said he could smell burning, and Freya hoped she wouldn't see him because she knew she'd be scared. Just like she'd been when Anna visited her for the first time.

Now Freya was used to Anna and she didn't mind her new friend playing with her toys. Although she sometimes wished she'd go away and let her sleep.

But Tom said that you don't need to sleep when you're dead.

Lexi Verity was beautiful. Everybody knew that, including Lexi herself. Top TV presenter, actress, and friend to the rich and famous, she had achieved it all. She was a familiar face and there were few places she could go without being recognised. But success can bring with it envy and criticism. And sometimes it attracts attention of the unwanted, and even dangerous, kind.

Lexi was now in her late forties and she knew that one day the edifice of her career would start to crumble with her looks. But for the time being her star remained in the ascendant and she was determined to make the most of fame while it lasted. And she was careful to hide all the doubts and insecurities of her past behind a confident mask.

Just over two years ago, on her forty-seventh birthday, her second husband, Milo Pilton, had finalised the purchase of a Georgian rectory in the beautiful village of Eaglethorpe in the North Yorkshire countryside, and before moving in, Lexi had added touches that the respectable churchmen who'd once lived there could only have dreamed of; a thorough refurbishment including a large swimming pool extension and a state-of-the-art hand-made kitchen she rarely ventured into because her housekeeper, Margaret, did the cooking.

In spite of her initial misgivings, Eaglethorpe had become her refuge, the house where she felt safe. Her happy place, where she could go make-up-free and don jogging bottoms and a T-shirt as she relaxed, away from the public gaze and the obligations of fame.

She'd been grateful that the locals were thoughtful enough to allow her a modicum of privacy, which

Killing in the Shadows

By Kate Ellis

Joe Plantagenet series:
Seeking the Dead
Playing With Bones
Kissing the Demons
Watching the Ghosts
Walking by Night
Killing in the Shadows

Wesley Peterson series:

The Merchant's House	The Cadaver Game
The Armada Boy	The Shadow Collector
An Unhallowed Grave	The Shroud Maker
The Funeral Boat	The Death Season
The Bone Garden	The House of Eyes
A Painted Doom	The Mermaid's Scream
The Skeleton Room	The Mechanical Devil
The Plague Maiden	Dead Man's Lane
A Cursed Inheritance	The Burial Circle
The Marriage Hearse	The Stone Chamber
The Shining Skull	Serpent's Point
The Blood Pit	The Killing Place
A Perfect Death	Coffin Island
The Flesh Tailor	Deadly Remains
The Jackal Man	

Albert Lincoln series:
A High Mortality of Doves
The Boy Who Lived with the Dead
The House of the Hanged Woman

Killing in the Shadows

KATE ELLIS

CONSTABLE

CONSTABLE

First published in Great Britain in 2026 by Constable

1 3 5 7 9 10 8 6 4 2

Copyright © Kate Ellis, 2026

The moral right of the author has been asserted.

*All characters and events in this publication, other than
those clearly in the public domain, are fictitious
and any resemblance to real persons,
living or dead, is purely coincidental.*

All rights reserved.

A CIP catalogue record for this book
is available from the British Library.

ISBN: 978-0-34944-299-0

Typeset in ITC New Baskerville by Easyset Ltd
Printed and bound in Great Britain by Clays Ltd, Elcograf S.p.A.

Papers used by Constable are from well-managed
forests and other responsible sources.

Constable
An imprint of
Little, Brown Book Group
Carmelite House
50 Victoria Embankment
London EC4Y 0DZ

The authorised representative
in the EEA is
Hachette Ireland
8 Castlecourt Centre, Dublin 15,
D15 XTP3, Ireland
(email: info@hbgi.ie)

An Hachette UK Company
www.hachette.co.uk

www.littlebrown.co.uk

For all the family – it can't be easy living with a writer!

Also thanks to Roger for fifty wonderful years.

meant she was able to walk into the village without being mobbed by selfie-seekers. In days gone by, fans would ask for autographs, but now they seemed to want photos featuring themselves within embracing distance of their favourite stars. Lexi found it intrusive, although she forced herself to smile and play along because it was all part of the job.

Since being targeted by a stalker, she had guarded her privacy fiercely. But that was four years ago, and the man was now safely behind bars. Even so, the whole incident still made her imagine threats in every shifting shadow. It had felt like a loss of innocence; the realisation that peril might lurk in the most unexpected places and strike at any time. Yet she kept telling herself that Milo had been right. She was much safer here in the countryside than in the streets of the capital.

That particular September day, her husband was away in New York on business and Margaret was out, so Lexi found herself alone in the house, relishing the peace in the elegant company of her Siamese cat, Horatia. She'd endured a busy couple of months filming, so solitude was just what she needed, and only birdsong and the buzz of a distant hedge trimmer somewhere in the village broke the blessed silence.

Very few people realised how Nathan Corde had changed her life, and memories of that terrifying time continued to gnaw away at the back of her mind, uncomfortable as a stone in a shoe. She'd first encountered Corde when he'd asked meekly for a selfie with his favourite star; it was something she was used to, so she'd thought nothing of obliging. After that, things had escalated and he'd turned up most days, stationed nearby in a restaurant, walking a few paces behind her in the street or staring from the edge of a crowd. In the end she'd lived her life looking over her shoulder, her eyes searching every scene for that familiar, hated face. Back then she'd felt anything but safe. She'd been terrified.

She was well aware that her stalker wouldn't stay behind bars for ever. He was bound to be freed from prison at some point soon, but this was something she couldn't bear to think about. Milo had told her that at least her nightmare was on hold for the time being, and she knew he was right. She had to try to banish the dark thoughts that had begun to plague her as Corde's inevitable release date drew nearer. If any threat arose in the future, she would let the police deal with it just like they had before.

She felt that a calming swim in the pure blue waters of her indoor pool would clear her head and provide a distraction, so after changing into a white swimsuit that showed off her gym-honed figure to perfection, she lowered herself into the water, taking deep relaxing breaths. She was about to begin her first length of the pool when she heard the sound of a door opening somewhere in the house. Suddenly alert, she stood up and listened.

There it was again. Definitely another door opening, closer this time. Lexi's body tensed and she sank down into the water until it covered her shoulders. Somehow she felt less vulnerable that way. She could hear steady footsteps getting closer, so in the end she decided to call out.

'Hello. Who's there?' she shouted as she climbed out of the pool and grabbed a fluffy white towel from a nearby sunlounger, wrapping it around her like a defensive shield.

But there was no reply. Just an ominous silence when even the birds seemed to stop singing. Then the door to the pool room opened very slowly.

Two

It had been a quiet day in Eborby's criminal investigations department. Until the call came in.

'Lady by the name of Margaret Cramp,' DS Sunny Porter announced loudly as he came to a halt by DI Joe Plantagenet's desk. Sunny, in spite of his name, always managed to look miserable, even when he was the bearer of good news. Joe wondered whether someone had called him Sunny as a joke once and the name had stuck.

Joe looked up from his paperwork. 'Margaret Cramp? What about her?'

'She's just called me. She's the wife's cousin, you see.'

The tentacles of Sunny's large extended family seemed to reach all over the area. But Joe had never come across the name Margaret Cramp before. 'So what did she have to say?'

'She's just found her employer dead. Drowned in her private indoor swimming pool, Margaret says.'

Joe took a deep breath. 'Where is this?'

'Eaglethorpe. It's a village ten miles north of here.

Very posh. Eborby's stockbroker belt – not that you find many stockbrokers around these parts.'

'Have uniform attended the scene?'

'They've been notified and they're on their way. Thought you and ma'am might want to go and see what's happening.'

Joe rose from his seat and peered through the window into DCI Emily Thwaite's office. It was empty, but his eyes were drawn to the colourful children's paintings decorating the walls, giving the space a comfortable family look.

At that moment Emily appeared, sweeping through the main office. She was a small, plump woman in her forties with wild fair curls and a pretty face. She'd transferred to Eborby from Leeds some years ago when her history teacher husband, Jeff Timmons, took up a new post in the city, and from the start, Joe had got on a lot better with her than he had with her predecessor, DCI Miller. Miller had been 'one of the boys' and Joe had never felt he'd fitted in, so Emily's arrival had come as a refreshing change. And he admired the way she somehow managed to combine her domestic life with Jeff and their three children with her career as detective chief inspector in Eborby CID. He never ceased to wonder how she managed to do it so successfully.

Emily looked from Joe to Sunny. 'What's up? Something happened?'

It was Joe who answered. 'Sunny's just taken a call. A woman's been found dead in a private swimming pool in Eaglethorpe.'

Emily raised her eyebrows. 'Eaglethorpe. Don't they call it the Yorkshire Cotswolds, where the celebs live? Suspicious?'

'Not sure yet.'

'OK, let's get over there.' Things had been quiet in Eborby over the past few months, with all the crime seeming to be of the petty variety, and she sounded eager for a challenge.

'It might be an accidental death,' said Joe.

Sunny chipped in. 'I don't think so,' he said, shaking his head. 'Margaret said there are signs of violence. Blood.'

'Who's Margaret?' Emily asked.

'The wife's cousin. She's the dead woman's housekeeper. She got back from visiting her friend in hospital and found—'

'OK,' said Emily, tossing Joe her car keys. 'You drive, Joe. I had two glasses of Pinot Grigio with my lunch.'

Nathan Corde had done his homework while he was inside. He'd already found out that she'd moved up north to a village near Eborby. He'd got a place in a hostel in the city, but even there he hadn't felt near enough to her, so he'd made his own arrangements.

While he'd been inside he'd read everything he could about survival, and he was now confident about living off the land. This meant he could watch from the bushes outside the large and luxurious pool room

8

as she'd swum length after length in that white swim-suit of hers. Perfect.

Some of the lads inside said Lexi Verity was past her best. But to Nathan she'd be for ever young. For ever beautiful. For ever his.

Three

Joe and Emily sat down on the pristine white leather sofa opposite Margaret Cramp. The housekeeper was nursing a cup of tea provided by one of the uniformed officers who'd been first on the scene. She looked as though she was in shock – and she didn't appear to be the type who'd shock easily. A sturdy Yorkshirewoman with steel-grey hair and shoes that could only be described as sensible.

She had already been through what happened. She'd left the house at one o'clock and returned from the hospital around half past four, the time she'd specified to her employer.

'I panicked and called Sunny because I thought he'd know what to do.' She took a tissue from her sleeve and blew her nose. 'Ms Verity was a lovely woman. And really down to earth for someone that famous. When I asked for time off to visit my friend, she told me to take as long as I liked and she gave me some money to buy chocolates. I've heard that she didn't hesitate to sack people who worked for her if they weren't pulling their weight, but she's always been very good to me.'

Joe made a note of her last statement. If the dead woman had made an enemy of a former employee, that might be a good place to begin the investigation.

'What about her husband?' Emily asked.

'Lord Pilton's gone to New York on business. He's in the antiques trade.'

'Lord Pilton?' said Emily.

'He's the fourth Baron Pilton. But Ms Verity, or rather her ladyship, doesn't use her title or her married name in her professional life.'

Joe noted the use of the present tense. The reality of Lexi Verity's death hadn't yet sunk in. 'When did he go?'

'Last week. He's due back in a few days.' Margaret put her hand to her mouth. 'Oh dear. Someone ought to let him know.' She sounded nervous, as though she imagined that making the painful phone call would be her responsibility.

'Don't worry,' said Emily quickly. 'We'll see to that. Who else works here?'

'There's Andrei and Maria. He drives for her ladyship because she lost her licence last year, and Maria helps with the cleaning. They're from Romania but they speak good English.'

'How did they get on with Ms Verity?'

Margaret hesitated. 'All right, I think.'

'You don't seem too sure,' said Emily sharply.

'Well, I did overhear Andrei asking Ms Verity for a pay rise. She said she'd think about it.'

'When was this?'

Margaret frowned. 'It was last week. Between you and me, I think Maria's keen to get back to Romania. She said they want to open a business there.'

Emily caught Joe's eye. The last thing they wanted was a pair of potential suspects fleeing the country.

'Where are they now?' Joe asked, trying to sound casual.

'They've gone to Eborby. It's their day off and Andrei took the Merc in for a service this morning. He said they'd be spending the rest of the day in town. Shopping, I suppose.' Margaret sniffed. 'Maria likes shopping. Andrei moans about how much she spends.'

'So you know Andrei quite well?' said Emily.

'Not that well, but he's always ready to chat. He likes to practise his English.'

'We'll need to speak to them. What time are they expected back?'

'Not until this evening. Andrei told me they were planning to go for a meal.'

'So Ms Verity pays her staff quite well?'

Margaret's cheeks turned red. 'I suppose . . . I've no complaints.'

'But Maria wanted more?' Emily watched Margaret's expression closely.

'I think Andrei was embarrassed to ask for more money, but Maria rules the roost in that house.'

Joe could tell that Margaret liked Andrei but she didn't feel the same about his wife. But he knew it would be unwise to form any opinion until he'd actually met the couple.

Emily gave him a small nod. It was time to move on. 'Does anyone else work here apart from yourself, Andrei and Maria?'

'A company comes in to see to the gardens twice a week. Coming Up Roses, they're called. They seem very good,' Margaret added.

Joe made a note. Anybody who'd had dealings with the victim had to be interviewed and eliminated from their enquiries.

'What about recent visitors to the house? Someone new, perhaps?' said Emily.

Margaret pressed her lips together in a disapproving line, and Joe suspected they were about to learn something interesting.

'If I'm in my flat or out of the house her ladyship sometimes answers the door herself. The only visitor I've actually seen is that man who calls himself a psychic. But if you ask me, he's just a con man.'

Joe saw Emily nod eagerly. He knew she was a sceptic. Joe would never have considered himself gullible or easily taken in, but he did prefer to keep an open mind, to allow for the possibility that some things people couldn't explain or understand might still be real.

Emily leaned forward, a hungry look in her eyes. 'What's this psychic's name?'

*   *   *

'I believe this building used to be a pub.'

'So we've been told,' said Elspeth Greengrass, trying to hide her impatience. Her neighbour, Penny, had done her a favour by taking in her parcel, so it had seemed churlish not to invite her over the threshold. But she wished she'd hurry up and leave.

Penny was still clutching the parcel, as though she was unwilling to relinquish her excuse for calling round. Elspeth saw her gaze wandering around the room, taking in the improvements the builders had made before the family had moved in three weeks before.

'I've heard the pub shut years ago, long before I moved in next door,' Penny said with a faraway look in her eyes. 'I can't help thinking of all the good times people must have had in this room.' She sounded as though she was eager to keep the conversation going, but Elspeth had things to do.

'Hopefully we'll be able to keep up the tradition.' Elspeth's husband, Ben, was standing near the new wood-burning stove, enjoying the warmth on his legs. It was a warm mid-September day, but there always seemed to be a chill inside Church Cottage. 'In fact we wondered whether we should have a housewarming.' He looked at Elspeth, but her expression gave nothing away.

Ben and Elspeth Greengrass had sold their box-like modern house outside London and moved north when Ben was offered a new job at Eborby University. The seventeenth-century former pub in a quiet street near the city centre, situated opposite a small, pictur-esque medieval church, had seemed a dream come true. The price had been ridiculously low for such a substantial building, and at first they'd assumed this was because of the dilapidated state of the place coupled with the fact that property was a lot more affordable up north. However, since moving in, Ben had begun to suspect that there were things about the house that hadn't been mentioned in the estate agent's details. It had been a busy time for them, so the whole transaction had been done online. Now he was angry with himself for not visiting before they made their offer.

'Well I must say, you've done wonders with the place,' said Penny.

'Thanks,' said Ben. 'But we can't claim all the credit. Our architect had most of the ideas. Wish he'd managed to keep some more of the original features, though,' he added softly, earning himself an admon-ishing glance from his wife.

There was no trace now of the building's origins – the builders had seen to that – but Elspeth visualised a gleaming mahogany bar where their new three-seater leather sofa now stood. The estate agent had empha-sised the generous size of the living room in the sales literature, along with the historic nature of the build-ing. That was what had attracted them to the property in the first place. Although the fact that it was Grade II listed had scuppered some of Elspeth's more ambi-tious interior design plans.

'Your builders were here a long time, but I expect there was a lot to do,' Penny said as she finally handed the parcel over with a nervous smile. 'I only moved here five years ago and the house was empty then. I was told it had been that way for years.' Her smile vanished. 'I was never really comfortable living next door to an empty building.'

Elspeth caught Ben's eye. 'Any particular reason?'

'Oh, er, just that empty buildings tend to attract vandals and drug users . . . that sort of thing.'

'Is there much of that kind of thing around here?' Elspeth asked, a challenge in her voice.

'Well, er . . . it's everywhere nowadays, isn't it? But you're here now, so . . .' Penny took a deep breath. 'How do the children like their new home?' she asked, as though she was desperate to prolong her visit in the hope of being granted the guided tour.

'They're fine,' said Ben, although the statement didn't sound very convincing.

'I expect they'll enjoy the little garden at the back.'

'Once we're cleared all the rubbish away,' said Elspeth. 'Well, thanks for bringing the parcel over.' She took a step towards the door in the hope that their visitor would take the hint.

Penny was all smiles as she said her goodbyes, assuring her new neighbours that if they needed anything they shouldn't hesitate to knock on her door. She managed to hide her disappointment well, but Elspeth suspected she was smarting at the curt dismissal.

Once she'd gone, Ben turned to his wife. 'You made it pretty obvious that you were keen to get rid of her. I think you hurt her feelings.'

Elspeth shrugged. The last thing she wanted to do was encourage a nosy neighbour.

'We could have mentioned the—'

'Why? It's none of her business.'

'But she's lived here longer than we have. And did you notice the way she asked about the children? I wonder whether we should have told her what's been going on.'

'I don't want people poking their noses into our business.'

Ben shook his head. 'Well, if you're not worried about what's been happening, I am.'

Elspeth sighed and sat down heavily on the new sofa. The children, Tom and Freya, were at their after-school club, but it would soon be time to pick them up. Then they'd have to start dealing with the problem all over again.

'Freya said the girl kept her awake all last night wanting to play. She was exhausted this morning. And Tom refuses to stay in his bedroom.'

'So he came into our bed. Kids do that sometimes,' Elspeth said, turning her head away. 'They've been unsettled by the move. And Freya's always had an over-active imagination.'

'You can't wish this away, Elspeth. There's definitely something odd going on in this house.'

Elspeth knew that her ability to ignore the problem was starting to irritate Ben. Ever since they'd moved into Church Cottage she'd felt a barrier forming between them. And she knew in her heart of hearts that their new home was responsible.

Four

'Nice,' Emily whispered to Joe as they made their way through the thickly carpeted hall to a large swimming pool extension that resembled the sort of orangery Joe had only seen in glossy magazines and the grounds of stately homes.

A cat appeared, an elegant creature with a lithe body and smooth creamy fur. Pedigree Siamese. Joe thought he spotted a smudge of dried blood on its flank, but the creature disappeared so quickly he couldn't be sure.

'Bit flashy for my taste,' he said. 'I think I would have preferred it when it was a shabby old rectory with a bit of character.'

'Yes, it is a bit bling. All that white and gold.' Emily grinned. 'Rather *Footballers' Wives*. Not that I've ever met a footballer's wife as far as I know.'

Joe took a deep breath as they entered the pool room, now buzzing with activity as the CSIs in white overalls busied themselves around the scene of Lexi Verity's death. Large arched windows took up the entire far wall and afforded a magnificent view of the manicured garden. The pool was surrounded with sunloungers and large, healthy-looking plants. There was a round spa at the far end, still bubbling. Nobody had bothered to turn it off. But the main space was occupied by a rectangle of discoloured blue water; the pool where Lexi Verity had met her death.

One surprising feature of the pool room was the huge mirror that occupied the entire wall opposite the window, at first glance doubling the size of the space. Joe wasn't a particularly vain individual – his short time in the seminary training for the priesthood had drilled into him that pride and vanity were sins – but even so his eyes were drawn to his reflection.

In his late thirties, he had wavy black hair, blue eyes and a pale freckled complexion inherited from his Irish mother. In his youth he'd never had any trouble attracting women in his native Liverpool, and it was a woman who'd put paid to his priestly career. He'd met his wife, Kaitlin, when she'd sung at the church where he'd been posted during his training. Shortly afterwards they were married. The life of a priest being closed to him, he'd chosen to join Merseyside Police. But when Kaitlin died in tragic circumstances not long after their wedding, he'd decided to make a new start by moving to Eborby, where his father had his roots. There had been relationships since Kaitlin, but experience had taught him to be wary. Sometimes he envied Emily her chaotic but happy family life.

Although he knew she'd had problems of her own in the past.

As he looked at his reflection, he noticed streaks of dried blood on the glass of the mirror. There was more blood on the pool side, and splashes of water as though someone had jumped – or fallen – in.

'Joe. Stop admiring yourself and come and have a look,' Emily shouted over to him.

'Sorry, ma'am. What have we got?' His attention was drawn to the side of the pool nearest the house, where the CSIs had gathered like wasps around a jam pot.

Emily didn't answer. Instead she led the way towards the hub of activity, and the CSIs parted to allow her and Joe a view of the woman on the ground.

A CSI photographing the scene turned to Emily. 'The housekeeper found her floating face-down in the pool. One of the uniforms first on the scene fished her out.'

Joe and Emily studied the body. She was lying on her front so they couldn't see her face, but even so, they knew what she'd looked like in life. Lexi Verity had been a ubiquitous presence on the TV screen and social media. A celebrity.

They could see that she had a perfect figure, and Joe's first thought was that she must have worked hard to keep herself in shape. She wore a white swimsuit, and the plunging back revealed tanned flesh. Immersion in water had turned her long blonde hair a mousy brown.

At that moment Sally Sharpe appeared, looking a little overawed. The pathologist was already wearing her crime-scene suit; hardly a flattering garment, but Joe thought she still looked good in it. They'd shared a kiss once at a Christmas party and there'd been a thin veil of embarrassment between them ever since.

They watched as Sally examined the body, finally asking for the dead woman to be turned over. Joe took a step back, an involuntary reaction to the horror before him. The beautiful face he'd last seen, full of vitality, on the TV screen was ashen, and the wide, staring eyes looked as though they were gazing into hell. There was a gash on her slender neck, washed clean of blood but clearly visible.

After a few seconds of stunned silence, he heard Emily mutter, 'I think she's had some work done. Not a wrinkle on her.' It sounded like a genuine observation rather than bitchiness. 'Poor woman. She had riches, fame and adulation and she ends up like this.' She bowed her head. 'I learned a poem at school once about the paths of glory leading to the grave. This must be what it meant.'

'Any ideas, Sally?' said Joe, tearing his gaze away from the corpse.

Sally pointed to the deep gash on the woman's neck. 'Looks like someone stabbed her there. It hit the artery and she bled out into the pool – as you can see, the water's tinged with blood. I wouldn't fancy a swim in it at the moment,' she added solemnly.

'There are blood splashes on the mirror glass over there, and on the side of the pool. Just next to that bloodstained towel on the ground,' said Emily, resuming her professional persona.

Sally considered this for a moment, trying to calculate the likely sequence of events.

'At a guess, she was killed when she got out of the water. She grabbed the towel to dry herself, and while she was doing that the attacker struck and pushed her straight back into the pool, which would explain all the water splashes.'

'She would have been trying to stop herself going under – fighting for her life,' said Joe, imagining the woman's panic.

'That's highly likely,' Sally said, suddenly business-like. 'But she probably bled out pretty quickly and lost consciousness. I'll be able to tell you more at the post-mortem. Tomorrow morning OK?'

'It's a date,' said Joe automatically.

Sally gave him a quizzical look and he immediately regretted his words. 'Nine-thirty, then.'

Emily clearly wanted to get away from the crime scene and Joe followed her back into the living room. Margaret Cramp had returned to her flat in the attic after giving a statement to a uniformed officer, and Emily sat down in the seat she'd vacated.

'According to the housekeeper, this psychic, Caradoc Karling, called several times. He last visited yesterday afternoon. We need to speak to him.'

'I've asked Jamilla to trace his address.'

'We won't have to warn him we're coming. If he has psychic powers he's bound to know in advance.'

Joe laughed dutifully. Emily always had a nose for anything she thought might be a scam to deceive the unwary.

'Andrei and Maria – we need to speak to them too. Check they were in Eborby all day like Margaret said.'

'They're top of the list. Have we ruled Margaret out?'

'She was visiting her friend in hospital, so that should be easy to confirm. And she's Sunny's wife's cousin.'

'We all have dodgy relatives, Joe. But you're right. I can't really see Margaret Cramp killing her employer. But we still need to confirm her alibi.'

Joe thought for a moment. 'She lives on the premises, in her own flat. She said that Ms Verity didn't hesitate to get rid of employees if she thought they weren't pulling their weight. What if Margaret fell out with her for some reason and had been threatened with dismissal? If she lost her job here, she'd be left homeless. Desperation can drive people to do things that are completely out of character.'

'And she called Sunny instead of dialling 999.'

'That might have been because she was in shock. Not thinking. But I think we have to consider her as a suspect.'

Emily sighed. 'I agree, Joe. We can't rule anyone out at this stage.'

When Emily's phone rang, she saw Jamilla's name on the caller display. She pressed the speaker so Joe could listen in to the conversation.

'Ma'am. I haven't managed to find Caradoc Karling's address yet. But the good news is that he's doing a performance tonight at the White Swan on Gallowgate.'

'Performance?'

Jamilla hesitated. 'I'm not sure what else to call it, ma'am.'

'Thanks, Jamilla. What do you know about Lexi Verity?'

'My mum's a great fan. So are my aunties.'

A mental picture of the women in Jamilla's large Indian family gathered round the TV, hanging on Lexi Verity's every word, popped into Joe's head. He imagined a lot of families all around the country did the same. Lexi's death would come as a devastating shock to so many.

'Mum read an article about her in a magazine at the dentist's and it said she was getting over the trauma of being targeted by a stalker.' Jamilla let the statement hang in the air.

'A stalker. Are you sure?'

'Oh yes. Mum said it was all over the papers a few years ago. Lexi Verity was living in London at the time. Maybe that's one of the reasons she moved up here.'

'What happened to this stalker? Do you know where he is now? I presume it was a man?'

'I think so.'

Emily suddenly regretted not taking more interest in celebrity news and social media. She looked at Joe and he shrugged.

'Well, if she had a stalker that's where we need to begin,' she said. 'Find out all you can about the case, will you, Jamilla. We have to find out where this stalker is now.'

'Will do, ma'am.'

Emily ended the call and frowned, deep in thought. Then she turned to Joe.

'Fancy a visit to the White Swan tonight? It's not far from your place, is it?'

Joe smiled. 'OK. Let's see what fate has in store.'

Elspeth announced that she was going out to pick the kids up from their friends' houses, leaving Ben alone. His job teaching at the university didn't start for another couple of weeks, so he had some time on his hands to sort their problem out.

Once his wife had left the house, he made a decision. Locking the front door behind him, he walked the short distance to Penny Harding's house.

Penny seemed surprised to find him on her doorstep. She was a slim woman in her early fifties with short brown hair and sharp blue eyes, and Ben guessed that not much got past her. All he knew about her was that she was single and worked as a solicitor, and he suspected she'd turn out to be a good neighbour, in spite of Elspeth's misgivings. Her house was a small brick-built cottage separated from the Greengrasses' new home by a narrow passageway. A climbing rose rambling up a trellis at the side of the door still bore a few late blooms.

'Hello, Ben. How can I help you?' she asked. The question sounded wary, and Ben wondered whether she was still stung by Elspeth's rather brusque dismissal.

'Look, Penny, I'm sorry Elspeth was a bit . . . short with you before. We've got a lot on our plates at the moment. I didn't thank you properly for bringing that parcel over.'

Penny appeared to relax a little. 'It was no trouble. And I quite understand. You must feel overwhelmed by the move,' she added with cool politeness, as though she wasn't quite sure of his motives. 'They do say moving house is one of life's most stressful experiences, don't they?'

'May I come in?'

She hesitated for a moment before standing aside. Once they were in her small, low-ceilinged sitting room, she offered tea. Ben glanced at his watch and estimated that he only had twenty minutes before Elspeth returned with the children, so he refused politely. He suspected Elspeth wouldn't approve of him fraternising with the woman she'd already labelled as an interfering neighbour, and he didn't want to be late back and have to lie to her.

'I just wanted to ask a couple of questions about our house.'

Penny looked puzzled. 'What sort of questions?'

'Our builders found evidence that there'd been a fire there at one time.'

She paused before replying. 'I did hear that there was a fire back in the 1990s. I wasn't here then, of course. I moved up from Birmingham five years ago after my mother passed away. New job, new start,' she said with a hint of sadness.

'Do you know whether anyone . . . died in the fire?'

Penny appeared to be making a decision. Eventually she took a deep breath and lowered her voice. 'Someone at work did mention that the people who used to live there had more than their fair share of tragedy. The mother was killed in a car accident, leaving the father to care for a little girl. Then later there was the fire and . . . the little girl died, and the father took his own life. Poor man.'

'That's really tragic.'

Ben couldn't help wondering whether he'd have bought the property if he'd known about its disturbing history. On the other hand, Elspeth would tell him that was ridiculous. The place had been a real bargain – and thanks to the builders, they'd got it exactly how they wanted it.

'Was it still a pub when all this happened?'

'Oh yes. I've heard it used to be called the Smithy because the building was a blacksmith's at one time. I believe that after the fire the brewery couldn't find anyone else to run it, so they sold it to a developer, who changed the name to Church Cottage because it's opposite St Nicholas's. The church is fourteenth century,' she added. 'Eborby has almost as many medieval churches as it has pubs. Anyway, the developers let the building go to rack and ruin and it lay empty until you bought it.'

'I know. The heritage people gave us a lot of grief during the renovations. We weren't allowed to do this and that.'

Penny nodded in understanding, and there was a long silence. Ben found what he had to ask next deeply embarrassing. He was a man of science, who wasn't meant to believe in this sort of thing. 'Have you heard anything about the place being . . .' He shook his head, realising how stupid his question would sound. 'It doesn't matter.'

A smile appeared on her lips. 'You're not going to ask me if it's haunted, are you?'

Ben didn't reply.

'I've heard some silly people say it is, but Eborby's got as many ghost stories as it has pubs and churches. I'm sure you've got nothing to worry about. People love to make these things up, don't they?' She gave him a sweet smile, but he thought he could see a knowing look in her eyes.

'You're right. It's ridiculous. I was just a bit concerned about what the builders found. I was hoping it wouldn't lead to any structural problems, that's all,' he added, suddenly wishing he hadn't been so open about his worries. The last thing he wanted was to look foolish in front of this woman he hardly knew.

He thanked her awkwardly and left. As soon as he returned to Church Cottage, he opened his laptop and looked over his shoulder before typing in a question. He tapped the keys surreptitiously, as though he feared being contaminated by what his wife would dismiss as a ridiculous superstition.

On the cathedral website he found a name and phone number. Canon George Merryweather, Diocesan Consultant on Deliverance and the Occult.

He snapped the laptop shut. Elspeth would be back at any moment.

Five

Joe didn't arrive home till seven that evening, giving him just enough time to grab a bite to eat before meeting Emily outside the White Swan. As Emily said, the pub wasn't far from his modern flat, which was situated just outside the city walls. There was a view of the walls from his living room and that was what had swayed him to buy the place when he'd first arrived in the ancient city seven years before.

He liked Eborby, and loved the history of the place. Once a Roman legionary headquarters, it was then, after the Romans abandoned Britannia, occupied by Anglo-Saxons before becoming a thriving Viking centre. Later it had become the home of the Council of the North, and Richard III's power base during the Wars of the Roses. Joe's father was originally from Eborby, and he'd always reckoned the family had acquired its regal name because an ancestor of theirs had been an illegitimate child of that King Richard. Joe's Irish mother had taken the story of her husband's royal origins with a pinch of salt. But Joe knew his father had believed it.

The flat seemed quiet as he walked in. Usually a low hum of traffic noise managed to seep through the double glazing, but at this time of night the rush hour was over. He was hungry, so he made straight for his tiny kitchen off the living room. An omelette and a banana would fill the gap for now. A couple of pints of Black Sheep in the White Swan would do for dessert.

He beat the eggs absent-mindedly as he wondered how the evening at the White Swan would turn out. He'd been to a psychic evening before and it hadn't taken him long to figure out how the trick was done. The combination of cold reading, leading questions and lucky guesses had impressed the more trusting in the audience, but Joe had seen right through it. He recalled that his former partner Maddy Owen once told him that her mother had consulted a psychic medium in the hope of contacting her dead daughter, Maddy's sister, who'd died out in Cambodia, where she'd been an aid worker. The tragedy had brought Maddy back to Yorkshire from London because her grieving parents needed her support. Whether the psychic had offered them any comfort, he didn't know.

After he'd eaten, he walked back into the living room and noticed that the red light on his answerphone was flashing. He rarely used his landline because, like most people, he relied on his mobile, so he pressed the button, assuming it was a cold call or even a scam, but instead he heard a familiar voice.

His sister-in-law, Kirsten, sounded softer and more reasonable than he remembered. 'Joe, I'm sorry to be calling you,' she said. 'I know we haven't spoken for a while. I'm in Devon and . . . there's something important I want to talk to you about. Please can you call me back?'

She went on to recite a number. A new one he didn't recognise. There was something contrite about her tone that was a change from her usual belligerent attitude to the man she'd once accused of killing her sister, motivated by a desire to get his hands on her inheritance.

At the time of Kaitlin's death, Kirsten had been gallivanting around the world and getting into all sorts of worrying and risky situations, so Joe suspected those wild accusations against him had been born of her own guilt. And she'd been wrong about the money; the substantial sum he had inherited from his late wife had been given away to charity, because in his grief he hadn't been able to bear the thought of benefiting financially from the tragedy.

He listened to the message again and decided not to do anything about it. He'd had enough of Kirsten's mind games. Besides, it was time to go out and meet Emily at the pub. He couldn't help feeling curious about the psychic who, according to Margaret Cramp, had become a regular caller at Lexi Verity's Eaglethorpe home in the weeks running up to her death.

The past few days had been fine; bright sunshine and a warm breeze as the trees began to fade from brilliant green to their autumn gold. While he was walking to the White Swan, however, it began to rain. A fine drizzle from a darkening sky. When he'd crossed Wendover Bridge on his way to work that morning, he'd noticed that the river was high. Eborby suffered from regular floods, and he hoped they weren't in for another. Although, thankfully, his own flat and the police station were far enough from the river to be protected from any influx of filthy water.

He found Emily waiting for him outside the pub, a half-timbered hostelry that was reputed to date back to the fifteenth century. Her umbrella was up, and as soon as she saw him, she raised her free hand in greeting.

'I thought you'd be in there getting the drinks in,' Joe said as she lowered her umbrella.

'Nice try, Joe. It's your turn.'

Once inside, they saw posters announcing that the psychic evening was to be held in the snug at the back. Joe ordered the drinks at the bar, a pint for himself and a large white wine for Emily. He knew her well enough not to have to ask what she wanted.

The pub was filled with the buzz of conversation and the chinking of glasses, and once they had their drinks, they made their way to the snug. It struck Joe that the room had been misnamed. Rather than being a cosy little anteroom, it was spacious, with comfortable red velvet seating and polished tables. In one corner a small stage had been set up with a throne-like chair behind a table draped in a dark blue cloth. The room was three quarters full and the atmosphere was one of nervous anticipation. They found a free table and waited.

At half past eight precisely, a man entered the room. He was smallish, around five foot five, and wore a maroon velvet jacket with a dark silk cravat at his neck. His movements were confident and youthful, although his mop of snow-white hair gave him a mature look. There was no smile of greeting on his thin lips. He appeared deadly serious. Joe caught Emily's eye. They were there to observe. The questions would come later.

The bar staff must have arranged for the lights to be dimmed, because all of a sudden the room descended into an atmospheric gloom.

'Very theatrical,' Emily whispered before taking a large swig of wine.

They waited as Caradoc Karling sat down and surveyed his audience as though he was trying to see into their very souls. There was a heavy silence, as if they were holding their collective breath.

'There's someone here who's recently lost someone close to them,' he began, scanning the faces for a sign of recognition. 'I see the letter J.'

A woman in the corner raised a nervous hand. 'My mother's just passed. Her name was Joan.'

Karling gave a satisfied nod and proceeded to probe until he knew the ins and outs of the late Joan's life. It was a technique Joe had witnessed before. Judging by what he'd seen so far, the man was a complete fraud.

The evening continued in the same vein, and Joe suspected they were wasting precious time watching Karling in action. They should have brought the man in for questioning and had done with it. One look at

Emily's face told him that her thoughts matched his. He sneaked out to the bar to get more drinks, but when he returned a couple of minutes later, things became more interesting.

Karling appeared to go into some sort of trance. Then he spoke in a voice that didn't seem to belong to him; a breathless voice that sounded like the crunch of dried leaves on an autumn day.

'There are people here who want to know about a death.' There was a long silence, then, 'Burning. I can see flames.' He clutched at his throat and began to cough. 'Smoke. I can't breathe.'

To everyone's shock and amazement, he let out an agonised cry and slumped off his stool.

The lights went on and a woman rushed forward to take charge, announcing that she was a nurse. She helped Karling to his feet. The man looked stunned and disorientated, as though he was as surprised by what had happened as everyone else in the room.

The nurse addressed the audience. 'I think that's it for this evening. Mr Karling's been taken ill and he needs to rest. Can someone please get him some water?'

The group dispersed as the water was fetched. A backwards glance told Joe and Emily that a cluster of people, led by the nurse, was fussing over Karling, who was now seated at one of the tables, apparently recovering and assuring everyone that he was fine.

'What did you make of that?' Emily said as they found a free seat in the lounge bar.

'Either he's a very good actor or it wasn't faked. Something spooked him.'

'But could it have anything to do with Lexi Verity?'

'She didn't die in a fire.'

'Well, we won't know what it was all about unless we ask. Another pint? My round.'

Joe and Emily didn't have to wait long before Caradoc Karling appeared, now wearing his overcoat and looking pale. The nurse had taken it upon herself to walk beside him, observing her charge in case he experienced a relapse. When Emily stood in their path, the woman gave her an admonishing look.

'Mr Karling, do you feel up to a chat?' Emily produced her ID with a sweet smile, trying to appear unthreatening, mainly for the benefit of the nurse, who was hovering like a lioness protecting her cub. 'Just routine. Nothing to worry about.'

Karling turned to the nurse. 'Thank you so much, my dear. I'm very grateful for your help, but I'll be fine now.'

'Are you sure?'

'Of course. Thank you again.'

The nurse wavered for a moment before joining a friend who was waiting by the pub door. At last Joe and Emily had Caradoc Karling to themselves.

They led him to a seat and Joe took his drink order – something stronger than water. Once he was served, he placed the double whisky on the table in front of Karling and watched him down it in one.

Emily came straight to the point. 'Mr Karling, we wanted to speak to you because according to a witness, you've been visiting Lexi Verity in recent weeks.'

'That's right. But I really can't discuss her case. Client confidentiality, you understand.'

Lexi's name hadn't yet been released to the press, so Joe knew that they had the advantage of surprise. When her death became common knowledge, as it would once her next of kin had been informed and the formalities of identification were completed, the station press office would be inundated.

'I'm afraid I have some very bad news,' said Emily, watching Karling's face carefully. 'Ms Verity was found dead earlier today and we're talking to everyone who's been in recent contact with her.'

Joe was tempted to observe that the psychic hadn't seen that one coming. But he stifled his irreverent Liverpool humour. There was a time and a place for everything. And the shock on the man's face seemed genuine.

'I only saw her yesterday.' Karling sounded perplexed. 'Surely there's been a mistake?'

'It's true. I'm sorry,' said Joe. 'Do you feel up to talking to us?'

The colour had drained from Karling's face and he shut his eyes. 'The news has come as a terrible shock. Please can we talk about it tomorrow? I'm feeling rather . . .'

'Would you like us to call a taxi?'

'Thank you, I'll walk. I only live nearby.'

Emily looked at Joe. The man seemed so shaken that it might be unwise to let him go home alone. 'We'll walk with you.'

Joe had half expected him to refuse, but instead he nodded. 'That's very kind of you. I'd be grateful.'

They left the pub and walked down Gallowgate and through the old iron gate leading to the famously haunted St Leonard's Church. Passing the church and its overgrown graves, Joe sensed a sudden chill in the air, but they carried on out into the maze of narrow snickleways leading to Boargate. When they'd been walking a minute or two, Karling came to a halt by a little door in the side of a tall half-timbered wall.

'My flat,' he announced, taking a key from his coat pocket. 'I think I'll retire to bed, so I won't invite you in. Now that you know where I live, I'll expect you tomorrow. I have a doctor's appointment in the morning, so would two-thirty suit you?'

'Two-thirty it is,' said Emily.

As they were turning to go, Karling spoke again. 'I hoped it wasn't true – what I saw.'

'What did you see?' Joe asked as he turned back.

'I saw death. Death by fire and water.'

He opened the door and disappeared into the darkness of the building.

Six

The next morning Joe knew he had the post-mortem to face, and it was something he wasn't looking forward to.

When he'd returned home from the White Swan the previous night, he'd switched on his computer and watched clips of Lexi Verity's TV appearances. She'd looked so vibrant, so full of life, and the thought of her lying on a slab in Sally's mortuary seemed wrong – almost obscene. After a while, he'd brought up her website and familiarised himself with some basic facts about her background.

She was born in Hong Kong, where her father had been working, and had moved to England in her late teens shortly after both her parents were killed in an accident in Thailand. There was no mention of any other family. It seemed young Lexi had been left alone in the world. Once in the UK, she'd taken various casual jobs, and at the age of twenty-two she'd started working in a lowly capacity for a TV company, starting at the very bottom of the career ladder.

Over the next few years she'd taken on various roles on the production side before moving in front of the camera to fill in when a junior presenter on a commercial TV breakfast show was taken ill. The powers-that-be decided she was relatable: the girl next door only with added beauty and vivacity; the smiling friend who was always there in the corner of people's living rooms.

After that initial break, her rise had been meteoric, graduating from weather girl to presenter followed by a number of consumer and investigative programmes. Soon she'd become a household name and the offers had flooded in: adverts, guest appearances on long-running drama series and even modelling work. Everybody knew Lexi Verity, and she'd been seen at every high-profile award ceremony. Now in her late forties, she'd become one of the Great and the Good. In a few years' time, no doubt, she would have been promoted to National Treasure.

She'd been married twice, climbing the social ladder with each set of vows, and according to her Wikipedia entry, her divorce from her first husband, a well-known actor, had been amicable. Her current husband, Milo Pilton, was a member of the aristocracy and dealer in high-end antiques. She had the right to call herself Lady Pilton, but being a woman of the people, she rarely used her title.

As he walked beside Emily on the way to the hospital, he discovered that she too had done her homework.

'She was a successful woman,' Emily observed as they crossed the railway bridge leading to the hospital. 'To some people that's like a red rag to a bull.'

'Which people?'

'Men. But only some – not the ones I choose to know,' she added quickly. 'No offence.'

'None taken,' said Joe, hiding his amusement at her embarrassment. 'To return to our victim, people in the public eye, particularly beautiful women, can attract the attention of all sorts of misfits and weirdos.'

'I'm well aware of that, Joe. I've asked Jamilla to find out all she can about this stalker who targeted her. Hopefully he's safely locked up, but if he isn't, once we've traced his whereabouts . . .'

'We bring him in.'

'Got it in one,' Emily said as they reached the swing-doors leading to the mortuary where Sally Sharpe carried out her gruesome business.

Fifteen minutes later, they were standing behind a glass screen watching Sally at work. Joe was glad of the barrier between him and the action, and he knew Emily felt the same. He wasn't a particularly squeamish man, but he couldn't help visualising the Lexi Verity he'd seen on his screen the previous night; Lexi as she'd been in life. Beautiful, confident and bright. The dead flesh lying on Sally's mortuary table seemed to bear no resemblance to the woman known and loved by her millions of viewers.

Sally gave her ultimate verdict in terms Joe and Emily could readily understand. The victim's carotid artery had been penetrated by a thin, stiletto-type blade, result-ing in the loss of a great deal of blood. The ultimate cause of death, however, was drowning, as she lost consciousness in the water. Sally had found bruising on Lexi's right arm, suggesting that she'd been grabbed before the knife went in. It was possible she'd been taken by surprise when she'd climbed out of the pool to dry herself, and was then shoved back into the water by the killer as she reeled from the shock of the attack. Most of her blood had gone into the pool, although some had sprayed onto the mirrored wall and the poolside tiles.

'Not a nice way to go,' said Emily.

'True, but it must have been fairly quick.' Sally thought for a moment. 'He might have waited some-where until she'd finished her swim, maybe hidden behind those huge potted plants. Then struck while she was getting dry.'

'You're sure it was a he?' said Joe.

She weighed up the possibilities. 'I suppose a woman could have done it. But I think it's more likely to be a man, don't you? If she'd attracted some crazed fan who thought she'd rejected him, or . . .'

Joe could see the sense behind Sally's theory, but he resolved to keep an open mind until they knew more.

'What about time of death?'

Sally rolled her eyes. 'Now you should know better than to ask me that, Emily. It depends on so many factors, including room temperature, and in this case the temperature of the pool water. You know it's hard to be exact.'

'Go on. Have a guess.'

'OK. When was she last seen alive?'

'Around one o'clock. That's when her housekeeper told her she was going to visit a friend here in Eborby General. She got back at four-thirty, found the body and called it in.'

'She'd probably been dead between one and two hours when I examined her at the scene, which means she was killed between two-thirty and three-thirty.'

'Thanks, Sally.'

'But that's purely a guess, Joe. It's still possible the housekeeper killed her before she went out – or if she came back earlier than she said. But I'll leave that to you.' Sally gave Joe a knowing look, then changed the subject. 'She's wearing a wedding ring. What about the husband? Isn't the spouse usually the first person you suspect?'

'He's in New York,' said Emily. 'We've contacted him and he's coming back.'

'Well if you find he sneaked home . . . I know she's famous, but I must confess I don't know much about her. I don't read gossip magazines. Even at the hairdresser's,' Sally added with a grin.

Emily thanked her and they took their leave. They needed to get back to the station to see whether anything new had come in. Joe was impatient to hear what Caradoc Karling had to say for himself, but they'd have to wait until their appointment at two-thirty to find out if Lexi had confided in him, maybe told him about some threat to her welfare she hadn't revealed to anyone else. Sometimes waiting was hard.

As soon as they entered the office, they were greeted by Sunny. He looked fidgety and Joe guessed that he was craving a cigarette. He'd tried vaping but he still longed for the real thing. Joe was glad he'd never got hooked himself. Sunny's face was prematurely lined and he was always moaning about lack of money. But he was a good cop and a good family man, devoted to his wife, Pauline, and his teenage kids, Craig and Leanne.

'I spoke to Pauline's cousin Margaret while you were out. She wanted to know whether we'd made any progress. Poor woman sounded a bit jumpy if you ask me. Oh, and she said that Andrei and Maria made a statement to a constable last night. I've had a look and it doesn't say much. They were out in Eborby all day yesterday. They heard nothing and saw nothing.'

'Even so, I'd like to speak to them myself. Anything else?'

'The CCTV cameras at the rectory haven't worked for a while. And Ms Verity never switched the alarm on while she was at home. Only when she was out.'

'Pity,' said Emily. 'It might have saved her life.'

'Margaret reckons the killer had been watching the house and waited until all the staff had gone out.'

'Any idea how he got in? Could the victim have let him in herself?'

'There's no sign of a break-in, so it's possible. But if she answered the front door wrapped only in a towel

45

and brought the visitor through to the pool room, it must have been someone she knew really well.'

'A lover, perhaps?' Emily suggested, scenting a new lead.

Sunny hesitated before answering. 'The forensic team found the French windows in the dining room unlocked.'

'So if the killer wasn't admitted by the victim, he might have gone round the house looking for means of access and found his luck was in. What about fingerprints?'

He shook his head. 'There were several unidentified prints that aren't on the database, but apart from that there was nothing you wouldn't expect. Of course, our man might have worn gloves.'

Emily gave a snort of disgust. 'They know too much about forensics these days. I blame all those TV detective shows,' she muttered before making for her office.

Joe followed her. 'Are we going to speak to Andrei and Maria?'

'Why not?' said Emily with a sigh.

By the time they arrived at the rectory it had started to rain. Emily hesitated before getting out of the car, saying she hoped it was only a passing shower. But her optimism was short-lived. The rain continued, and she manoeuvred her umbrella into position as she swung her feet onto the gravel.

'Can't get my hair wet. It goes all frizzy and I look like I've been dragged through a hedge backwards,' she said to Joe, who was watching her antics with some amusement. 'Can't interview suspects looking like a wild woman, can I?'

'I suppose not . . . ma'am.'

'You're making fun of me.'

'Would I do that?'

'Yes. Let's go and see what this pair have to tell us.'

The long drive was lined with tall rhododendron bushes, perfect concealment for any intruder with evil intent. With her umbrella held high, Emily stood behind Joe as he knocked on Andrei and Maria's door. They lived in a small cottage near the drive's gated entrance, and Joe couldn't help thinking that rectors of the past must have been considerably more prosperous than present-day clergy. Their social standing back then guaranteed them entry to the upper echelons of local society. Things had changed a great deal in the intervening years. When he'd been planning a life in the priesthood, he'd resigned himself to an existence of relative austerity. At least the police were better paid. Even so, he could never see himself or Emily being able to afford anywhere like the rectory.

It was Andrei who answered the door. He was a stocky man in his mid thirties with short black hair and a small beard. His expression was solemn and he was dressed in black from head to toe. Joe wondered whether he usually dressed like that or if it was out of respect for his late employer. When they introduced themselves, he opened the door wide and let them in without a word as Emily folded her umbrella and left it at the entrance.

Andrei looked nervous. But an encounter with the police affected some people that way.

'We are shocked. Miss Verity was a very fine woman. We don't know who would want to kill her.'

Joe noticed the use of the word 'we' and wondered where Maria was. According to Margaret Cramp, she was the one who ruled the roost. He didn't have to wait long before his curiosity was satisfied. A woman entered the room, arms folded and a challenge in her eyes. She was dark-haired and beautiful, like the famed Italian actresses of the mid twentieth century. She looked at Emily with something approaching disdain, and focused her smouldering eyes on Joe.

'You are detectives. Last night I tell your policeman all we know.'

'I realise that, but I'm afraid we need to ask you some more questions,' said Joe.

Andrei shot his wife a nervous glance and invited Joe and Emily to sit. The room was neat and spotlessly clean, but every surface seemed to be covered with lace cloths and knick-knacks. It was too fussy for Joe's taste, but Emily looked round admiringly.

'This is a nice cottage,' she said.

Joe saw Maria give a resentful nod, and wondered whether the couple's future there was now uncertain.

Emily looked straight at Andrei. 'Mr Popescu, we've heard that you argued with Ms Verity.' She tilted her head, awaiting a reply.

It was Maria who answered. 'Whoever tell you this is lying. Who tell you this?'

Andrei cleared his throat and gave his wife a wary glance. 'We did not argue. I ask for more money and madam say she think about it. No argument. I tell truth.'

Maria folded her arms more tightly. There was no mistaking the anger on her face. 'I tell you who Miss Verity really argue with. I clean yesterday morning and I hear madam shout at that Margaret. She tell her to ring man about cameras many days ago but Margaret forget. Miss Verity very angry.'

Joe caught Emily's eye. This was certainly a different version of events from the one Margaret Cramp had given them.

'We'll certainly talk to Ms Cramp again,' Emily said, trying to calm the atmosphere. 'I understand you were in Eborby yesterday. What time was this?'

It was Maria who answered. 'We go out at eleven after I finish cleaning and return at half past six.'

'Did you buy anything or eat at a restaurant?' In view of Maria's combative attitude, Joe thought Emily was right to avoid asking for proof of their alibi directly.

'We buy sheets, bedding, and I buy shoes. Then we go to have pizza and come back to find police all over house. It was big shock.'

'Of course. I don't suppose you have receipts?'

The question was apologetic, but Maria still bristled with indignation.

'We are not thieves.'

'I didn't mean to imply . . .' Emily took a deep breath. 'Nobody's accusing you of anything. It would help if we had proof that you were in Eborby, that's all. It's just routine.'

Maria stormed out of the room as though she didn't believe the statement. But Andrei found his wallet and produced four receipts. One for bedding from a chain store timed at two-thirty. One for shoes from a well-known outlet an hour later. One for lunch from a café near the market: two sandwiches and two coffees. And one from a pizzeria on Boargate timed at five o'clock. Joe examined them and returned them with a smile.

'That's fine,' he said. 'Thank you.'

Andrei took a deep breath, as though he was making a decision. 'Maria is right. You should speak to Margaret. Miss Verity very angry with her.'

As they took their leave, Emily asked Joe what he thought.

'Their alibi seems watertight. But I'd still like someone to visit the pizzeria and speak to the staff. A meal for two doesn't necessarily mean it was Andrei and Maria. He could have dined with someone else.'

'And I suspect that Maria has a temper. They seemed very keen to point the finger at Margaret.'

'Now we've been told about this argument, we need to speak to her again.'

'No time like the present.'

Emily raised her umbrella again as they walked up to the house and knocked at the door.

The first thing they noticed was that Margaret looked tired and haggard, as though she hadn't slept since she'd found her employer's body. Joe suspected that she might be facing an uncertain future and the strain was starting to tell. Instead of taking them into the drawing room, she led them up the wide staircase, then up another set of stairs, much smaller and narrower, into her little flat, created from what must have once been the rectory's servants' quarters.

The ceilings here were low and sloping, but the flat had a cosy feel and was filled with personal belongings. This was her home. And depending on the whim of Lexi's widower, Lord Pilton, she might be in danger of losing it.

Joe came straight to the point. 'We've spoken to Andrei and Maria. They say you had an argument with Ms Verity shortly before her death.'

He let the question hang in the air as Margaret bowed her head. Then she looked up. 'It's true. She did admonish me that morning for not calling out the company to repair the CCTV, but the truth is, I forgot. With my friend being ill in hospital, I've had a lot on my mind. Hilary and I . . . well, we've always been very close.'

'And Ms Verity was angry?'

'She said I'd put her personal safety in jeopardy.' She looked away. 'Maybe she was right. Maybe it's all my fault. Four years ago she was . . . harassed by a man. Since then she's been rather nervous, especially in the house on her own.'

'There was no sign of a break-in, but the French windows in the dining room were found unlocked. Could Ms Verity have unlocked them herself? Or did you leave them like that because you were distracted?' Emily's question was blunt, but it had to be asked.

'Is that how he got in?'

'It's possible.'

They watched as Margaret burst into tears, her shoulders rising and falling as she sobbed. Emily tore a tissue from a box on a side table and handed it to her.

Margaret blew her nose and recovered a little. 'I must have left it unlocked when I went out. I never thought to check. To think that he might have got in because of my negligence.' The tears started to flow again. 'What's his lordship going to say when he finds out?'

'Why didn't you call the security company?' Emily wasn't going to let her off lightly.

'I told you. I've had so much on my mind that I forgot.'

That didn't sound like much of an excuse to Joe, but he said nothing.

'Besides, the man who stalked her is safely in prison. All that's over and done with, and Eaglethorpe's hardly a crime hot spot, is it?' It sounded as though she was trying to convince them – and maybe herself – that she couldn't possibly have foreseen what had happened.

'Did Ms Verity threaten to dismiss you on the morning of her death?' Emily asked.

Margaret looked down at the carpet. 'Er, no. Nothing like that. I always got on well with her ladyship. She relied on me.'

Joe suspected she wasn't telling the truth.

Emily stood up. 'We might need to speak to you again,' she said.

They saw themselves out and made for the car.

The previous night, Ben Greengrass hadn't been able to sleep. Elspeth, in contrast, was snoring gently beside him.

If he mentioned to Elspeth the possibility of consulting George Merryweather, he knew she'd say he was losing his mind. The very word *exorcist* would make her sneer, and she'd ask him how he could believe in anything so ridiculous. But Ben was sure that something was wrong in their house, and if Canon Merryweather could help, he was prepared to put up with his wife's mockery. Although for the time being it was probably for the best if she didn't know he was thinking of summoning that sort of assistance. Ben was a man who preferred a peaceful life.

In the silence of the night he'd been acutely aware of any sound, and he'd strained to hear the soft voice coming from Freya's room. He'd slipped out of bed. He needed to see what was going on and it was preying on his mind.

Freya's door had been ajar and he could hear her talking in a quiet mumble, as though she was comforting someone. He hadn't been able to resist putting his head round the door.

'You still awake, love?' he'd said softly. 'Why don't you get back into bed? I'll tuck you in.'

The child had been kneeling in the far corner of the room, holding out her favourite doll like an offering. She'd carried on talking to the darkness as though she hadn't heard her father's words.

He'd tiptoed over to her and put a gentle arm around her shoulder. 'Who are you talking to, darling?'

She'd turned her head and given him a puzzled look. 'Anna's upset. She's crying.'

'Why is she crying, love?'

'She wants Tilly.'

'Well, give her the doll and come back to bed. You've got school in the morning.'

'Tilly isn't the doll's name. She's called Rose,' the child said, as though her father should have known this.

Ben hadn't argued. He'd guided his daughter to bed, tucked her in and kissed her forehead. 'Sleep tight.'

'What about Anna?'

He'd smiled and blown a kiss into the air, thinking that perhaps there was nothing to worry about. Perhaps Anna was just an imaginary friend after all. Maybe Freya would grow out of it without any help.

But as he'd crossed the landing, he'd been sure he could smell burning. There for a moment, then gone.

'I think Margaret Cramp was lying through her teeth when she said Lexi Verity didn't threaten her with the sack,' said Emily as they set off back to Eborby.

'I agree,' said Joe. 'She's a lousy liar and she had a hell of a lot to lose. I don't care if she is a relative of Sunny's wife, we need to double-check that alibi of hers.'

Emily's phone rang. It was Jamilla with the news that Lexi Verity's stalker, Nathan Corde, had been released from prison a week ago. And nobody knew where he was.

Seven

Now they knew Nathan Corde was at large and his victim, Lexi Verity, was dead, finding the stalker was their top priority.

Joe was studying the case and it made for disturbing reading. Corde's campaign of harassment had begun innocently enough. He had sent Lexi emails and letters telling her how much he admired her. He'd turned up at public events, always making a determined effort to talk to her and request selfies. Then he'd started sending her gifts and flowers and had pursued her, turning up everywhere she went. But it was once he was warned off that things began to turn nasty. She started receiving messages, increasingly threatening. If she didn't go out with him he'd harm her. Acid in the face, kidnap and imprisonment. Eventually he'd been caught with chloroform, cable-ties and various other items that suggested he was about to put his threats into practice.

He told her that she belonged to him. She was his and nobody else could have her. He said that once the acid had done its work on her beautiful face, nobody else would want her, including her rich husband, Lord Pilton. Corde was the only man who really loved her, and he didn't care about her appearance because they were soulmates. He knew she returned his feelings, and once she'd obtained a divorce from Lord Pilton, they could live happily ever after. The judge at his trial had observed that it was a horrible and sinister way of expressing love.

Corde had received a prison sentence and Lexi had been keen to tell the press that it wasn't long enough. After her ordeal she'd been careful about her security, and reading the details of the case, Joe understood why Margaret's negligence had made her so angry. Lexi must have lived in constant fear of history repeating itself – even in the apparently secure location of Eaglethorpe.

On his release, Corde had moved to a hostel in Eborby, just ten miles away from his victim. And when everyone had access to a vehicle and could travel anywhere they liked, nowhere was absolutely safe. In addition, traffic cameras recording journeys in the Eaglethorpe area were frustratingly non-existent.

Sunny was at his desk near the window, speaking on the phone. Joe waited until he'd finished before walking over to him. He had some questions to ask but he wasn't sure how to begin. It all depended on his sergeant's relationship with his wife's cousin. If it was close, he'd need to use tact.

'Sunny, we've just been speaking to Margaret Cramp. How well do you know her?'

Sunny pulled a face. 'We see her at weddings, funerals and christenings. Pauline used to see more of her years ago before we got married, but they were never that close. Margaret's ten years older than she is and I don't think they had much in common.'

'Margaret never married?'

Sunny shook his head. 'Nah. She's what they used to call an unclaimed treasure – although Pauline reckons she's never been the marrying kind, if you get my meaning. Not to a man anyway.'

'This friend she was visiting in hospital yesterday . . .'

'Hilary. I think they've been an item for a while.'

'What's wrong with Hilary?'

'Women's troubles, according to Pauline.'

'Is it serious?'

Sunny shrugged. 'Pauline hasn't said – and she usually has her finger on the family pulse. You'd have to ask Margaret herself.'

Although Pauline might appear to fill the role of a traditional housewife, Joe knew she held all the power in the Porter household. Sunny had once described his wife as 'an iron fist in an oven glove'.

'If Margaret did lose her job and had to move out of her flat at the rectory, could she move in with Hilary?'

'Doubt it. Hilary lives with her old mother and I don't think she approves of Margaret and Hilary being . . . you know. Some people aren't as open-minded as we are.'

Sunny was a copper of the old school and it had taken him a while to adjust to having a woman in charge of CID. Joe would hardly have described him as open-minded. All the same, he nodded in agreement.

As he was returning to his office, Jamilla called him over. 'I've checked with Eborby General. The ward sister told me that Hilary Jones had a visitor fitting Margaret Cramp's description yesterday but she didn't stay long. She left after half an hour.'

'That's not what Margaret told us.'

'Then she was lying.'

Joe headed straight for Emily's office. She needed to know.

Emily reckoned Margaret Cramp wasn't going anywhere. Where else could she go? Her home was at the rectory and the person she apparently cared most about was in hospital. Hilary Jones had suffered some complications following her operation but now she was on the path to recovery, which meant she was up to a visit from the police. Jamilla had gone to her bedside to speak to her. They needed to know whether Margaret had mentioned anything during yesterday's visit; something Hilary might not have realised was important at the time.

Joe went to Emily's office, where they ate the sand-wiches that had been brought in for them. A working lunch. They had an appointment with Caradoc Karling that afternoon. He claimed to have 'seen' Lexi Verity's death, and yet the news had seemed to surprise him. They really needed to find out what he had to say.

Luckily it had stopped raining by the time they left the station. As they crossed Wendover Bridge, Joe glanced down at the choppy river beneath and saw that it was worryingly high and lapping the top of the steps leading down to the water. The pubs on the riverside had already started taking precautions against floods with sandbags and barriers placed at the doors.

Once over the bridge, they reached the narrow streets at the heart of the medieval city. The cathedral's massive towers dominated the skyline. When Emily had first arrived in Eborby, she'd observed that it was almost impossible to get lost there. All you had to do was look up and walk towards the towers peeping over the rooftops.

Joe suspected that they might have trouble finding Caradoc Karling's small front door again in the maze of narrow streets and snickleways, and although Emily usually had an excellent sense of direction, they decided to walk to the White Swan and retrace the route they'd taken the previous night. In the afternoon gloom, St Leonard's churchyard no longer looked like the set of a zombie movie, just an overgrown area with worn gravestones protruding from the ground like rotting teeth. The church door was open for visitors; curious tourists as well as those who cared for the little stone church. Joe had been in there many times. It was a peaceful place filled with old box pews and heavy with history. But today there was no time for exploring.

Caradoc Karling looked a lot less exotic in the cold light of a Yorkshire day. Instead of the velvet jacket and cravat, he was wearing jeans and a plain black sweatshirt, a marked contrast to his theatrical appearance of the previous night.

'How are you feeling?' Joe asked. After Karling's collapse at the White Swan, he was afraid the man might claim he didn't feel up to questioning.

'Quite recovered, thank you, Inspector.' Karling paused. 'That sort of thing happens from time to time when strong emotions are involved. Of course, I didn't know that Lexi had passed over to the other side then, but I did sense something was wrong. Very wrong indeed.'

He led them upstairs into a tidy white living room filled with modern furniture. Joe had expected something more Gothic, and he felt mildly disappointed. Karling invited them to sit and made himself comfortable on the armchair opposite, leaning forward, hands clasped in front of him, as he awaited their questions. Joe could see that he was younger than he'd first thought. He was one of those people whose raven-dark hair turned white at a young age. Either that or he'd dyed it to fit in with his image.

Emily began by asking how he came to be in contact with Lexi Verity.

'She heard about me from Harry.'

'Who's Harry?'

'I'm sorry, I thought you might have spoken to him. He's her gardener. Well, strictly speaking he works for a gardening company. He visits the rectory twice a week. Harry's a relation by marriage – my sister's husband's brother.' He gave a little laugh. 'Oh dear, that all sounds rather complicated, doesn't it.'

'What was Ms Verity's relationship with Harry?' Joe asked, wondering if they'd stumbled across a Lady Chatterley situation.

'I know what you're thinking, Inspector, and I wouldn't be surprised if you're right. Harry's a personable, good-looking man and Lexi's husband spends a good deal of time away on business. In spite of her wealth and fame, I had the strong impression that Lexi was a lonely woman.'

'Did Ms Verity contact you, or . . .?'

Karling turned to Emily. 'Oh yes. I don't tout for business. All appointments are by recommendation. Even the odd session I do in the more reputable public houses of Eborby.'

'Like the White Swan?'

He nodded.

'When did she contact you?'

He thought for a moment. 'It must have been about a month ago.'

'Did she say why she needed the services of a psychic?'

'She said she'd consulted several psychics in the past. I think I was just one in a long line. Some people like the reassurance.'

'Can you tell us where you were yesterday afternoon?'

'Ah, you want an alibi? That's easy. I was visiting my mother. She lives in Ripon. I realise that an alibi given by a doting mother probably won't count for much in your world, but my aunt was there too. She's a retired headmistress, pillar of the community, and she'll back up my story. I'll give you their details and you can check.'

He walked over to the sleek modern sideboard and tore a sheet out of a notebook. Once he'd handed the address to Joe, it was time for more questions.

'Tell us about your dealings with Lexi Verity,' said Emily. Joe knew from experience that she normally treated anything she regarded as supernatural with heavy scepticism. When he'd revealed his past intention to become a priest, she'd looked at him as though he was mad. And he rarely mentioned his friendship with George Merryweather to her. To Emily, a diocesan consultant on the occult was only one up from a Druid or a witch doctor.

'I sense you're not a believer, Chief Inspector.'

Joe decided it was time to take over. The last thing he wanted to do was antagonise the witness. He gave Karling a sympathetic smile. 'Did she ever indicate that she was troubled about something?'

Karling nodded. 'I'd say that, contrary to appearances, Lexi was a very troubled woman. But before you ask me what she was troubled about, she never revealed that to me. She gave hints, that's all. It's my policy never to ask direct questions. My gift is knowing.'

'Knowing? I didn't see much of that last night at the White Swan,' said Emily. 'Someone whose name begins with J.'

Karling had the grace to look embarrassed. 'My gift doesn't always manifest itself straight away, so I have to resort to . . . well, let's call it tried and tested techniques. People expect a bit of showmanship.'

Joe was sitting next to Emily on the sofa, and he gave her arm a subtle nudge. She should leave the questioning to him.

'But later you did actually sense something, didn't you?' he said.

Karling nodded and suddenly his face clouded.

'You said last night that you saw death by fire and water. Can you explain?'

It was a few moments before Karling answered Joe's question. 'I sensed that someone in that room was connected to a death. A death by water. I saw blue. And white. Someone was wearing white. Then I saw fire. And I felt a terrible pain in my throat. And terror. Real fear.' Articulating the words seemed to be an effort. He sounded breathless.

'What did you see when you had your meetings with Lexi Verity?' Joe asked quietly.

Karling stood up and walked to the room's tiny window. He turned and stared at the view outside – the blank brick wall of the building on the other side of the snickleway. There was a long silence before he answered. 'I saw exactly the same thing. The blue water. The white garment. The pain in my throat. The flames were new, but the rest . . .'

'You told Lexi all this?' Emily chipped in.

'I have to use tact. I asked her whether these things meant anything. She said she had a pool and favoured white swimsuits. As for the throat, she said she'd had a sore throat the week before; had some antibiotics from the doctor. Of course that couldn't explain the terror I experienced, but I didn't want to frighten her.'

'How many times did you visit her?' Joe asked.

'Three times in all.'

'And that's all you got? Water. A white garment and throat pain?'

Karling swallowed hard. 'Not exactly.' He paused. 'I felt hatred. A bitter jealousy stemming from many years ago. And I sensed very strongly that she'd once experienced another life.'

'Reincarnation?' Emily couldn't keep the disbelief out of her voice.

'These things aren't always clear.'

'Or could it be that she was hiding her past?'

'That's another possibility, of course, but . . .'

'But what?'

'I had the impression that at one time Lexi Verity might have been another person altogether.'

'What did you think?' Emily asked as they made their way back to the station. The sun had come out and the clouds had cleared, and with them the imminent threat of rain and flooding.

'I don't know what to think.'

'Oh come on, Joe. All this reincarnation business. The man's a fraud.'

'He knew about the water and the white swimsuit she was wearing when she died. And the throat wound.'

'He'd been to the house. Probably seen the pool and maybe spotted the swimsuit hanging up. And she might have mentioned that she'd had a sore throat. These things can all be explained.'

'The circumstances of her death haven't been reported yet.'

'He knows she was found dead at her house. She might have told him that she went for a swim every day. He could have put two and two together.'

'And the fire?'

'The scattergun approach. If she didn't actually drown in her luxury pool, the house might have caught fire. But it didn't, did it? He got that wrong.'

'What about her having led another life?'

'She was a celebrity. Of course she led a completely different life before her rise to stardom. Nobody's born famous – unless they're a member of the royal family. Honestly, Joe, you can be so gullible some-times.' She paused. 'But just in case he didn't make up those details, we'd better get his alibi checked.'

'You think he might have known about them because he killed her?'

Emily considered the question for a moment. 'I can't think he'd have a motive, but you never know. I don't think he's in the clear just yet.'

Joe found it hard to imagine Karling as a killer. But he knew that Emily was right. They couldn't rule anything out at this stage.

They walked in silence all the way back to the police station, a modern building situated behind the train

66

station. On a clear day with the office window open, you could hear the platform announcements.

He was still smarting from Emily's remark about his gullibility when they reached the office and Jamilla greeted them, looking pleased with herself.

'I've spoken to Hilary Jones at the hospital, but she didn't say anything particularly useful. She just confirmed what we already knew about Margaret cutting her visit short on the day of the murder.' She took a deep breath. 'The better news is that we've got Lexi Verity's phone records.'

'Anything interesting?'

'We've been through them and there are a lot of calls to her agent and various other people associated with her working life. I've spoken to the agent, Artemis James.'

'Artemis – the goddess of hunting. Did she have anything interesting to say?'

'She's in France on holiday at the moment with non-existent internet access, and her phone signal wasn't good so we couldn't speak for long, but she sounded really upset. In view of what's happened, she's going to cut her holiday short and come back. As soon as she gets to London on Saturday she's promised to speak to us on a video call.'

'I suppose that'll have to do,' said Emily. She wasn't a great fan of technology, preferring to conduct interviews face to face so that she could sense when someone was lying. But in view of the fact that the agent was abroad at the time of the victim's death, she could hardly be treated as a suspect. 'Anything else?'

'I spoke to some of Lexi's friends too, mostly fellow celebrities,' Jamilla added. 'I had to tell them why I was calling and they all seemed shocked by the news that she was dead.'

'Did you ask them where they were yesterday?'

'Of course, and all their stories seem to add up.' Jamilla consulted her notes. 'And someone's spoken to a Harry York, who turns out to be the victim's gardener.'

'Harry the gardener. We've heard all about him,' said Joe, catching Emily's eye.

'Lexi rang his number several times and he called her too. Do people usually call their gardeners that much?'

'If they want work doing,' said Emily. 'But probably not if you're a celeb who has people to arrange that sort of thing on your behalf. What did he say?'

'He said he was working somewhere else at the time of the murder – another address in Eaglethorpe – but he sounded a bit cagey. I think someone should go and have a word with him.'

'I agree,' said Joe, recalling Karling's comment that Harry might or might not have provided solace to the beautiful and possibly lonely victim. 'Thanks, Jamilla. Good work.'

But Jamilla hadn't finished. 'There were a few calls to and from an unregistered mobile. I've tried the number but there's no answer. And a month ago, shortly before she contacted Caradoc Karling, she received a call from the offices of a company – Eborby

Gaming. The person I spoke to didn't know anything about it, but they said it might have been someone from the firm trying to tout for a bit of publicity.'

'Seems likely. Keep trying.' He gave her an encouraging smile. Jamilla Dal was a good officer. She deserved promotion, but Emily was reluctant to lose her to another department.

He followed Emily into her office and sat down. She looked up and gave a wary half-smile. 'OK, I was rude to that psychic, but con men like that make me sick, preying on the vulnerable and lonely. Convincing people their dead loved ones are trying to get in touch.'

'He doesn't claim to be a medium.'

'Same difference.'

'Something he said has got me thinking. We need to follow up Lexi Verity's background.'

'You think the killer could be someone from her past with a grudge?'

'Karling mentioned bitter jealousy. What about the husband? I assume he's on his way back from New York.'

'Last I heard he needed to tie up some important business deal, but he should be back any time now.'

Joe frowned. 'Odd that he didn't get on the next flight after we broke the news. Does that say something about their relationship, do you think?'

'Maybe. But one thing's for sure. If he was definitely in New York when Lexi died, he couldn't have killed her. Let's consider other possibilities, shall we. People might be jealous of success like Lexi's, I suppose. As for her past, the brief biography on her website sounds routine enough. Have a look for yourself.'

The biography didn't contain any information they didn't already know, and any reference to her early life – the childhood spent abroad and the loss of her parents – was annoyingly vague. Maybe, Joe thought, her past didn't fit with the image she'd been trying to nurture. Although nowadays rising from a mundane background was usually thought of as authentic and inspirational. Unless there was a reason for her reticence. Unless there was something she'd been trying to hide.

Sunny came rushing in. He looked strained and tired, and Joe wondered whether there was something wrong. Maybe he was worried about Margaret's situation. Or maybe something else was bothering him.

'I've had a call from one of the uniforms at the crime scene, ma'am. Lord Pilton's just arrived back from New York and he wants to speak to the detective in charge.'

Emily stood up. 'That'll be me.' She looked at Joe. 'We'd better get over there.'

Eight

Joe had never met a member of the aristocracy before and he wasn't quite sure what to expect. He'd looked Lord Pilton up online and found pictures of the man. Some made him look every inch the country squire, in tweed suit and hand-made brogues, and in others he appeared as an urbane dealer in high-end antiques in his Savile Row suit. There were a lot of pictures of his lordship with his glamorous second wife, Lexi Verity, and Joe discovered that his first wife was still alive and lived in Bristol, where according to the internet she did a lot of work for charity. There was no mention that she had remarried, and Joe wondered what she thought of her ex-husband's second wife. Someone would need to speak to her at some point, and no doubt they'd discover her opinion of Lexi in due course.

The house was still sealed off with crime-scene tape; hardly a welcoming sight to greet Lord Pilton on his return home. To Joe's surprise, it was the man himself who greeted them at the front door.

Even though the police usually treated the partner of a victim as a suspect, the normal procedure didn't apply in this case. Lord Milo Pilton had been thousands of miles away when his wife met her end, with plenty of witnesses to vouch for him. However, on their way there Emily had observed that he was a wealthy man so perhaps he could afford to get others to do his dirty work. She wasn't going to let him off the hook quite yet.

With impeccable politeness, Pilton led them to the drawing room where they'd first talked to Margaret Cramp. There was evidence of the CSIs' fingerprint powder on the door frame, and stickers here and there indicating places of possible interest.

'I've been informed that your forensic people have finished in this part of the house, but I can't face staying here for the time being so I've booked into the hotel in the village,' Pilton said as they sat down. 'I've just been to the mortuary to identify my wife's body, but it still doesn't seem real. I keep expecting to wake up and find the whole thing was a nightmare.'

To Joe, the shock on his face seemed genuine. But Emily had often accused him of being too trusting.

'We're very sorry for your loss, your lordship,' he said. 'Do you feel ready to answer some questions?'

There was a short silence before Pilton replied. 'I suppose so. Anything to find the madman who killed Lexi. A few years ago she had a lot of trouble with that terrible man. Nathan Corde. He's safely locked away now, thank God, but it seems he wasn't the only one she needed to worry about. Have you any idea who did this?' His voice was shaking, as though he was close to breaking down in tears.

Joe caught Emily's eye. There was no way they could keep the truth from him.

'I'm afraid Nathan Corde was released a week ago.'

For a few moments Pilton appeared to be lost for words. When he eventually spoke, his voice cracked with emotion. 'Surely you've arrested him? Surely you're questioning him about Lexi's death?'

'It seems he didn't report to his local police station when he was supposed to. He told the authorities he was staying in a hostel in Eborby, but he hasn't been there for several days.' Emily sounded truly contrite.

Up until then Lord Pilton had been a model of self-control, but now he rose from the white leather armchair like an avenging fury, glowering at Emily as though he held her solely responsible for the decision to free his late wife's tormentor. 'You mean you've lost him. The man is dangerous. He's a monster. Did nobody foresee that he'd come after her again? Are you all totally stupid?'

Emily looked him in the eye. 'If it had been up to me, sir, I'd have locked Corde up and thrown away the key, but sadly, that's not how these things are done. I don't know who made the decision that he was no longer a danger, but it certainly wasn't me and it wasn't Inspector Plantagenet here either. If I were you, I'd bring it up with the Home Office and raise a bloody stink. I promise you we're on your side. And we'll get him. All our patrols are on the lookout, and I've got a team tracing his contacts as we speak.'

Pilton subsided back into his seat. 'I'm sorry, Chief Inspector. I realise it wasn't your fault. I'm sure you'll do all you can.'

'We will,' said Joe. Pilton's anger had been genuine – and, in Joe's opinion, justified. The reaction served to convince him that the dead woman's husband most likely had nothing to do with her death. If they wanted a culprit, they had to look elsewhere. And Nathan Corde seemed the most likely candidate.

Pilton took a deep, calming breath. 'I suppose you'll release Lexi's name to the press now she's been formally identified. And after you do, all hell's bound to break loose.'

'I'm afraid so,' said Emily. 'We'll provide you with a family liaison officer who can hopefully shield you from intrusion. Once Lexi's name is out there, it might bring witnesses forward. It can be a positive thing.'

Pilton looked sceptical, but Joe knew Emily was right. The press had already been sniffing around once word had got out that there'd been an 'incident' at an address in Eaglethorpe in which a woman was found dead in suspicious circumstances. Once the name of the victim was released, the media would be circling like seagulls around a trawler. The upside was that the police expected to be inundated with information. Then it would be a case of sorting the useful from the totally useless.

'We've obtained Lexi's phone records, but can you tell us about her friends, anyone who knew her well she might have confided in?'

'Lexi didn't have many people she could trust. When someone's a celebrity they appear to have a lot of friends, but fame tends to attract all sort of sycophants and hangers-on. There were lots of invitations to parties and awards dinners and everyone wanted to be seen with her, kissing and arms entwined as though they were best buddies. But I know, and I think Lexi did too, that most of those so-called friends would vanish in an instant if her fame ever began to fade. Do you know what I'm trying to get at?'

'I think so,' said Joe. 'What about her family?'

'Lexi had no family. She was an only child and her parents died before she became famous. She always said she was sorry they never got to see her on TV.'

'She was brought up in Hong Kong, I believe?'

'That's right, and when her parents died in a traffic accident on holiday in Thailand, she returned to England to live with her grandmother somewhere in the Home Counties. Then sadly the old lady passed away, leaving Lexi on her own in the world. Eventually she got a job at the TV studios and the rest is history, as they say.'

'Whereabouts in the Home Counties did her grandmother live?'

'I'm not sure. She always said her background was very boring. Suburban was the word she used.'

'What about friends from the years before she was famous?'

'I'm not aware of any. As I said, she was brought up in Hong Kong but she didn't keep in touch with anyone out there.' Pilton thought for a moment. 'I think the person she was closest to was Artemis, her agent. I suspect she was the nearest Lexi had to a genuine friend.'

'We know about Artemis. She's abroad at the moment but we've arranged to speak to her as soon as she gets back. Lexi had been married before, I understand.'

He hesitated. 'That's true. But she said the split was amicable.'

'What can you tell us about her former husband?'

Pilton looked a little embarrassed as he cleared his throat. His wife's failed foray into marriage before she met him was probably something he preferred not to think about. 'He's an actor. Connor Nuffield. He's best known for that TV detective series. *Holly and Ivy*. Not that I've ever watched it.'

Joe saw Emily nodding. *Holly and Ivy* was a light-hearted crime drama featuring Nuffield as DCI Chris Holly, partnered by DS Ivy Noel. He remembered Maddy enjoying it when they'd been together. And he wondered whether it was one of Emily's guilty pleasures.

'You say the split was amicable.'

'So she told me. They were married for nine years, but according to Lexi, they gradually grew apart and they'd been leading their own lives for a long time before their separation became official.' He gave a sad smile. 'When we met, she said that she was fed up of spending all her waking hours with people connected to the world of TV and that being with me was like a breath of fresh air. And before you ask, I don't have a current address for Connor.'

'That's OK,' said Emily. 'Given his high profile, it shouldn't be hard to find him. I'm sorry to have to ask this, but do you know of any other significant relationships Lexi had?'

'Lexi and I were quite open about our pasts, and she did tell me about someone she lived with when she was in her early twenties. He was a chef. French. His name was Pascal. Pascal Allard.'

Joe thought the readiness with which he came up with the name suggested he was more bothered about the relationship than he'd admitted.

'Do you know where we can find Mr Allard now?'

'I'm sorry. I have no idea.' The answer sounded final.

Pilton seemed to have recovered from his initial shock and his manner was becoming more confident, like a man who was used to taking charge and commanding respect.

'I'm afraid there's nothing more I can tell you. As far as I'm aware, nothing unusual has happened recently. Nothing that caused me any concern about leaving Lexi on her own here, although if I'd known about Nathan Corde's release, things would have been quite different. I confess I was rather preoccupied with a major deal I've been negotiating with a New York gallery, so perhaps I took my eye off the ball. Perhaps that's why it never occurred to me that my wife might be in danger.' Joe could see tears welling in the man's eyes.

'You mustn't blame yourself, sir.' Somehow he couldn't bring himself to call him 'your lordship'. 'Nobody could have predicted—'

Pilton looked up, suddenly angry. 'I don't blame myself. I blame whoever decided to release Nathan Corde. You need to find him and lock him up for good this time.'

'We'll find him. I promise,' said Emily with determination. 'We'd like to have another word with your housekeeper, Margaret Cramp. Is she in?'

Pilton raised his eyebrows. 'As a matter of fact, I haven't seen her since I arrived. I did expect to find her here, but . . .'

'Her close friend's in hospital,' said Joe. 'So maybe she's visiting her. Are you aware that your CCTV system isn't working? Your wife blamed Margaret Cramp for not contacting the company to get it fixed.'

'Quite right. It's Margaret's job to see to that sort of thing. And if the lack of security contributed to Lexi's death . . .'

Joe immediately regretted bringing the subject up. He'd feel bad if Pilton used it as an excuse for dismissing Margaret. Although her omission was bound to come to light sooner or later, with or without his contribution.

'The cameras might have provided us with some useful evidence but they wouldn't have prevented your wife's death,' he said quickly, deciding not to mention the unlocked French windows.

They took their leave, saying they'd keep in touch, and Joe rang the hospital to ask whether Margaret

Cramp was at her friend's bedside. He was told that Hilary had received no visitors that day.

'Strange,' said Emily. 'If she wants to get on the right side of his lordship and keep her job, she'll need to turn up pronto. Where the hell could she be?'

'That's what we need to find out.'

Emily was right about the media. The release of the victim's name had started a frenzy of speculation. Representatives of news channels and other media outlets were camped outside the police station and metal barriers had to be erected so that staff could come and go unmolested by news-hungry people with microphones pressing for statements. A press conference had been arranged for half past five, just in time for the evening news broadcasts. The death of a celebrity like Lexi Verity was a story that would dominate the headlines for days, if not weeks.

Emily had appeared in front of the cameras on several occasions and she'd always seemed to take it in her capable stride. But she'd never led such a high-profile investigation before and Joe thought she looked uncharacteristically nervous.

'You'll be fine,' he assured her when he found her in her office touching up her make-up.

Emily turned. 'I don't have time to go home and change. Is this top all right?'

'Looks fine to me.'

'The whole country's going to be watching.'

'You've done it before.'

'But that was mainly on local news. This is . . .' She searched for the right word. 'Big.'

'People won't notice what you're wearing. They'll be concentrating on what you've got to say. Just be yourself.'

Emily began to laugh. 'What am I like? Stage fright at my age. I'd better call Jeff and tell him to watch my performance.'

'You don't think we should have asked his lordship to appear. Appeal by the grieving widower?'

'I have a feeling Lord Pilton might come across as a bit . . . aloof. We need the public onside.'

She checked the time. 'You get off home, Joe. We'll make an early start in the morning. We'll be inundated with calls coming in overnight. Most of it's bound to be dross, but who knows?' She checked the time. 'I'd better get ready for my moment in the spotlight.'

'What is it they say in the theatre, ma'am? Break a leg!'

Nine

Emily was right. All hell broke loose after the press conference. The office phones hadn't stopped ringing and the night shift looked more exhausted than ever as they handed over the following morning.

Joe found a pile of paper on his desk when he arrived; leads they needed to follow up. He felt overwhelmed. But his priority had to be finding Lexi Verity's killer and there was always a chance that the heap of messages might contain a vital clue.

When he walked into Emily's office, he found her talking on the phone and he could tell from her expression that it was the superintendent on the other end of the line. When the conversation was over, she slammed down the receiver with a bang.

'He's just given me a long lecture about Lexi Verity's murder being a high-profile investigation that will attract a lot of public interest and how the way we tackle it will reflect on the whole force. He wants us to pull out all the stops. Talk about stating the bleeding obvious.' She looked up. 'Sorry, Joe. Just having a rant.'

'I don't blame you for letting off steam,' Joe said as he took a seat.

'It's not been a good morning. I realised I hadn't washed Sarah's PE kit for school and had to send her in with Daniel's old shorts, which are far too big for her.' She laughed. 'But you don't want to hear about my domestic problems. I'm wittering on.' She stood up, once more assuming her professional persona. 'We'll be able to speak to Artemis James tomorrow morning. Let's hope she'll have something useful to tell us. And there are over a hundred calls to follow up. Luckily Sunny appears to have things organised.'

'It's more than the usual response to an appeal for information.'

'Lexi Verity was very popular. A face off the telly who appeared in people's living rooms on a regular basis. I suppose they feel a sense of ownership. She must almost seem like a member of their families.'

Joe nodded. He knew Emily was right. 'And I suspect people like to be associated with celebrity – to experience a bit of reflected glamour. We really need to sort the wheat from the chaff.'

'That's one way of putting it.'

Emily looked out of the window to where the sergeant was sitting staring into space. 'Sunny's been a bit quiet recently. Not his usual ebullient self.'

'Could be pressure of work. Or Pauline's cousin's connection with the case. It can't be easy when a family member turns up on the suspect list.'

'Do we suspect her?'

'She lied about her visit to the hospital. And she has free access to the house and the victim.'

'Agreed. Odd that she wasn't there to welcome his lordship home. Why don't you call the family liaison officer at the rectory to see whether she's turned up.'

Joe made the call and was told that Margaret Cramp still hadn't returned to her flat in the attic at Lord Pilton's Eaglethorpe house and that her whereabouts were a mystery. He asked the family liaison officer to take a quick look through her flat for any clue as to where she might be and to ring him back. Once the call came, he returned to Emily's office to tell her the news, closing the door so Sunny couldn't overhear.

'Margaret lied to us and now she's gone AWOL,' said Emily when he'd finished speaking. 'So as far as I'm concerned, she needs to be classed as a suspect. I doubt if Lexi would have seen her as a threat, so she would have been off her guard, and Margaret had a strong motive. Lexi could have made her homeless; wrecked her cosy little world. And who knows what people are capable of if their security's under threat.'

'We need to find her, but where would she go?'

Within the next hour Hilary was spoken to, but she either couldn't or wouldn't tell them anything. All hotels and B&Bs in the area were being checked and all patrols had been instructed to be on the lookout for Margaret Cramp. If she had lost control and killed her employer, Joe feared that she might harm herself out of remorse – or the fear of punishment.

But until she turned up, as Emily seemed confident she would, they had other leads to follow. The most promising one had just landed on Jamilla's desk, and she entered Emily's office after giving a token knock.

'Ma'am. Thought you'd like to see this. Could be important.' She handed Emily a piece of paper. Jamilla's handwriting was good and legible, but even so, Emily donned her reading glasses, a recent concession to age she liked to hide from her underlings whenever possible.

Joe gave Jamilla an encouraging smile and waited for Emily's verdict. She said nothing, but passed the note to Joe with a raise of her eyebrows.

A Caroline Frederick who works at the museum says her colleague, Fleur Chandler, once mentioned that she used to work for Lexi Verity and that she hated her because she'd been dismissed for a trivial mistake. Caroline suggests we speak to her.

'No time like the present,' said Joe, standing up. 'Let's go have a word with this Fleur Chandler.'

The museum was somewhere he knew well. His former partner Maddy worked there as deputy director. Joe had backed away from commitment with her, although there had been times when he wondered why. Officially they were still friends, but he hadn't seen her for a while and the prospect of another meeting made him a little nervous; something he hadn't expected to feel. But he told himself he'd be going there to speak to Fleur Chandler, not Maddy.

'Good idea,' Emily replied. 'And we need a word with the gardener. He and Lexi called each other a lot. Maybe their relationship wasn't purely professional. Maybe that's what all this is about. Jealousy and dirty secrets. They do say sex is one of the main motives for murder, don't they?'

Joe didn't answer.

'Anyway, let's hope Fleur Chandler will be willing to spill some grubby little beans about her former employer. We need a bit of luck.'

The museum was housed in an impressive classical building, complete with columns at the entrance and rows of Georgian windows. It had once served as a prison and was the most impressive one Joe had ever encountered; more like a stately home than a place of punishment.

Once past the pay desk, where they flashed their ID, Joe asked a member of staff wearing a polo shirt with the museum's logo and a lanyard where he could find Caroline Frederick, and was told she was in the street. He knew what this meant. The museum was famed for its impressive reconstruction of a Victorian street, complete with alleyways, workshops, shops and even a horse and carriage driving down the middle. It was one of Eborby's major attractions for adults and children alike.

Caroline was easy to find. She was talking to a group of visitors, telling them about the old-fashioned pub on the corner of the street, authentic in every way apart from the lack of beer in its well-polished hand pumps. She looked young enough to belong to the cocktail bar generation; energetic and far too youthful to remember that variety of spit-and-sawdust establishment. And yet she still managed to conjure a vivid picture of the traditional inn, bringing the past to life with considerable enthusiasm. Joe and Emily waited until she'd finished before approaching her, IDs to the ready.

'Caroline. You contacted us about a colleague of yours. Fleur Chandler,' Emily began. She waited for a response.

Caroline looked round to make sure she couldn't be overheard and lowered her voice. 'I thought you should know, that's all. Fleur used to work for Lexi Verity and I get the impression she really hated her. I was in the canteen with her one day after Lexi had won some award; it was all over the TV and social media. She said people didn't know what a bitch she really was. Fleur used to be in her PR team and Lexi put in a complaint against her and got her sacked. She made a minor mistake and Lexi accused her of being stupid and incompetent. Made it personal. Fleur was devastated.'

'What's Fleur like?'

Caroline hesitated. 'Well, er . . . she is a bit . . . eccentric. She's only my age but she . . .' She stopped mid sentence. 'Well, you'll see for yourselves.' A sudden flash of panic appeared in her eyes. 'Look, I'm not accusing her of anything. Let's be clear about that. I just thought she might be able to tell you something about Lexi Verity; something people who put her on a pedestal might not want to mention.'

'We understand,' said Joe.

'It's about time we heard the unvarnished truth,' Emily added softly. 'Where can we find Fleur?'

'I haven't seen her for a couple of days, but she usually works in the prison wing. You can't miss her. She's got purple hair.'

Joe was about to point out that he'd seen lots of people out and about with purple hair so Fleur was hardly unique, but instead, after thanking Caroline, they followed the signs to the prison wing.

Here the whole atmosphere changed, from the street's cosy ambience of Victorian nostalgia to the cold reality of nineteenth-century prison life. Damp and despair seemed to ooze from the network of stone cells with their tiny barred windows and hard stone bed platforms. According to the signs, this was the debtors' section, where desperate people who couldn't pay their bills were housed. The real criminals' accommodation was even worse, apart from the condemned cell, where prisoners were afforded a modicum of comparative comfort during their last days on earth before they faced the hangman's rope.

As Joe walked through the gloomy passageways, looking for the woman with purple hair, he felt a little depressed. His job entailed putting people in places like this, but it was something he rarely thought about. Emily, in contrast, looked unconcerned as she peered into each dimly lit cell and alcove. Eventually they found a young man wearing a staff polo shirt, but when they asked him where they could find Fleur, he said she hadn't been in for a couple of days. She'd called in sick so he was covering for her.

They retraced their steps to the reception area, Emily marching ahead with a determined look on her face. Joe followed, suddenly feeling apprehensive. Maddy was likely to be in her office and he knew she'd be a good person to ask about one of the employees. He spotted a room with her name on the closed door and took a deep breath before knocking.

When he opened the door, she looked up, surprised. 'Hello. What brings you here?' He found it hard to tell whether she was pleased to see him.

'Work, I'm afraid.'

'Come in then. Sit down. How can I help?'

He felt his initial nervousness vanishing. Maddy seemed completely relaxed, and the embarrassment he'd feared he'd feel at seeing his ex faded as he introduced Emily and stated the purpose of their visit.

'Oh yes, Fleur with the purple hair,' she said with a smile. 'She's off today. Called in sick a couple of days ago. She said she had a stomach upset. I didn't ask for details.'

'We need her address,' Emily said.

Maddy hesitated for a moment, then looked at Joe, who gave her a small nod. After finding the address in

88

her filing cabinet, she handed it to him, and as their hands touched, he drew his away as though he'd experienced an electric shock.

Emily left the office without a backward glance, but Joe lingered by the open door. 'You OK, Maddy?'

'Never been better. You?'

Before he could reply, a man pushed past him without knocking, as though he had every right to be there. 'Maddy, I . . .'

When he saw Joe was still standing there, he stopped mid sentence. He was tall, with a gaunt, handsome face, the sort of looks sometimes described as 'Byronic', and his dark ponytail and single earring gave him a slightly bohemian appearance.

'Silas, this is Joe Plantagenet, a . . . friend of mine. Joe, this is Silas Sellie, he's designing a new exhibition for us.'

'Pleased to meet you, Silas,' said Joe, noting how Maddy couldn't take her eyes off the man. 'What sort of exhibition?'

It was Maddy who answered. 'Eborby's famous murders. Right up your street. Joe's a detective, Silas. Maybe he can help with your research.' There was something eager, almost needy, in the way she said it that made Joe uneasy.

'I've got everything under control, thanks,' Silas said. 'Just going home for a while. Something to see to that won't wait.'

He winked at Maddy and Joe noticed her blush. He had the sudden and unexpected urge to punch the man. He swiftly suppressed the thought and joined Emily outside.

Ben had never been inside the cathedral before. For one thing, he'd never considered himself a particularly religious man. And for another, unless you were actually attending a service, the great church charged a massive entrance fee, which seemed wrong somehow.

But this time he had an appointment, so he'd be able to take in the famed glory of the medieval architecture for free. He explained to the friendly woman on the pay desk that he was there to see Canon George Merryweather and she allowed him through after providing him with directions; if he crossed the nave, he'd see a sign to the chapter house and Canon Merryweather's office was the fourth door on the left, just after the toilets.

Holding the directions in his memory, Ben began his quest, halting to look up at the spectacular ceiling. The wandering tourists rather ruined the peace of the place, taking selfies against the backdrop of the carved figures on the great stone screen that separated the nave from the choir. He was surprised by how irritated he felt at the visitors' irreverent behaviour as he headed for the canon's office.

He wasn't sure what to expect of a diocesan consultant on the occult and hoped he wasn't about to make a fool of himself. He stopped by the entrance to the octagonal chapter house, wondering whether he should turn back. Church Cottage could seem perfectly normal during the day. Then he thought of the nights. That was where the problem lay.

Canon Merryweather's name was on the door, so Ben knew he'd arrived at the right place. He knocked lightly.

'Come in, whoever you are,' a cheerful voice called out.

When Ben pushed open the heavy oak door, he was greeted by the sight of a small, round man, bald as a snooker ball, wearing a shabby black cassock and sitting on an antique captain's chair among a chaos of books and papers. A print of Holman Hunt's *Light of the World* hung askew over a cast-iron fireplace. The man looked up at his visitor with a benevolent smile.

'Mr Greengrass, I presume.' He rose to clear a pile of books from a chair by his desk. 'I do apologise for the mess. Please take a seat.'

Ben did as he was asked. He'd thought Canon Merryweather would be tall, cadaverous and sinister. He was surprised to find that he looked positively jolly, and his initial misgivings were rapidly melting away.

'Are you the exorcist?' he asked, wondering if he'd come to the wrong place.

George Merryweather smiled. 'We prefer not to use that word nowadays. My title is Diocesan Consultant on Deliverance and the Occult. It sounds a lot less . . . dramatic, I suppose. Now tell me, Mr Greengrass, how can I be of assistance?' He sounded rather like a sympathetic doctor enquiring about a patient's symptoms.

'It sounds stupid, but . . .'

'Allow me to be the judge of that. Something's bothering you or you wouldn't be here. Am I right?'

Ben sat in silence for a few moments before speaking. 'I think my new house might be haunted. That sounds ridiculous, doesn't it?'

'Not at all. But there's probably a perfectly rational explanation for what you're experiencing. Why don't you tell me about it?' George sat back, preparing to listen carefully to what his visitor had to say.

'It started almost as soon as we moved in, a couple of weeks ago. There was a lot of building work to do before the place was habitable and the builders said they'd found evidence that there'd once been a fire in a couple of the upstairs rooms.'

George waited for Ben to continue, as though he knew there was more to come.

'My son, Tom, won't sleep in his new bedroom. He sneaks into bed with me and my wife every night. He's eight and he hasn't done that since he was a toddler. He says he's scared of someone called Jack who comes into his room. And my daughter, Freya . . .' Ben paused, fearing that what he was about to say might sound foolish. 'She has an imaginary friend who keeps her awake all night playing. She's called Anna, and Freya describes her in detail. Apparently she wears pink pyjamas and she's told Freya that she's dead.'

George sat back. 'Oh dear. Poor children. What do you know about the history of the house?'

'Only that it started life as a blacksmith's in the seventeenth century before it became a pub. One of

92

my neighbours said she'd heard there'd been a fire there in the 1990s. Apparently a child died and a man killed himself.'

George nodded slowly and waited for Ben to continue.

'We've come up from down south because I'm due to take up a new post at the university, and I'm afraid we didn't actually see the place before we bought it. We found it online and it looked like an absolute bargain, so we put in an offer and hired an architect to carry out the alterations. It's in a small street off Gallowgate, not far from the city centre – a lovely situation and convenient for everything. There's even a little garden; bit overgrown at the moment, but it has potential. It seemed perfect, but now we're beginning to wonder whether it was cheap for a reason.'

'What's the address?'

Ben recited the address and postcode. 'It used to be known as the Smithy when it was a pub, but now it's called Church Cottage because it overlooks an old church, St Nicholas's. There's a small graveyard, but it's quaint rather than creepy.'

George nodded again. 'I know it. It might be helpful if I visited the house. Is that OK with you?'

Ben suddenly looked wary. 'I don't mind, but I'm not sure whether my wife would . . . She's a sceptic, you see. She puts everything down to the children being unsettled by the move.'

'She may well be right. But perhaps I could call when she's out . . .'

A conspiratorial smile passed between the two men. 'That might be for the best. She's got a job at the theatre, assistant general manager, and is out most of the day and some evenings. My appointment at the university doesn't start for another couple of weeks, so I'm home a lot at the moment.'

'Very well. I'll give you a call to arrange a suitable time. And in the meantime, I'll do a spot of research. But as I said, your wife is probably right and it's nothing to worry about.'

Ben left the cathedral feeling reassured. Some people you met in life could surprise you – and Canon George Merryweather was one of them.

Fleur Chandler lived in a converted warehouse overlooking the river. Joe knew the apartments there were expensive, and as they entered the atrium he sensed an atmosphere of quiet affluence. He couldn't help wondering how she'd acquired the funds to live in such an expensive place.

He pressed the lift button but Emily said she'd rather take the stairs. She didn't get enough exercise and she saw climbing a couple of flights as the perfect opportunity. Better than the gym, she observed. And free into the bargain.

The flat door was opened by a small, thin woman with purple hair wearing orange harem pants and a T-shirt proclaiming the virtues of a band Joe had never heard of.

When they introduced themselves, her expression

changed from curiosity to hostility and she folded her arms defensively. 'What's this about?'

'It would be best if we discussed it inside. Can we come in?'

'No.'

'We can get a warrant,' Emily said sweetly. 'Up to you.'

Realising she couldn't win the argument, Fleur stood to one side. Her combative attitude had immediately made them suspect that she had something to hide. And they needed to find out what that something was.

To Joe's surprise, the stark modern flat with exposed brickwork walls was cluttered with ethnic knick-knacks, Indian throws and brightly coloured cushions. There was a strong smell of patchouli, and the remnants of joss sticks protruded from a vase on the dusty coffee table.

'Do you live here alone?' he asked, unable to contain his curiosity.

'It's my brother's flat. He's away for a year so I'm looking after it for him.'

'We're investigating the death of Lexi Verity. You've heard about it?'

Fleur nodded, avoiding their eyes.

'You used to work for Ms Verity?'

'I worked for a PR agency and she was a client. Then I was asked to join her team and I was flattered at first. Big mistake.'

'Be honest,' said Emily. 'Don't worry about speaking ill of the dead. We need to know what she was really like.'

Fleur hesitated. 'She was all sweetness and light on TV and with her fans but a complete bitch with people who had to work with her. She was queen bee and we were just the workers. She didn't respect personal boundaries – used to message us at all hours of the day and night. If she wanted something, it was our job to provide it. And it's not as though we were paid well. In the end, I quit.'

There was a short silence before Emily said, 'We've been told you were dismissed after you made a mistake.'

Fleur looked away. 'It wasn't my fault. There was a message from her agent, Artemis, cancelling an appearance. Someone left it on my desk but it got covered by a file so I didn't see it until it was too late.'

'What was this appearance?' Emily asked.

'She was booked to open a supermarket, but they had a problem with the building so it had to be postponed. She turned up to find the builders still working there. When she got back, she was furious. Bawled at me in front of everyone. I told her someone must have dumped the file on top of the message, but she wouldn't listen. She called me all sorts of vile names and said she never wanted to see my stupid face again.'

Fleur's voice shook as she recounted the incident and Joe could see tears of frustration and anger forming in her eyes. He couldn't help sympathising. If he'd had to endure such public humiliation, he knew he might have felt the same.

96

'How did you react to that?' he said.

'I was in shock. I mean, she'd always been a thought-less cow, but to be so vindictive . . .'

'When was this?'

'Almost four years ago.'

'About the time when she was being bothered by a stalker?'

Fleur nodded. 'Someone said the stalker was really getting to her and that's why she was so . . . ratty. But that's no excuse, is it?'

Joe caught Emily's eye, but neither of them answered the question.

'Sorry I have to ask, but where were you on Wednesday, the day before yesterday – in the after-noon?' said Joe.

Fleur hesitated. 'I was here. I rang work that morn-ing to say I had a stomach bug.'

'Was that true?' said Emily sharply.

'Don't you believe me?'

Joe wondered why the woman was being so defen-sive. 'Is there any reason why we shouldn't?' he said.

They watched as Fleur slumped down into a saggy sofa by the window and stared out at the river below as though her thoughts were elsewhere.

After a few moments, she broke the expectant silence. 'If you want the truth, I was trying to avoid someone at work.'

'Who are we talking about?' said Emily.

'His name's Silas Sellie. He's setting up an exhibi-tion of famous Eborby murders and his work will be finished by next week, when it opens. I'll go back to work when he's gone.'

'What's he done to make you feel like that?' Emily asked.

Fleur's cheeks flushed. 'He just makes me feel uneasy, that's all. He cornered me in one of the exhibition rooms and said something that made me uncomfortable. He's an arrogant prick. Thinks he's God's gift.'

'You could have reported him,' said Emily. Joe could hear the indignation in her voice.

'I couldn't. I think there's something going on between him and the deputy director, Maddy Owen. I didn't feel I could tell on him because I didn't think I'd be believed.'

Joe's heart sank. He remembered the way Sellie had winked at Maddy – and her reaction. Fleur had just confirmed what he'd feared.

'I know Maddy,' he said. 'You might be misjudging her.' He felt a sudden impulse to defend his former partner. He'd always had a high opinion of her judgement, but what Fleur had said made him uneasy. He and Maddy were no longer involved; they'd made that mutual decision long ago. But his disappointment that she should choose to be with someone described as an arrogant prick was growing by the moment.

Fleur shook her head. 'He's what some describe as charismatic. The type who mesmerises people.' She paused. 'Lexi Verity was the same, and that sort of person can get away with all sorts, can't they,' she added bitterly.

'What do you know about Silas Sellie?' Joe asked, glancing at Emily.

'He's the director of a company called Sellie Creative Media. They specialise in exhibitions. That's all I know really. That and the fact that he's a pretentious creep.'

'Do you know if he ever had any dealings with Lexi Verity?' Emily asked.

'Yes. He did a project for her production company while I was working for her, and when he saw me at the museum he said he recognised me.' She paused. 'He asked me how she was, but there was something about the way he said it . . . Sort of mocking, as though he knew about my falling-out with her and wanted to see me squirm.'

'What was his relationship with Lexi?'

'Oh, they had a fling. What is it they say? Like attracts like.'

Ten

Lexi's agent, Artemis James, was due to arrive back in England later the following morning and she'd arranged to speak to them on a video call. Emily was impatient to find out what she had to say, but in the meantime she suggested that they pay Silas Sellie a visit. According to Fleur Chandler, he'd once been involved with the dead woman and she wanted to find out what he had to say about her. And where he'd been at the time of her murder.

She'd called the offices of Sellie Creative Media, and although Silas's assistant had been reluctant to provide his home address, Emily's official rank had eventually swayed things in their favour. He lived in the centre of the city, only fifteen minutes' walk from Fleur's flat.

'You OK?' she asked Joe as they headed through the narrow medieval streets to Sellie's flat.

'Why shouldn't I be?'

'Just that you don't seem too chuffed about Sellie and Maddy being an item.'

'You're right. I'm not. But I won't let it cloud my judgement.'

'Good,' she said. 'Let's see what he's got to say for himself.'

They reached Boargate, one of Eborby's main tourist streets, lined with both quirky and high-end shops to attract the wealthier sort of visitor to the historic city. Sellie lived above an antique shop, and when Joe looked up, he saw a painted red devil, about two feet tall, peering down at him from above the shop doorway.

Emily noticed it too. 'What the hell does this shop sell? Things to do with Satanism?' she said, half joking.

'I think it's the old sign for a printer's shop. But don't ask me why printers were associated with the devil.'

She stood back and looked at the building. 'Even if it used to be a printer's at one time in its life, it doesn't explain why they left that horrible thing there.'

'It's probably been there for centuries. It'll be listed or protected, like so many other things around these parts,' said Joe as he rang the bell beside the little door next to the shop.

Emily glanced up at the horned figure again and pulled a face. 'Still gives me the creeps.'

They waited in the pedestrian street teeming with tourists for the door to open. The commentary of a guide addressing a Japanese tour group in their own language drowned out any sound from inside the building so it was impossible to hear footsteps on the stairs.

Joe wondered whether his office had called to say they were on their way. Forewarned or not, it took Sellie a long time to answer the door, and once it had opened a fraction, he made it quite plain they weren't welcome visitors.

'I'm busy. What do you want?' he began, a note of hostility in his voice.

Emily put on her sweetest smile. 'We need to ask you some questions relating to the death of Lexi Verity. I don't like talking on the doorstep, so may we come in?'

Sellie obviously decided it was no use arguing in the face of Emily's determination, and he opened the door wider, leading them into a large living room with a low ceiling and bare white walls. It was as though someone had tried to transplant a modern loft apartment into a historic building; Joe noted the sleek Scandinavian furniture and tall, slim radiators. In his opinion the contrast jarred.

Emily sat on the black leather corner sofa without being invited and looked as though she was making herself at home, emphasising the point that she was in charge here. Sellie sat down opposite. He obviously wasn't comfortable, which gave Joe a small frisson of satisfaction.

'You knew Lexi Verity, I believe.' Emily's words were a statement rather than a question.

'Who told you that?'

'Is it true?'

'Yes. I knew Lexi.'

'You've heard about her murder?'

'It's been on the news.'

'You don't seem very shocked,' said Joe. 'I know I would be if someone I knew had been murdered.'

'I'm not a hypocrite or someone who posts mawkish messages of sympathy on social media. It's not my style.'

'Where were you the day before yesterday? In the afternoon?'

Sellie took out his phone and consulted it ostentatiously. Emily wasn't the only one who could make a point. 'I was here, working on the final designs for the museum exhibition.'

'Can anyone confirm that?'

'I'm a creative person. I prefer to work alone.' He thought for a moment. Then he smiled suddenly, switching on the charm. 'Actually, I did have a visitor later, around five-thirty. The deputy director of the museum came round and we went out to that new Italian place in Hussgate. You can ask her. And if you still don't believe me, I kept the receipt. Have you tried Luigi's?' he added. 'I can definitely recommend it.'

Joe said nothing. He was trying very hard not to imagine Sellie and Maddy, heads bent together, sharing private jokes over an intimate Italian meal. Emily shot him a look, as though she could tell what he was thinking, and understood.

'We're more interested in what you were doing earlier in the day,' she said.

Sellie gave her his most co-operative smile. 'So sorry, Chief Inspector, but I can't really help you there. I was working here alone, you see. Rather lost track of the time, to tell the truth. I was almost late for my date.'

'What was your relationship with Lexi Verity?' said Joe before the man could say any more about his evening with Maddy.

Sellie steepled his fingers as though he was giving Joe's question serious thought. 'We met a few years ago when I did some design work for the TV company, and I'd describe our relationship as physical. She was older than me, of course, but she was an attractive woman. It wasn't serious and she dropped me like a hot brick as soon as she got fed up. That's it really. It was after her first marriage broke up and before she got together with his lordship.'

'Did you resent her ending the relationship?'

Sellie shrugged. 'Not really. We didn't part on particularly good terms and I told her she was a self-obsessed bitch. I might as well come clean about that, because if I don't tell you, I'm sure someone else will.'

'Who?'

Sellie smirked. 'Have you spoken to the Huntress yet?'

Joe caught on fast. 'If you mean Artemis James, we're due to speak to her tomorrow.'

'Named after the goddess of hunting. Very appropriate. She might seem warm and cuddly, but she doesn't take prisoners. She seemed to dislike me for some reason, and I wouldn't be surprised if she whispered poison into Lexi's ear.'

'When did you last see Lexi?'

'Must have been last year. We ended up at the same party in London. And before you ask, we didn't speak to each other.' He raised his hands. 'Not my decision. Anyone who knows me will tell you I'm a man of peace.'

Joe and Emily exchanged a look.

'You haven't seen her since then?'

'No.'

Joe stood up. As he glanced towards the window, he caught a glimpse of the little red devil's horns. He wanted an excuse to take a wider look at the apartment, so he asked to use the toilet.

Following Sellie's directions, he walked down a narrow corridor, white-painted like the living room. Before reaching the bathroom, he opened a door to his right, and what he saw made him gasp.

The room was filled with what appeared to be shop dummies, fully dressed. One in particular caught his attention. A woman with staring glass eyes. And a cord around her slender neck.

Eleven

On their way back to the station, Joe told Emily what he'd seen in Silas Sellie's flat. When he asked her whether she wanted to go back and ask some further questions, she pointed out that the dummies were probably to be used in the museum's forthcoming exhibition of famous Eborby murders. Besides, it would hardly be wise at this stage to let the man know they'd been snooping without a warrant. Joe suspected she was right, but he still felt uneasy.

When Emily suggested that he was biased because Sellie had mentioned his dinner with Maddy, he denied it. But he could tell from the half-smile on her lips that she didn't believe him.

'I thought he was rather charming, in an arty sort of way. He didn't appeal to me, of course, but I can see why some women might find him exciting.'

'Really?'

Emily smiled. 'We'll get him checked out and find out if any vehicle registered to him was caught on camera driving towards Eaglethorpe at the relevant time.'

'Good,' said Joe. 'I'll set that in motion.'

When they arrived at the station, they were greeted by the news that there was still no sign of Margaret Cramp. Sunny admitted that his wife was worried she might have 'done something stupid', as she put it.

Something else was worrying the team far more, however, and that was the whereabouts of Nathan Corde. It seemed he'd gone to ground at the same time as the woman he'd stalked had been murdered. Emily observed that you didn't need to be Sherlock Holmes to see a connection.

All patrols were on the lookout for him, and once they had him in custody, Emily seemed confident that the case would be wrapped up quickly and they could all get home early for a change. Joe said nothing. He knew Corde was their most likely suspect, but somehow he found it hard to share the DCI's certainty.

He returned to his office and examined the list on his desk. There was someone he wanted to speak to; someone who, according to the psychic Caradoc Karling, had been more than friendly with the dead woman. Harry York, the gardener employed by Coming Up Roses may or may not have been Lexi's lover. But in Joe's opinion, it was a question that needed asking.

He rang the number they had for Harry and he answered almost immediately. As it was raining, he couldn't work as planned that afternoon, so he was free and offered to come to the station right away. Having such a co-operative witness made a pleasant change.

Fifteen minutes later, Joe and Emily were sitting in one of the interview rooms facing a young man wearing a hoodie and jeans. Caradoc Karling had been right. Harry was a remarkably good-looking young man. He was tall, with thick fair hair, cornflower-blue eyes, freckles and a fetching smile. His lithe body suggested strength, and he had the healthy look of someone who worked outdoors. He seemed relaxed, although Joe noticed that one finger was drumming on his thigh, a telltale sign of nerves.

'You managed to get past the press pack outside OK?' Joe said pleasantly, trying to put the young man at his ease.

Harry nodded. Ever since Lexi's name had been released, a crowd of reporters had been camped outside the station entrance, hungry for information. The murder of a TV celebrity was huge news. It dominated all the bulletins, so even at home the team couldn't escape it.

'I believe you introduced Lexi Verity to Caradoc Karling?' Emily began, getting down to business.

'That's right. She said she was interested, so I gave her his details.'

'What was your relationship with Ms Verity?'

There was a long silence, as though Harry was deciding how much to reveal. 'It wasn't serious. Just a bit of fun.'

'Your relationship was sexual?'

He exhaled. 'Suppose it was. But I liked her. She had no airs and graces once you got to know her.'

He stopped talking. This was a different version of Lexi Verity from the one Fleur Chandler had given them, and it made Joe curious to know more.

The two detectives let the silence hang there between them, hoping Harry wouldn't be able to resist filling it. Eventually their patience was rewarded.

'She might have been famous and all that, but underneath the gloss and glamour I think she was lonely. She didn't have many proper friends, and his lordship was away a lot and was quite a bit older than her, so . . . We got talking one day and we ended up in bed. Just a bit of fun,' he repeated.

Emily looked at Joe, and he could see an almost imperceptible smile playing on her lips, as though she understood the temptation.

'What can you tell us about her private life?' Joe asked. Now that Harry seemed to be in a confessional mood, he wanted to make the most of it.

'Not much. I know she'd been married before she met his lordship. She said it took her a while to realise that first marriage had been a mistake. She told me they broke up because he'd changed. Became quite nasty in the end.'

'This was Connor Nuffield.'

'That's right – the one who plays Inspector Holly on TV.'

Joe glanced at Emily. They were going to have to speak to Nuffield sooner rather than later, but when they'd contacted his agent, they'd been told that he was busy filming in Kent.

'What about her relationship with his lordship?'

'She never said much about it, but . . .'

'But what?' prompted Emily.

'One time we were in bed and she panicked because she thought he was on his way home. I got dressed fast and I was going to help her make the bed but she told me to get down to the garden so it would look like I'd been there all the time. She told me that her husband could be really jealous. He'd found out his first wife was having an affair and had the man beaten up. He ended up in hospital, I believe.' He hesitated. 'To be honest, I think Lexi was a bit scared of him.'

'It would be natural to panic about your husband finding you in bed with another man, surely,' said Emily.

Harry shook his head. 'I know, but I got the impression there was more to it than that.'

'You mean he's capable of violence?'

'Not him personally. He wouldn't get his own hands dirty, would he? He has people to do that sort of thing for him – for a price.' He paused again, looking Joe in the eye. 'After that afternoon, I lost my nerve and told Lexi that we should keep our relationship strictly professional from then on. She didn't seem too cut up about it and we stayed on good terms. As I said, I liked her. She didn't deserve to die like that.'

'Do you think her husband might have had something to do with her death?'

He considered the question for a few moments.

'Let's just say I wouldn't rule it out. I think he saw Lexi as some sort of trophy, a possession, and if he thought she was betraying him, maybe laughing at him behind his back . . .'

'You mean he'd hire a hitman?' said Joe.

Harry shrugged.

'Do you know if she had other lovers?' Emily asked.

'I don't know, but it wouldn't surprise me. And all I can say is she might have appeared confident on the surface, but underneath she was as vulnerable as the next person.'

There was something honest and open about Harry York. Either he was an expert actor or he was telling the truth as he saw it.

'You were in Eaglethorpe on the afternoon of the murder, I believe,' said Joe.

'Yes, I was doing Mrs Payne's garden. She's elderly. I go in once a week.'

'You didn't visit the rectory?'

Harry shook his head. 'Not that day. I was due there today, but his lordship rang my boss and cancelled.'

His answer sounded reasonable, but they'd still check his alibi with Mrs Payne.

After telling Harry he could go, adding that they might need to speak to him again, they returned to the CID office.

'I can't see him as the killer, can you?' Emily said as they walked down the corridor.

'Are you sure you're not dazzled by his good looks?'

'Wash your mouth out, Joe Plantagenet. I'm a married woman.'

They allowed themselves a moment of light relief before Joe told her that he agreed with her verdict. Harry York was an unlikely killer. But they both knew they couldn't rule out any possibility at that point in the investigation.

'What he told us puts his lordship in the frame, don't you think?' said Emily. 'I know he was thousands of miles away in the States at the time of the murder, but you heard Harry York. The man's quite capable of getting someone else to do his dirty work for him. Always question the partner; first rule of murder investigation.'

'Has Pilton got a secretary?'

'Probably. Might help if we could check his diary and his contacts. But we need to be discreet. If he thinks we're asking too many questions, I wouldn't put it past him to complain to the chief constable.'

'Nobody should be above the law.'

'I couldn't agree more, Joe. But you know as well as I do that sometimes things don't work like that. We'll have to tread carefully.'

When Emily reached her office, she slumped down in her chair and Joe sat opposite. 'Nathan Corde's still our best bet, but we've had no luck finding him so far, which in my humble opinion is suspicious in itself. We really need to bring him in. Margaret Cramp's still missing and we know she argued with the victim. So many possibilities, Joe.'

'Then there's Andrei and Maria.'

'Can you really see them being involved?'

'Probably not, but we ought to keep an open mind. It looks as though Lexi was a woman who made enemies; Fleur Chandler, for instance – she hasn't got an alibi. And the victim didn't part on good terms with Silas Sellie. Fleur described him as a creep, and he hasn't got an alibi either.'

'But Sellie and Lexi had their fling years ago – before she got together with Lord Pilton. Surely he wouldn't still be nursing resentment after all this time. No, I think Nathan Corde's our man. He moved into the area as soon as he was released. He left the hostel where he was supposed to be staying and he's out there somewhere on the loose. How likely is it that the first thing he'd want to do on leaving prison is track down the object of his obsession?' Emily gave a heavy sigh. 'Sadly we don't have the resources to flood the whole of North Yorkshire with officers, much as we'd like to. All we can hope is that he surfaces soon. He's a danger-ous man, Joe. The public could be at risk.'

Joe thought she looked defeated. And the investiga-tion had only been running for a couple of days.

When he returned to his own office, he was surprised to find a message waiting on his desk. *Can you ring Canon George Merryweather for a chat? Nothing urgent. Says he just wants to pick your brains.*

He put the note to one side. Much as he liked George Merryweather, he had too much on his plate at that moment to embark on an inevitably long catch-up with his old friend.

However, after an hour spent on the Lexi Verity case, he suddenly felt bad about not returning George's call. It had been George who'd helped him when he'd first arrived in Eborby after losing Kaitlin and being shot in the line of duty in Merseyside; a tragic incident that had killed one of his colleagues. George had made him want to carry on. George had given him hope. Joe knew he owed him a lot.

'Sorry for the delay in getting back to you, George. I've been busy with the Lexi Verity case. You've heard about it?'

'You can't miss it. I believe there's going to be a special tribute programme on TV tonight. Have you any suspects?'

'Too many. And our prime suspect's gone missing.'

'Oh dear. Look, Joe, if you want to talk . . .'

'Thanks, George. I might take you up on that, but not just yet. How can I help you?'

'It's just an idea I had. A gentleman came to see me with a problem. He and his family have just moved into a new house.'

'So what's the problem?'

'He thinks there's a strange atmosphere there and his children seem to have acquired imaginary friends – only I have a feeling they may not be imaginary, if you see what I mean.'

'More your territory than mine, George.'

Joe held George in very high regard. He was one of the only truly good people he'd ever met in his life. However, that meant he sometimes saw too much good in others, which gave him an innocence, a naïvety that allowed some to take advantage. Joe suspected that he himself had been like that at one time – until life and a career dealing with the evil side of human nature had taught him otherwise.

'I'd like to tell you about it; get your opinion. Are you free for a drink tonight?'

Joe felt the pull of temptation. But he knew he had to refuse.

'Sorry, George. I might be working late. We're rushed off our feet at the moment.'

He felt bad about disappointing his friend, but he knew he had no choice.

They were lined up, their plastic faces expressionless and their empty eyes staring ahead. As Silas Sellie walked among them like a general inspecting his troops, he stopped at one particular figure at the back of the room. A female, smooth and naked, chosen because of her strong resemblance to Lexi Verity, with her blonde hair and perfect features. Only the dummy's hair was artificial and the features a bland, blank canvas for his creativity.

It was growing dark outside, so he switched on the dim bare overhead bulb. He needed to see what he was doing. The only window in the room overlooked the blank wall of the shop next door, so there was nobody to watch him. He hadn't shown the room of dummies to Maddy when he'd invited her for dinner. He'd told her he kept props and equipment in the flat but hadn't specified where – or what sort of props he meant. He didn't know what he'd have done if she'd showed more curiosity. He suspected he would have made an excuse. Some things were personal. Some things were hard to explain.

A knife would do damage, so he had to find another way. He took hold of the cord that had been placed loosely around the dummy's neck. Then he pulled.

Twelve

Joe sat in his office, thinking about the conversation he'd just had with George. He hated letting his friend down, but he knew he ought to be concentrating on the case, not on some vague story about a haunted pub.

He stood up and strode into Emily's office. 'Anything new?'

She looked up from her computer screen. 'Still no sign of Nathan Corde, and we're widening the search for Margaret Cramp. I've had to give the job of ringing round hotels and B&Bs to three DCs and two civilian investigators.' She gave a little laugh. 'Didn't know there were so many places to stay in North Yorkshire.'

'It's a popular place to visit. Especially at this time of year.'

Emily glanced out of the window. 'Just wait till the fog comes down and the river starts to flood. That'll send the tourists packing.'

Joe shook his head. 'I doubt it. That's when they head for the museums and the Viking Centre.'

Emily sighed. Like many Eborby residents, she'd become weary of the tide of tourists meandering through the narrow medieval streets, getting in the way of those who had a living to make in the city. Joe himself had lived there long enough to feel quite protective of the place. But tourists brought money in and provided a lot of employment, so the residents couldn't complain too much; it was the price that had to be paid for living in a place with so much history and stunning architecture.

'Do you think Margaret's OK?' he asked, feeling a sudden rush of concern for Lexi's housekeeper. He couldn't shake off the feeling that if she'd witnessed something, even if she didn't realise it at the time, she might be in danger.

Emily looked up, suddenly interested. 'She left the hospital earlier than she told us on the day of Lexi's murder. And now she's vanished, so . . .'

'You don't think she could have killed Lexi?'

She considered the question for a few moments. 'Either that or she came back and witnessed something? What if she could identify the killer?'

'Surely she would have told us.'

'Not if she was frightened. Or she was protecting him for some reason.'

'Who would she lie for? Her friend Hilary's in hospital, and I can hardly see her covering up for Nathan Corde. Or anyone else we've questioned, for that matter.'

'What about Andrei and Maria?'

'They've got an alibi. Besides, there's no evidence that Margaret would want to protect them. They don't seem that close.'

'I hoped Sunny might have some idea about where she's gone, but he says he doesn't know much about her private life, apart from the fact that she and Hilary are an item.' She hesitated. 'Mind you, Sunny's seemed a bit preoccupied over the past few days. Do you agree?'

Joe had been thinking the same. 'I'll have another word with him – maybe ask him to do a bit of family research. If we discover that Harry York is Margaret's secret love child, it might explain everything.'

'You're not serious, Joe?'

'Of course not.' Their eyes met and they exchanged a grin, a rare light moment in a few days of intense gloom.

'We're putting out a TV appeal about Nathan Corde tonight. You know the sort of thing. We ask the public to help us find this man who's wanted for questioning in connection with the murder of TV presenter Lexi Verity, but we warn them that he's not to be approached. If you see him, call this number.'

'Are you doing the appeal?'

Emily sat up straight and smoothed her unruly curls. 'Yes. It's my second appearance this week. Could get used to all this fame and fortune.'

Joe laughed dutifully.

'I'd better drag a comb through my hair and slap some make-up on. Make myself look presentable.

And I'll have to think about what I'm going to wear.'

'I'll watch your performance if I'm home in time. In the meantime, I'll have that word with Sunny.'

When he entered the main office, he glanced up at the clock. Five p.m. The day was still young in the CID office but there was no sign of Sunny. When he asked Jamilla where the sergeant was, she said he'd received a phone call and rushed out. Some sort of family emergency.

DS Sunny Porter had been christened Samson by his parents, who'd clearly had hopes of him growing up tall and strong enough to make the local rugby team. Instead Sunny had ditched his biblical name at the first opportunity, fearing it would lead to mockery at school, as he'd only reached the height of five feet six inches and the kindest thing anyone could say about his physique was that it was wiry rather than muscular.

Sunny drove home to his semi-detached house in the suburb of Hasledon, not far from the university campus. He often moaned about the influx of students at the start of each term. His wife, Pauline, more cheerful by nature, thought they livened up the area.

But as soon as he opened the front door, Pauline rushed up to him, clutching at his coat. 'There's no sign of her. I expected her back by four o'clock and I've been calling her phone but she's not answering.'

Pauline was a pretty woman, with a turned-up nose and a youthful face, but when Sunny looked at her standing there, he couldn't help noticing that the recent strain had piled on the years.

He put a comforting arm around her. His wife wasn't usually one to panic. He took a deep breath, knowing that one of them at least needed to keep calm. He was a police officer, used to dealing with taxing situations. But the non-appearance of his daughter, his own flesh and blood, made him feel helpless. He pulled Pauline towards him and she buried her face in his coat, seeking comfort.

Sunny looked up as his son, Craig, emerged from the front-room doorway.

'What's going on?'

'Your sister was supposed to be home two hours ago. She's not answering her phone.'

'Have you called her mates?'

He sent up a small prayer of thanks that at least one of his children was level-headed and gave them little cause for worry. Leanne, on the other hand, had seemed troubled ever since her teenage years began. Now seventeen, she appeared to have rejected study and wholesome, parent-approved pursuits. Instead she hung round with her mates, very few of whom Sunny and Pauline had met, and bunked off school. She had become secretive, and Sunny hated the effect her behaviour was having on Pauline. They'd both tried to talk to their daughter. But they might as well have been speaking to a stone.

'Give her another couple of hours, then I'll report it,' he said. 'It's not as if she hasn't done this before.'

'I know, but it's Craig's birthday. I've made a nice tea. And a cake. I told her to be in early.'

The tears started up again and Craig put a comforting arm around his mother's shoulder. 'It's all right, Mum. I'm not bothered. Honest.'

'Good lad,' Sunny patted his son's arm. He'd given him his present that morning before he'd gone to work. A season ticket to Eborby United. The boy deserved it.

'It's past six. The tea's going to be spoiled,' said Pauline, trying to distract herself with domestic matters.

'In that case, let's eat now. I'm starving,' said Sunny, nodding to Craig, who ushered his mother into the kitchen.

They were halfway through their first course, the cake with its fourteen candles standing unlit in the centre of the table, when they heard the front door open.

There was no greeting from the hall, just the sound of footsteps running up the stairs as tears of relief began to trickle down Pauline's cheeks.

The following morning, Ben Greengrass watched his wife climb into her car wearing her smart grey work suit. It was Saturday, one of the theatre's busiest days, with two performances scheduled. It was left to Ben to take the kids to their weekend activities; ballet for Freya and swimming for Tom. In this short interlude of leisure between leaving one job and beginning another, he felt rather like one of the 1950s housewives he'd seen in old black-and-white films, seeing their man off to work with a cheerful wave. He couldn't help smiling at the thought that all he needed to complete the picture was a frilly apron. In some ways he couldn't wait to get back to work once term began.

He returned to the kitchen, where the children were picking at their cereal. Freya was looking particularly tired and pale and Elspeth had commented in passing that she might be sickening for something. But Ben thought he knew the real cause. And he needed to do something about it.

The previous day he'd been to Eborby's central library and spent a couple of hours looking through old local newspapers held in their archives. When he came across a report from 1997 of a fire at the Smithy, a pub on Kirkgate, he read it closely, taking in every detail. A little girl aged six, the same age as Freya, had died in the blaze, but the father had managed to escape. Trawling through later issues, he'd discovered a disturbing development in the case. An older child, who hadn't been on the premises when the fire broke out, had gone to live with relatives down south. Then a few days later the father had hanged himself in one of the pub's undamaged upstairs rooms after being accused of starting the fire deliberately for the insurance. His name was Jack Halliday.

Ben had frozen when he'd seen it there in black and white. A man called Jack had died in the building he now called home. And his son Tom's night-time visitor was called Jack. Jack with the sad face. It had to be more than a coincidence. And it was really time he did something about it.

Thirteen

On Saturday morning it was business as usual in the CID office. There'd be no weekends off until the case was wrapped up.

Joe noticed that Sunny seemed to be taking more cigarette breaks than usual. He knew that he'd been trying to give up, trying vapes instead. But each time he returned to the office, he reeked of tobacco smoke. Joe overheard Jamilla asking him if everything was all right. His answer was non-committal. If there was a problem, it wasn't one he felt he could share with his colleagues, and Joe wondered again whether it had something to do with Margaret Cramp.

Emily appeared to have recovered from her fifteen minutes of fame the previous evening. Jamilla congratulated her warmly on her performance but Joe said nothing. He'd missed seeing her on TV. Instead he'd gone out to the pub because he couldn't face being alone in his flat. He'd downed three pints of Black Sheep and woken up that morning with a slight headache.

Calls relating to Emily's appeal were already coming in thick and fast. Nathan Corde had been sighted at a takeaway in Leeds, on a bus in Sheffield, at a car wash in Doncaster and in a fish and chip restaurant in Whitby. All these sightings would be followed up and CCTV footage examined where possible, but Joe wasn't feeling optimistic. He was sure the man would have gone to ground. He was into survival, and if he had those skills, he'd be able to avoid human contact until the fuss died down.

At ten o'clock, Joe received a message. Lexi's agent, Artemis James, had scheduled the promised online meeting for ten forty-five, reiterating that she was far too busy to travel up to Yorkshire. When Joe broke the news to Emily, she reckoned it was better than nothing and at least they'd be able to watch the woman's reactions on screen. Body language, she observed, gave a lot away. Particularly lies. She seemed optimistic that the agent would be able to throw some light, not only on Lexi's professional life, but on her private life as well. She'd been described as a friend; and friends tended to know your secrets.

At the allotted time, Joe and Emily shared the screen at their end. Artemis James wasn't at all what they'd been expecting. It was hard to assess her age, but Joe thought the small, round woman with short greying hair was probably in her sixties. There was nothing glamorous about her apart from her name. She looked like the classic gran of popular imagination. Although a lot of the grans Joe knew were more youthful and fashion-conscious than their title would suggest.

'Sorry I can't come up to see you,' she began. To Joe's surprise, she had a strong Lancashire accent and sounded genuinely regretful. 'But I've only just got back from France and there's a lot of urgent stuff here that needs sorting. Lexi's death has come as one hell of a shock, I can tell you. Is it true that she was murdered?'

'I'm afraid so, Ms James.'

'Oh, call me Artemis. Everyone does. I don't stand on ceremony. My dad was a classics professor and he named me after the goddess of hunting. My sister's Athena, goddess of wisdom, but she's the silliest woman I know,' she added with a twinkle in her eye. 'Turns out the name's come in useful in my professional life. That sort of thing goes down well in the world of show biz.'

There was something refreshingly straightforward about Artemis and he guessed that her greatest professional strength was keeping her celebrity clients grounded and in touch with the harsh realities of life. Tough love, they called it.

He sensed that the DCI and Lexi's agent were kindred spirits, down-to-earth women who took no nonsense from anyone, so he let Emily do most of the talking while he listened carefully.

'Tell us about Lexi,' she said. 'What was she really like?'

Artemis considered the question for a few moments. 'She was a grafter – a hard worker. She worked her way up from nothing. Started off making the tea and running errands before being promoted to production assistant. Then one day she stood in when one of the presenters on a flagship show was taken ill and they couldn't get anyone else at short notice. She did a really good job, so they asked her to present the weather and it became a regular gig. The camera loved her, as they say, and after that she went from strength to strength; she did more presenting and eventually fronted her own programmes, even making cameo appearances in drama series. She became a household name, and to give her her due, she stuck by me through the good times when others might have ditched me and gone for someone more . . . high profile. Our Lexi was a trouper, and in this business that's high praise, I assure you.'

'Anyone that successful is bound to make enemies,' said Joe.

'You're right, of course. And her relationship with her ex-husband, Connor Nuffield, became very stormy. They were married for about nine years and they'd been together for a couple of years before that. Not many people know this, but the split was more acrimonious than the tabloids made out. I was her shoulder to cry on – not that she did much crying. She was glad to get rid of him if you ask me. He'd got heavily into gambling, you see. Not just a flutter on the gee-gees; he hung out in casinos and in the end he owed some very dodgy people a lot of money. Poor Lexi had to bail him out a number of times, and he turned nasty when she said she'd had enough.' She gave a meaningful nod.

Emily looked surprised, and maybe a little disappointed. Artemis glanced at her as though she'd read her thoughts. 'I can promise you that Connor Nuffield isn't the jolly, squeaky-clean character he appears to be on screen. I know his agent and even she has to acknowledge that he isn't a nice man in spite of all the cosy charm he oozes. I'm surprised he and Lexi lasted for so long really. They met early on in her career at some showbiz shindig when he was presenting the awards. He was flavour of the month at the time – very much in demand – and she fell for him hook, line and sinker.' She sighed. 'I believe he has his fangs into another victim now – an up-and-coming young actress. Maybe someone should warn her.'

'Would he have any motive for killing Lexi?'

'Well, I know he has a temper, and his star's on the wane, which might make things worse, so if Lexi did something to annoy him . . . Have you spoken to him?'

'He's filming in Kent and we're still trying to get hold of him.'

'Lexi got annoyed when she saw fawning articles about how wonderful Connor was and how he'd made a lovely home with his new partner. She said she'd like to dish some dirt on him – go to the press with her story about their time together. His gambling and the rows and all that. I sympathised, of course, but I advised against making anything public.'

'Did she take your advice?'

'I thought she'd see sense. I told her that revealing anything about their life together would only make her look vindictive and probably wouldn't do her own career any good. She had some good projects in the pipeline so she'd be stupid to rock the boat and cause a tabloid feeding-frenzy. In my opinion she was just letting off steam. Anyway, I pointed out that she was married to his lordship, who was a much better bet. He's in antiques, you know. Very high-end furniture and art for billionaires and galleries; more Sotheby's and Christie's than your local antiques warehouse.

'What was her relationship with her present husband like?'

'OK as far as I know. Why?'

'We've spoken to someone who thinks she was scared of him. Did you ever suspect he might have been violent or controlling?'

There was a long silence. 'Not violent, but she did mention once that he was possessive. She said she found it flattering at first. That it made her feel safe after . . . after what happened with Nathan Corde. But I think the novelty was wearing off. I'd say she was wary rather than actually scared. But there might have been things she didn't tell me. Lexi wasn't one to admit to weakness. She was very much "the show must go on".'

'Did she mention that she was having a fling with her gardener?'

For the first time a smile lit up Artemis's round face. 'Was she really? She kept that one quiet. Naughty girl.'

'According to the gardener, Lord Pilton had somebody beaten up when he suspected they were having an affair with his former wife. He was out of the country at the time of murder, but it's possible he hired someone else to do his dirty work for him,' said Emily.

'You mean he arranged to have her killed?' Joe could hear the disbelief in the agent's voice. 'That sounds a bit far-fetched.'

Emily decided to change tack. 'Tell us about Lexi's work. These projects she had in the pipeline. What were they?'

'She'd been asked to present an antiques programme but she didn't seem too keen, even though I told her that sort of thing was very popular and would be good for her profile. Then she was going to front a new TV series. Filming was due to begin next month.'

'What was that?' Emily asked.

'It was a series about crimes that have never been solved. People who've escaped justice.'

'There are lots of those sort of programmes on the TV,' Emily observed. She'd often told Joe she was sick of them – and their underlying implication that the police were as incompetent as the Keystone Cops.

'Oh, this one was going to be different,' said Artemis. 'It was going to be about tragic accidents that turned out to be murders. Cases of people who did terrible things and got away with it for some reason or other. The working title was *The Killers Among Us*. I anticipated that the main problem would be the legal aspect. But there are ways of getting round these things. There's been a lot of publicity about it, and she said she was even going to feature a crime that was personal.'

'What crime was this?'

'Her stalker, I presume. Although she never actually said as much in the publicity interviews. Keeping the punters in suspense.' She smiled. 'Just like our Lexi – show biz through and through.'

'Could someone who featured in one of the cases have been afraid that the series would uncover something they didn't want bringing to light?' Emily asked. Joe could tell the way her thoughts were going.

'You mean was Lexi killed to stop the series going ahead? I doubt it. It's a great concept, and if she backed out, they'd only get someone else to do it. Mind you, if someone didn't know how these things work . . .'

Artemis didn't have to finish the sentence. It was another possible motive to add to their list.

Joe wanted to change the subject. 'You know all about her stalker, Nathan Corde?'

She gave an exasperated sigh. 'It left her traumatised, which didn't surprise me. She put up a good front, but I knew how it affected her deep down. She didn't want to stay in her London flat, so his lordship bought a place in the wilds of Yorkshire, hoping it would provide her with more privacy. She had a lot of followers on social media and some thought they owned her, if you see what I mean. Whenever she went anywhere, they could be so intrusive, sending her constant messages, wanting selfies and demanding her attention. I don't know how she kept her patience sometimes, but I did my best to keep them at bay. Obsessed fans can be an occupational hazard for someone in Lexi's position. Nathan Corde was just the most extreme example, but I suspect there are quite a few would-be Cordes out there, just waiting to be pushed over the edge.'

Joe's spirits sank at the thought of other crazed fans.

'Has she kept her London place on?' Emily asked, realising this was the first time it had been mentioned.

'No. She eventually decided to give it up. I think that after the Nathan Corde incident, the idea of living in the capital lost its appeal. She wasn't keen on moving up north at first, but after they got married, his lordship insisted.'

'Why wasn't she keen?' Emily asked, as though she was unable to believe anybody wouldn't prefer Yorkshire over every other place on earth.

'She'd never say, even when I told her it was a lovely part of the country.'

'You'd think she'd be anxious to get as far away as possible from the place where her stalker targeted her.'

'You would, wouldn't you, but I think she took a lot of persuading. Corde used to follow her around when she lived in Mayfair – used to lurk in the little park opposite her flat with binoculars trained on her windows. The thought of something like that happening again terrified her, and I told her the countryside would be safer – less . . . anonymous. But it seems I was wrong.'

'A village like Eaglethorpe is certainly less anonymous. On the other hand, there are far more places to hide in the North Yorkshire landscape.' Joe hesitated. 'Actually we've just found out that Corde's been released. He told the authorities he was staying up here at a hostel in Eborby, but he hasn't been there since last Tuesday and he failed to report to the local police station as arranged. I'm afraid he's gone missing.'

'You mean you don't know where he is? You've lost him?' Artemis sounded alarmed.

'All our patrols are on the lookout,' said Emily. Joe thought she sounded defensive. 'I made a TV appeal last night. We're hoping he'll be in custody soon.'

'I presume it was Corde who killed her? He's the man you're looking for?'

'We need to speak to him.' Emily wasn't going to commit herself or give too much away. 'Do you know a woman called Fleur Chandler?'

Artemis looked surprised by the sudden change of subject. 'Oh yes, I remember her. She worked on Lexi's PR team at one time. Messed up badly, so Lexi had to let her go. She gave the girl a really hard time. Fleur left in tears.'

'Was Lexi often like that?'

Artemis shook her head. 'One thing you have to realise about Lexi, along with a lot of other high-profile people, is that in her professional life she was a perfectionist, and that meant she could be tough. But in her private life she could be generous. She was human, just like you and me.'

'What about a man called Silas Sellie?'

'He did some publicity work for Lexi many years ago, but I can't say I took to him. I understand he has his own company now and it's doing well. But he had some very strange ideas. Macabre, you could call it. He was very good-looking and rather charismatic, but a bit handsy, if you know what I mean. I know for a fact that he tried his luck with Lexi.'

'Did he succeed?'

'I suspect so. She'd just broken up with Connor and it was before she met his lordship, so I think she sowed a few wild oats around that time, if you get my meaning.'

'Who else did she sow them with?' Emily asked.

'Lexi and I didn't tell each other everything.'

'Is there anyone else you can think of who might be able to help us?'

'Well, I know her ex got in touch with her recently. He was asking for money.'

'Connor Nuffield?'

'Oh no. An ex-boyfriend from the very early days, before she met Connor. Bit of a blast from the past, as she put it. He's French and was a chef. Still is, I believe.'

'Pascal Allard?'

'That's the one. He went back to France after they split up, but now he's moved back to work here. They met when her career was only just starting and she was a production assistant on some daytime food programme.'

'And you say he'd contacted her recently asking for money?'

'He emailed me saying he needed investment for some new restaurant project, but I suspect that was code for he'd run out of cash. I forwarded the email but told her not to fall for it. She wasn't a charity for impecunious ex-partners.'

'What did she say to that?'

'She asked me to reply on her behalf and say she couldn't help. She was no pushover.'

'Did she ever mention her staff up here in Yorkshire? Her housekeeper, Margaret Cramp, and her driver and cleaner, Andrei and Maria?'

'No, I don't think so. Why would she?'

'Did she tell you she'd been consulting a psychic called Caradoc Karling?'

Artemis nodded. 'I believe she's consulted quite a few of them over the years. Some of these stars are very insecure. Always after reassurance.'

'Is there anything else you can tell us, Artemis? Anything at all, no matter how insignificant it may seem.'

The answer was a shake of the head. 'I can't think of anything. But if I do, I'll let you know.' She sighed. 'I've got a lot to sort out this end. People to inform. Contracts to deal with. But it all seems so trivial now Lexi's . . .'

Joe thought he saw tears forming in her eyes. Lexi had been with her since the start of her stellar career. And over the years Artemis had seen her client through good times and bad. They must have been close.

They thanked her and ended the call.

'What do you think?' Emily asked.

'The ex-boyfriend, Pascal Allard, is now in the picture – along with the former husband, Connor Nuffield. But he's been busy filming in Kent, which gives him an alibi.'

'Kent's two hundred miles away, but he could easily have driven up here and back.'

'We need to have a word with him, and with Pascal Allard. Find out where they both were at the time of the murder.'

'I'll ask Jamilla to track Nuffield down. It shouldn't be too difficult.' She looked at Joe and frowned. 'Pity we've mislaid Margaret Cramp. She might know whether the French ex has crawled out of the woodwork over the past weeks. If he's fond of asking for handouts, he might not have been willing to take no for an answer.'

The Serenity Guest House on the outskirts of Whitby had been visited by a uniformed female constable, who'd asked the proprietor whether a woman called Margaret Cramp was staying there. The answer had been no. There was nobody of that name registered.

During the constable's visit, Margaret stood on the half-landing above the entrance hall, keeping out of sight and holding her breath as she listened to the brief conversation. Feeling like a felon on the run was a whole new experience for her – and although she'd never have admitted it, even to herself, she was finding it rather exciting.

She was glad she'd had the foresight to check into the guest house under her mother's maiden name, Esme Cameron, and make her payment in cash. She knew that if she stayed away much longer, the police would gain access to her bank records and discover that she'd been using cash machines in Eborby and Whitby. She had also taken a bus to Whitby, and buses these days were kitted out with CCTV, so it was only a matter of time before they caught up with her. Besides, she needed to get back for the cat, Horatia. Maria was supposed to be feeding her, but Margaret didn't quite trust her.

That evening she summoned all her courage and made a phone call from her room. Sunny answered after one ring with 'Where are you? We've been looking for you.'

She didn't answer the question. She only said four words before ending the call: 'I'm coming back tomorrow.'

Fourteen

Margaret Cramp had been raised to be truthful and to have respect for the police. If her late mother could see her now, she'd be mortified at how her daughter had behaved. But self-preservation had trumped conscience. She'd been responsible for the death of Lexi Verity and the thought of what she'd done made her deeply ashamed.

She'd taken a taxi from the station, an unaccustomed extravagance she justified by telling herself that she shouldn't be late, and when she arrived back at the rectory, she saw that the police tape was still in place, fluttering around the entrance, a reminder of her wrongdoing. However, there was no sign of a police presence, which came as a relief.

She had her key, and she knew the code for the alarm, so she let herself in, feeling like an intruder in what had been her own home, her refuge from a world that had so often proved unkind. The silence in the house felt heavy, populated by the unseen spirits of past residents, including the woman who'd died so violently in the pool room a few days before.

She made for the kitchen and smiled when Horatia clattered through the cat flap in the back door, purring and rubbing herself around Margaret's legs. She found a pouch of cat food and filled her bowl. It was good to see Horatia again. In a household often filled with dark undercurrents beyond her comprehension, the cat was a straightforward if haughty presence.

As she climbed the stairs to her little flat, the memory of Lexi Verity's bitter words, with their threat of expelling her from her own personal paradise, still echoed in her head. In the guest house she had lain awake going over and over what had happened. But with Lexi dead, hope had returned. Lord Pilton was bound to need someone to keep house for him now he was alone. And if the police hadn't mentioned the cameras or the unlocked French windows to him, he might never find out about what Margaret had done – or failed to do.

Now she had to face the police and tell the truth – but not the whole truth. That would go with her to the grave.

She'd called Sunny as soon as she arrived back and he'd said someone would come round to the rectory to speak to her. He'd given her strict instructions to stay where she was. She'd tell the police enough to satisfy their curiosity. Then hopefully they'd leave her alone.

*   *   *

First thing the next morning, Emily told Joe about the call she'd received at home from Sunny the previous evening, disturbing her night in with Jeff and a nice bottle of Pinot Grigio. But she'd forgiven the intrusion because the news that Margaret Cramp was safe came as a relief. She'd feared that the woman might have stumbled into danger – or done something stupid.

She didn't consider it appropriate for Sunny to be present when she drove with Joe to the rectory to speak to the prodigal housekeeper. The woman had run away during a murder investigation, and that meant she had to fall under suspicion until their enquiries proved otherwise.

When they arrived at the house, Margaret opened the front door and led them upstairs to her flat. They could see that she was in the process of unpacking, and her half-emptied holdall lay open in the corner. Emily and Joe sat on the sofa, waiting patiently until she was ready to speak.

First she offered coffee – 'only instant, I'm afraid' – which they accepted gratefully. Joe hadn't slept well the previous night and was longing for some caffeine to set his brain in motion again.

, 'I needed to get away,' Margaret said as he took his first sip of coffee.

'Why? This is a murder inquiry and you could be a vital witness,' said Emily. 'You must realise how this looks.'

Margaret pulled a tissue from her pocket and turned it over in her fingers. 'After the shock of finding . . . I just couldn't face being here on my own.'

'Where have you been?' Joe asked.

'A little guest house just outside Whitby. I didn't want to stay away too long because of Hilary. I called the hospital yesterday. There's been a complication, so she has to stay in longer than expected, but they said she was making good progress and she should be discharged soon.' She gave a feeble smile.

'That's good to hear,' said Joe, playing good cop. 'She'll need your help when she gets out.'

Margaret frowned. 'Her mother will insist on looking after her. She doesn't approve of me, so until Hilary's able to get out and about, we probably won't see much of each other. Her mother thinks that us being together is ...' She searched for the word. 'Wrong.'

'Surely that's none of her business,' said Emily with a hint of indignation. 'You're both grown women.'

'The two of them have always been very close. Hilary's an only child and her father died when she was small, so she's all her mother's got.'

Emily and Joe exchanged a look.

'Sounds like a case of emotional blackmail to me,' said Emily.

'That sort of blackmail's not illegal,' said Joe. 'Not like the other kind.'

He might have been imagining it, but he was sure he saw Margaret flinch, and her pale cheeks flushed as she looked away.

'Have you anything new to tell us about the day Lexi Verity died?' said Emily. 'Something you failed to mention before?' She sounded as though she was losing patience.

If Margaret was as innocent as she claimed, her disappearance had been an unwanted distraction. But they couldn't forget that she'd lied about her movements on the day of Lexi's murder.

'I don't think so.'

Emily leaned forward, putting her face close to Margaret's 'We've found out that you lied about the time you left the hospital last Wednesday. You cut short your visit to Hilary. Why was that?'

Margaret opened her mouth to speak, but no sound emerged.

'Did you come back here early that day and find Lexi alone? Did you argue with her about your position here? It must have made you angry to see her living a life of luxury with a swimming pool and all the trimmings while you were in danger of being made homeless. I know how it would make me feel. Your security, everything you had was suddenly under threat. Did you lose your temper and stab her?'

'No.' The word came out as a cry of despair.

'Is that why you ran away?' said Joe quietly.

'I've already told you, I needed to get away. I found her. It was horrible. I just couldn't stay here.' She buried her head in her hands. 'I'm still having nightmares about it.'

'What did you do with the knife?' said Emily pleasantly, as though she was asking the woman whether she took sugar in her tea.

'I didn't do anything with it. I didn't kill her.' Margaret looked pleadingly from one detective to the other, desperate to be believed.

Emily's next question was more aggressive. 'Our forensic people have examined all the knives in the kitchen and none of them are an exact fit for the wound in Lexi's neck. Did you dispose of it after you'd killed her?'

'No. I've told you, I didn't kill her. Why don't you believe me?' Tears began to roll down Margaret's cheeks as she sobbed out the words.

'We don't understand why you won't tell us why you left the hospital early. What did you do in those lost hours?' Joe asked the question calmly. Even though the interview wasn't being recorded at this stage, the last thing he wanted was to be accused of bullying a suspect.

Emily stood up. 'We should carry this on back at the station. You're entitled to a solicitor, Ms Cramp.'

Margaret raised her eyes, teary and horrified. 'I haven't done anything, I swear.' A lengthy silence followed, as though she was making a decision. 'OK. I'll tell you where I was that afternoon.'

Emily glanced at Joe and sat back down.

'I went to a beauty parlour to have some injections. Botox.' Margaret spoke in a shamed whisper. 'Hilary's a lot younger than me and I thought . . . Afterwards I felt so stupid for thinking that some miracle would happen. I'm scared of losing Hilary, you see, and . . . I knew her ladyship had had it done, so I hoped . . .'

'Why didn't you tell us this before?' said Joe. He could tell the woman was seething with embarrassment and he couldn't help feeling some sympathy for her.

'Because as soon as I'd done it I realised how silly I'd been thinking I could look like her ladyship just by lying on a coach having needles stuck in my face.'

Joe looked at Emily and thought he could see her eyes twinkling with amusement. Margaret had confessed to a moment of vanity, something that had made her feel deeply awkward and perhaps even ashamed. Joe could understand why she'd wanted to keep it to herself.

'We'll need the details of the salon,' he said.

Margaret blushed and wrote something on a scrap of paper. 'It's hardly made any difference,' she said as she handed it over. 'I feel such a fool for thinking it would.'

Joe gave her a sympathetic smile. 'Is there anything you can tell us about the weeks leading up to Lexi's murder? Anything unusual that happened; something you might have forgotten to mention?'

Margaret appeared to relax a little, as though she was relieved to have got her embarrassing secret off her chest. 'There is something. It was one morning a few weeks ago when his lordship was away in London, but I didn't think it could have anything to do with . . . what happened.'

'What was it?' Joe wished she'd just come out with it, but he tried to hide his impatience.

'Lexi had a visitor. There was a terrible banging on the door and I went to answer it, but she told me she'd see to it so I went back into the kitchen.'

'Did you see who it was?'

She hesitated for a moment. 'I was curious, so I crept through to the dining room and peeped out of the window. I had quite a good view of the man standing at the front door. He looked angry. No, more than angry. Furious.'

'What happened?'

'Her ladyship let him in and they were talking but I couldn't hear what they were saying. He left about twenty minutes later and slammed the door behind him.'

'Had you ever seen him before?'

'He'd never been to the house, but I recognised him at once from the telly. It was her ladyship's ex-husband. Connor Nuffield.'

'Think carefully,' said Emily. 'Are you sure you didn't hear what they were talking about?'

'I heard her ladyship saying something like "How dare you try to get them to spy on me like that. I'm going to tell the police."'

'What do you think she was talking about?'

Margaret paused, as though she was making a decision. 'One day I saw a car parked outside Andrei and Maria's cottage. I'm sure it was the same one Connor Nuffield arrived in – a big black BMW.'

Joe caught on fast. 'You think Nuffield was paying them to spy on Lexi and report back to him?'

'I don't know. All I know is that she was furious with him. She told him to get out and leave her alone.'

'Just one more thing. Did Lexi ever receive a visit from a former boyfriend of hers? His name's Pascal Allard. He's French.'

Margaret shook her head, avoiding eye contact. Then she looked up. 'You didn't tell his lordship about the security cameras? I need this job, and if he finds out I've been negligent . . .' The words came out in a pleading whine.

Joe knew he'd done nothing wrong in revealing to Lord Pilton that the cameras hadn't been working, but he couldn't help feeling guilty. He was saved from having to answer by Emily.

'Thank you, Ms Cramp,' she said as she stood up. 'We'll be in touch.'

Joe had a suspicion that Margaret was lying about something. But he wasn't quite sure what it was.

The interview with Andrei and Maria proceeded more smoothly than Joe and Emily had anticipated. The pair were only too eager to give out the details of Connor Nuffield's visit to their cottage. They hadn't mentioned it before because it had happened a few weeks ago so they didn't think it was relevant. Besides, they couldn't imagine such a famous man, who seemed so charming and friendly when he spoke to them, having anything to do with her ladyship's death.

He'd admired the cottage, saying how he wished he had somewhere that cosy, and had seemed so sincere when he asked them to keep an eye on his former wife, saying he was concerned for her safety. He'd offered Maria a hundred pounds, but Andrei had said there was no need for payment. The two of them had argued about this after he'd gone. Andrei said it seemed wrong to spy on their employer, but Maria had no such qualms. Money was money and they needed it to go home and set themselves up in business.

Emily and Joe believed Andrei when he said he'd refused the offer. But they suspected that Maria might have been tempted to contact Connor later and agree to his terms without her husband's knowledge. She definitely looked cagey as Andrei described the encounter.

'We had nothing to tell this man anyway,' he said. 'I saw no danger. Nobody watching the house.'

'What about you, Maria?' said Emily sweetly.

Maria shook her head. 'Nobody. But we cannot see the house well from here.'

'So neither of you spied on Connor Nuffield's behalf – or his lordship's?'

This question caused a definite reaction from Maria. She shifted awkwardly in her seat.

'You told his lordship about the gardener, Harry York, didn't you, Maria?' said Emily, her voice harsher this time. She didn't like snitches – unless they were helping the police, of course.

'He is my employer. He ask me to tell him if his wife has lovers. I tell him about Harry. He is grateful. He give me money.' She looked at her husband defiantly.

'His lordship deserve to know. He is her husband and he is a gentleman. He no kill her. Madman kill her. Stalker, yes?'

'Did you tell Connor Nuffield about Harry too?' Joe asked, recalling what Artemis James had said about the actor's violent tendencies.

Maria shrugged. 'He want to know if she had boyfriends. I tell him yes.'

'You might have put your employer in danger.'

'No. Mr Nuffield a famous man. He is nice actor. No threat. He worry about her ladyship. That is all.'

'Did you see anyone who could be a stalker hanging around?'

But before Maria could answer the question, Emily's phone rang. It was the station. There'd been a sighting of Nathan Corde, and the team were closing in.

Fifteen

It was a major police operation. Drones, search teams, even the police helicopter disturbed the Sunday peace as it swept the Howardian Hills, the deafening noise sending frightened sheep scurrying for shelter.

Eventually, after all that effort, they struck gold. A shelter was spotted in a small copse, a green tarpaulin stretched between wooden posts to form a makeshift tent. It was camouflaged by foliage and would have remained undiscovered if a farmer hadn't spotted what might have been smoke from a campfire and reported it. Without that, the search might have taken weeks.

As the team searched the shelter, they came to realise how organised the suspect had been. He'd obviously obtained camping equipment from somewhere, and a couple of stained and well-thumbed survivalist manuals lay beside the sleeping bag. But there was no sign of Nathan Corde.

When Emily was told about the discovery, Joe could sense her frustration. 'Just get him found and bring him in,' she almost shouted into her phone. 'He's not the flaming invisible man. He must be somewhere!'

As they approached the station entrance on their return from Eaglethorpe, she turned to Joe 'Think we should go up there and give the search team a hand?'

'I think we'd only get in the way. What did you think of Andrei and Maria? Were they telling the truth?'

'I think he was. She's the bright one in that relationship. I think she took cash from Connor for information about Lexi, as well as from Milo Pilton. She might have told Pilton about Nuffield's visit and Lexi's carryings-on with Harry York. But whether Pilton would have paid someone to get rid of her for that, I'm not sure.'

'If Pilton hired a professional, it might be hard to prove,' said Joe. 'A hitman could be miles away by now, with no way of tracing him.' He paused. 'Maria didn't seem aware of any stalker.'

'If Corde's as good at concealment as he seems to be, he'll have been taken care not to be seen.'

They made their way to the CID office, and for half an hour there was no news. Then all the phones started ringing, and the news was good.

Nathan Corde had finally been cornered by a drystone wall when a frightened sheep gave away his hiding place with a startled bleat. One of the officers conducting the search suggested that the sheep should be given a medal.

Corde, wearing full camouflage, had resisted arrest. He was agile and strong and, thanks to hours spent in the prison gym, fully fit. It took four officers to restrain him, and even when the handcuffs were in place behind his back, he'd continued to struggle.

Joe could tell that Emily, normally so confident and unflappable when faced with a criminal, was a little apprehensive about facing Corde. He was a violent man, and Joe couldn't help imagining how frightened Lexi Verity must have been when he'd targeted her.

An hour later, Emily received word that their chief suspect was being brought in. In the meantime, Joe discovered that Lexi Verity's ex, Connor Nuffield, happened to be up north for the weekend to fulfil a long-standing engagement.

It was turning out to be a busy day.

Pauline Porter heard the front door open and close, followed by running footsteps on the stairs, the sound muffled by the thick carpet they'd had fitted six weeks ago.

Leanne had left the house an hour before, saying she was going to see a friend, but now she was back. Pauline gathered all her courage and made her way up the stairs, thinking how ridiculous it was that she should feel so nervous at facing her own daughter; the child she'd carried inside her body and cared for all her life. She knocked softly on Leanne's bedroom door and waited.

When there was no answer, she pressed her ear to the door. She thought she could hear gentle crying from inside the room.

She hesitated before pushing the door open. Leanne was face-down on the bed, her slim body shaking with sobs. Without hesitation, Pauline rushed over and took the girl in her arms, stroking her hair and murmuring soft words of comfort, just as she had when Leanne was tiny and she'd awoken from a nightmare.

Leanne clung to her for what seemed like an age before Pauline tore a tissue from the box on the bedside table and began to dab her daughter's eyes.

Once the sobs had subsided, she dared to speak. 'What is it, love? What's wrong? Tell me. Please.'

Leanne took a deep, shuddering breath as she recovered herself.

'Isabel's missing. She went out on Wednesday morning as usual but never arrived at school. Me and my mates have been trying to message her but she's not answering. That's why I've been out so much. We've been checking everywhere she goes and asking if anyone's seen her. Nobody knows where she is.'

'Have you told the police?'

'Her mum called them when she didn't come home, but they were useless. They said teenagers run away all the time and usually turn up safe and well. They said it was too early to worry but they'd keep an eye out for her. They didn't seem bothered.'

'So you and your friends have been doing your own detective work?' Pauline felt a thrill of pride.

'Well, the police said because she'd just turned eighteen and there was no evidence she'd come to any harm . . .'

'But you're worried?'

Leanne nodded. 'I've just been to Phoebe's, but she hasn't heard anything. We've looked everywhere she's likely to be.'

Pauline felt annoyed on Isabel's mother's behalf. Any young person going missing, even one who was eighteen and technically an adult, was surely a cause for panic, whatever the statistics might say. 'I'm going to call your dad, see if he can get things moving.'

'No, please. He'll only fuss – say I can't go out and . . .'

Leanne blew her nose on the tissue and Pauline's instincts told her that she hadn't been given the whole story.

'Is there anything you haven't told me, Leanne?'

Leanne looked away, suddenly regretting taking her mum into her confidence. She'd made a solemn promise. And a promise was something you couldn't break.

Connor Nuffield wasn't hard to find. He'd barely had time to recover from his intense filming schedule in Kent when he'd had to travel to Hull to open a super-market the previous day. They were still waiting for Nathan Corde to be brought in, so she sent a couple of constables to pick Connor up from the hotel where he'd stayed overnight and bring him to Eborby. She instructed the constables to ask him very nicely and assume that he'd be anxious to help the police catch whoever had killed his ex-wife.

As they waited for Connor to arrive, Joe and Emily had a sandwich in her office. A chance to sit down and gather their thoughts.

'I still think Nathan Corde's our best bet,' Emily said after a short period of amicable silence.

Joe didn't contradict her. Corde had obvious survival skills and was adept at concealment. He could have lurked unseen around the rectory's extensive grounds for a while, watching and waiting for his opportunity.

He might have seen Margaret Cramp and Andrei and Maria go out and known that Lexi would be there alone. Margaret had confessed to being distracted by Hilary's illness and leaving the French doors unlocked. In addition, the CCTV was out of action. Joe put forward the theory that Corde could have disabled the cameras himself a few days before the murder so he could watch Lexi without being detected. According to his record, he'd been apprenticed to an electrician at one point in his life, so he would have known how to do it. He'd also spent time in the army, where he'd lasted just long enough to learn his survival skills before going AWOL and leaving under a cloud. It all fitted. But Joe wondered why he had a strong feeling that they ought to explore other possibilities before they committed themselves to charging him with murder.

Once Corde was in the cells, though, the clock would be ticking, and if time ran out they'd have to release him if they couldn't gather enough evidence. Suspicion wasn't enough, however strong it was.

'Once we've got him in custody, I'd be reluctant to let him go,' said Emily as though she'd read Joe's mind. 'I think we should obtain an extension to hold him longer; we can say he's bound to slip through our fingers if he's released.'

Before she could say any more, her phone beeped. It was a message from the officers sent to pick up Connor Nuffield to say he'd be with them in fifteen minutes.

'Better get the kettle on,' said Emily. 'He's a celeb, so he'll expect to be treated like one. Once he thinks he's getting the soft treatment, we'll start asking some awkward questions.'

'The element of surprise.'

'Exactly.'

Connor Nuffield was all charm as he walked to Emily's office, smiling at people and asking how they were as he passed. Joe had to hand it to him. Anyone would think that the affable DCI Holly himself had arrived to take charge.

Jamilla brought the tea, in proper china mugs rather than the paper cups from the machine. She'd even managed to find mugs that weren't cracked, which was an achievement in itself. Joe made a mental note to congratulate her.

Connor looked completely relaxed as he made himself comfortable on Emily's visitor's chair.

'Do you know, I've never actually been into a CID office before,' he said casually. 'I've been a DCI for years in the fictional world, of course, but I've never experienced the real thing. Interesting.' He looked round, apparently fascinated. 'Do you watch *Holly and Ivy*?'

Emily admitted that she did whenever she got the chance. The programme bore little resemblance to reality, but she still secretly enjoyed the light-hearted investigations of DCI Chris Holly and DS Ivy Noel.

'How's your inquiry progressing?' Connor asked with a concerned frown. 'I must say, Lexi's death came as a terrible shock to me. I would have come up earlier, but filming waits for no man. Besides, I don't really see that I can tell you anything useful. I mean, Lexi and I had both moved on since our divorce, both remarried and leading new lives. Even so, I can hardly believe what's happened.' He shook his head sadly.

'Have you ever visited Lexi's Eaglethorpe home?' Emily asked pleasantly.

'No. I haven't.'

Joe caught Emily's eye. He could tell she was long-ing to call him a liar, but she smiled sweetly and said nothing.

'What would you say if we told you that you were seen by witnesses calling at Lexi's home and arguing with her?' Emily tilted her head to one side and waited for an answer.

For a split second Connor Nuffield's bright blue eyes flashed with alarm, no sooner there than gone and replaced with a look of mild disbelief. 'I'd say that whoever told you that was lying – probably in the hope of selling some salacious and totally false story to the tabloids. It's absolute rubbish. I hope whoever told you that is charged with wasting police time.'

'This was a few weeks ago. One of our officers checked with your agent and you were in Yorkshire at that time.'

'That's true. I was brought up in Leeds and have family there. I was visiting my sister. You can check. I have nothing to hide.'

'Where were you last Wednesday afternoon?'

Connor took his phone from his pocket and consulted it, looking remarkably calm for a man who was being questioned in relation to the murder of his former wife.

'I was in Kent filming an episode of *Holly and Ivy* in the morning and I spent the afternoon with my agent. Again, you can check. If you think I had anything to do with Lexi's death, you're making a huge mistake.'

He spoke with such confidence that Joe was inclined to believe him. Until he reminded himself that the man was an actor. Being convincing was his job.

'Do you know anything about Lexi's ex-partner, Pascal Allard?' Joe asked.

'Not much. She rarely spoke about him.'

'Do you know Artemis James?'

'She's Lexi's agent.' Connor pressed his lips together. 'In some ways I blame her for the break-up of our marriage. Always whispering poison into Lexi's ear, telling lies about me. Woman's a total bitch if you ask me.'

'She spoke well of you too.'

Emily was keeping up the sweet, unthreatening act. But Joe knew that in a moment this would change.

'When we spoke to Ms James, she suggested that you are heavily into gambling. She said that at one time you got yourself into serious financial trouble.'

Connor blustered for a few moments, clearly shocked. Then he smiled. 'That's absolute rubbish. I told you she didn't like me.'

'What about Lexi's chauffeur and cleaner, Andrei and Maria? They told us you'd offered them money for information about your ex-wife. Are they lying, too? Because I don't see why they would, do you?'

'Envy. People can be jealous of anyone who's success-ful, I'm afraid. Can I go now?' Connor sounded completely calm. If Joe hadn't learned cynicism over his time in the job, he might have believed him.

'Why did you offer them money?'

There was a long silence before he answered, as though he was considering his options. 'OK, I admit I did pay them a visit. I was concerned about Lexi's safety. She was stalked a few years ago and I wasn't comfortable with the idea of her living in such an isolated place. I knew her husband was away a lot so I thought it would be helpful if someone kept an eye on her. That couple seemed very . . . reliable.'

'Come on, Mr Nuffield, there was more to it than that, wasn't there?'

The actor nodded slowly, as though he'd realised that this real-life DCI couldn't be fooled. He took a deep breath before speaking. 'OK, there was another reason. I wanted to see whether there was any chance of Lexi helping me out . . . financially.'

'Blackmail?'

'I'd hardly put it like that.' He gave a nervous little laugh. 'Blackmail's illegal and I'd never . . .' He swallowed hard, his confidence fraying at the edges. 'If you must know, they're pulling the plug on *Holly and Ivy* after this season. I have debts, and Lexi has . . . had money. I thought she might give me a loan, that's all.'

'And you thought that if you knew something she'd rather Lord Pilton didn't find out, you could exert some pressure.'

'That's ridiculous.'

'Did you kill her when she refused to help you out?'

Connor shook his head vigorously. 'Of course not. No way. Anyway, I was down south when she died. I've told you before. Lots of people will back me up. Why don't you ask them?'

'We will. Don't worry.'

There was a question Joe wanted to ask, something that had been at the back of his mind. 'Was Lexi Verity her real name?'

Connor frowned. 'Yes. Why?'

The phone on Emily's desk rang. It was a message to say that Nathan Corde had arrived and was being taken to the custody suite.

Emily looked at Connor and gave him a businesslike smile. 'Thank you for coming in, Mr Nuffield,' she said.

'No problem. Anything to help the boys and girls in blue,' Connor said with strained bonhomie.

'Don't leave the country, will you. We might need to speak to you again.'

'Why did you ask him if Lexi was her real name?' Emily asked once the man had left.

'Just an idea,' said Joe, reluctant to say that Caradoc Karling had planted the notion in his mind. He knew she would only tell him that nothing the psychic said could be taken seriously. Besides, it was time to talk to Nathan Corde.

The first thing that struck Joe as he walked into the interview room behind Emily was the overpowering smell of sweat mixed with something even more pungent. He told himself that he'd soon get used to it. He noticed Emily take a tissue from her pocket and hold it to her nose for a few moments.

The suspect had refused the help of a solicitor and at first said little other than confirming his name. He sat with his head bowed, showing no sign of the violent tendencies they'd been warned about. Instead he seemed remarkably meek and resigned to the inevitable.

As soon as Emily switched on the recording machine, he looked up, suddenly alert.

'I want to make a statement,' he said in a hoarse whisper. 'I'll say what I've got to say then it'll be no comment from then on.'

'OK,' said Emily. 'What do you want to say?'

'I didn't do it. I didn't kill Lexi. Why would I? I loved her. I wouldn't harm a hair on her lovely head.'

'She got you sent down,' said Joe reasonably. 'That must have made you angry.'

Corde shook his head. 'I knew the signals.' A small, secretive smile appeared on his thin lips. 'Lexi and I had our own secret code.' He nodded, sure of himself. 'That's why I decided to come up north when they let me out. While I was inside, I heard she'd moved to Yorkshire. That's why I came here – so we could be together.'

Joe glanced at Emily. She was scribbling something on the notepad in front of her. He could tell she was trying to keep her temper. Corde had terrified Lexi Verity, but in his mind, they were star-crossed lovers. And it seemed a few years spent behind bars hadn't cured him of his delusions.

'How did you find out she was dead?' Joe asked, his eyes focused on the man's unshaven face. 'We only released her name a couple of days ago, and you've been living off the grid for a while.'

'I saw a newspaper in a shop. It was the headline.'

'When was this?'

'Can't remember.'

'Why did you leave the hostel.'

'It was too much like prison. Couldn't come and go without the bloody screws wanting to know where I was.'

'And you didn't want them to know because you were hanging round Lexi Verity's house. Watching.

Waiting for your chance. Did she scream when she saw you? She didn't welcome you with open arms like you'd hoped. Is that why you killed her?'

'I didn't kill her. Like I said, I loved her.'

'Where were you last Wednesday?'

Joe and Emily waited for an answer. But the only words they heard were 'No comment.'

Sixteen

'What time will Dad be back?'

Pauline Porter thought her daughter seemed several years younger since her return home earlier. The gobby, insolent teenager of recent weeks had been replaced by the young girl she'd been a year or so ago, before she'd started hanging round with her new friends, especially Phoebe and Isabel, the missing girl. She hadn't even objected when her mother had put her arms around her and given her a warm hug.

'I don't know, love. You know what it's like when he's working on a case.' Pauline stroked her daughter's hair. It was something she'd done when Leanne was little and she was trying to soothe her to sleep. Even now she seemed to take some comfort from it. 'Do you know something about Isabel's disappearance? If you do, you should at least tell her mum. She'll be worried sick.'

Leanne nodded, and Pauline waited for her to speak. Further prying would do no good. If the girl was going to confide in her, it would be on her own terms and in her own time.

Eventually Leanne broke the silence. 'I promised I wouldn't say anything to anyone.'

'Maybe it's time you broke that promise. Your friend's missing. She might be in danger.'

'Dad'll go mad.'

'Why would you think that? Your dad's a policeman. If Isabel's in trouble, he's the best person to help.'

But Leanne shook her head. 'She made me and Phoebe swear that we wouldn't tell anyone. You mustn't tell Dad. You've got to promise. Cross your heart and hope to die.'

Leanne's phone rang, the sudden noise making her jump. After a short conversation, she looked up at her mother with tears of relief in her eyes. 'That was Phoebe. It's OK. Izzy's come home safe.'

At the end of the interview, during which Nathan Corde had answered no comment to everything that Emily and Joe asked, he had been taken back to the cells and the super had agreed an extension to the time they could hold him. They didn't have any clear evidence yet to pin him to the murder, but his obsession with Lexi Verity and his past behaviour meant that he still had to be their chief suspect. Emily was pinning her hopes on the lab finding some forensic evidence from the makeshift shelter where he'd been camping out that would link him to the crime. But these things took time, so they needed to be patient.

Emily had wondered whether Connor Nuffield should be in the frame, until she'd called his agent, who readily confirmed that on the afternoon of Lexi Verity's death, they'd had a long boozy lunch. Connor had been drowning his sorrows about the loss of the most lucrative role of his career. There was no way he could have got to Eaglethorpe in time to kill his ex-wife.

Joe agreed with Emily that they should leave Nathan Corde to stew for a while, and he went around the office asking whether anything new had come in while Emily made a phone call. He could see her through her office window and he knew she was speaking to her husband and children, who were spending their Sunday without her. Her expression had softened and every so often she laughed. He'd always been surprised at the way she could switch from professional crime-fighter and formidable interviewer of suspects to mother of three, baker of cakes for school fairs and wrangler of lost reading books and PE equipment.

He remembered Kaitlin telling him that women were capable of anything. He'd laughed at the time, admitting that she was probably right. The memory gave him a jolt, as it always did. He'd almost forgotten about the message Kirsten had left on his phone a few days ago. He hadn't called her back, partly because he'd been too busy and partly because he preferred to put his sister-in law-out of his mind.

His phone rang again. Lexi's former partner, Pascal Allard, had been traced. He was working in an upmarket restaurant in Liverpool city centre. However, it turned out that for the past fortnight the restaurant had been closed for a major refurbishment and the staff had been given time off, which meant Pascal could easily have driven over the Pennines to North Yorkshire to kill his former partner. They needed to find out more about him and his relationship with Lexi Verity. Past and present.

They already knew that he and Lexi had met before she became famous, and she'd probably outgrown their relationship as her career blossomed and they began to move in different worlds. After the split, she had met Connor Nuffield, an up-and-coming TV actor who'd just landed the starring role in what was to become a long-running and popular series. The rest they knew.

After telling Emily about this new development, he rang Merseyside Police, who promised to find Allard's current address for him. It seemed strange to Joe to hear the familiar accent of his home city again, and it brought back memories of his own days in the force there; memories that weren't always happy ones, although there had been good times. Times before his colleague, Kevin, was shot dead and Joe himself was injured in the incident. Even now he experienced a degree of survivor's guilt. Why was it Kevin who'd left a grieving family and not him?

He thanked the officer and emphasised the urgency before ending the call, adding that if necessary he and Emily could drive down the M62 to interview Allard.

His phone rang again. Since the investigation had begun, it never seemed to stop, even on a Sunday. The person on the other end said that a member of the public wanted to speak to someone dealing with the Lexi Verity inquiry. Joe asked for the call to be put through at once.

It was a few seconds before he heard a woman's voice. She sounded nervous. In Joe's experience, lots of law-abiding people felt like that when dealing with the police. He knew she just needed reassurance.

'How can I help you, Ms . . .?'

'Mrs. Mrs Jackie Page.' There was a short silence before she spoke again. 'It's about my husband.'

'Would you like to tell me about it?' He tried to strike the right note between sympathy and curiosity. Sometimes his training for the priesthood came in useful.

'He said he was going away on Tuesday until the end of the week; something to do with work. I was expecting him back by yesterday, but he hasn't come home. I keep trying to call him, but there's no answer.'

'Did he say where he was going?'

'No. But he often doesn't if he's only going to be away a few nights.'

'What sort of work does he do?'

'He owns his own business. He usually lets me know if he's going to be away longer than expected. My sister's just been round and she said I ought to call you. I wasn't going to, but . . .'

'You did the right thing, Mrs Page. You haven't got the registration number of his vehicle by any chance?'

'It's a Jaguar but I don't know the number off the top of my head. Why?'

Joe didn't want to go into the ins and outs of number plate recognition so he told her it didn't matter. He was sure there were other ways of tracing the man if necessary.

There was another silence before Jackie Page spoke again. 'When my sister came round, she said we should have a look in Douglas's office at home. I told her we shouldn't, but . . . Anyway, she went in there and found some press cuttings about Lexi Verity – about things she'd been doing and where she'd been. My sister said I should let you know because he might have something to do with her murder.'

'And what do you think?'

She ended the call without answering the question.

Seventeen

While the police had been examining the rectory, his lordship had taken up residence at the Blue Boar. Once Eaglethorpe's village boozer, it had undergone an extensive modernisation programme some years ago and now boasted a gourmet restaurant and seven luxury rooms worthy of a boutique hotel. Margaret Cramp was sure her employer would be comfortable there, but she was disappointed that he hadn't seen fit to allow her to look after him in the time of his bereavement. It was her job, after all. She liked to feel she was needed, that she had her own special place in the world.

The police had allowed her to remain in her flat because it was separate from the rest of the house. His lordship had promised her that her position was safe; he needed someone to cook and clean for him, and take care of the place during his many trips away. It seemed that either he wasn't aware of her sin of omission or he'd chosen to ignore it to avoid the effort of finding another housekeeper. His words had reassured her, because the rectory was the only home she had.

She'd expected the new widower to show more signs of grief, but he seemed the same as usual, serious and unsmiling. But then she imagined that he'd been raised not to show his feelings; the old stiff upper lip.

A piece of good news distracted her from thoughts of her employer. Hilary was to be discharged from hospital after the weekend, and it crossed her mind that once things had settled down and the police interest in the house died away, maybe her friend could come and stay with her next time his lordship went away. The prospect gave her a warm glow. It was something she could look forward to now the threat of dismissal had gone and the lengths she'd been prepared to go to in order to survive were no longer necessary. Lexi Verity was dead, and so was the threat to Margaret's precious security.

There was something she needed to do urgently, and that was to destroy all evidence of her transgressions; the sins that had seemed so vital at the time but that had now become a source of guilt and regret. She walked to the corner of the room and moved the cane chair that stood there so that she could get at the loose floorboard, the hiding place she had discovered when she'd moved in and had used ever since. Her fingers found the small knothole and the board came up easily. Inside the cavity was a wooden box, and she drew it out, instinctively looking around to make sure nobody was watching. She opened the box and removed some papers. Her insurance; the evidence she'd intended to use to threaten her dead employer if it became necessary. They had to be destroyed. If the police decided to make a thorough search of her little attic flat, questions would be asked. And in spite of her relationship by marriage to one of the investigating officers, if her secret ever came to light, she would find herself in deep trouble.

'Do you think we should send someone to talk to this Jackie Page?'

Emily looked up from her paperwork.

'Her husband's been away from home since the day before Lexi's murder and she says he kept press cuttings about her. I think we should have a word. Even if it's only to eliminate him from our enquiries.'

'I agree. He might simply have been a big fan of our murder victim, but it's definitely worth following up. Just in case there's more to it. Has he any record of stalking? Any sexual offences?'

'No, nothing. I'll organise someone to find out whether the Jaguar registered in his name has cropped up on any of our traffic cameras. And we'll send one of the DCs to have a word with Mrs Page. She didn't give her address, but it shouldn't be hard to find. Leave it with me.'

'Thanks, Joe.' Emily looked him in the eye. 'Why don't you sit down,' she said as she checked the over-sized watch on her left wrist. 'Let's go over what we've got so far.'

Joe did as she asked and watched as she consulted a sheet of paper.

'Lexi Verity, star and TV personality, discovered stabbed to death in her swimming pool. Her house-keeper, Margaret Cramp, confessed that she forgot to contact anyone to repair the CCTV installed in the house, and also admitted that she'd failed to lock the French windows in the dining room when she went out to visit her friend in hospital that day. She cut the hospital visit short and went to a beauty salon. That's been confirmed, by the way, but she'd still have had time to go back to the rectory before she made the call to Sunny reporting the death.'

'Somehow I find it hard to see Margaret as our killer, but you never can tell. What about Andrei and Maria?'

'I can't see them as killers either. Besides, they've got an alibi. They spent all that day shopping in Eborby, with the receipts to prove it. No, my money's still on Nathan Corde. He's been our chief suspect all along. At least he's now in custody. Hopefully a night in the cells will soften him up nicely and he'll be keen to make a confession.'

'Optimist.'

Emily smiled. 'Well, even if he doesn't, the lab might come up with something; Lexi's DNA in his shelter or a microscopic speck of her blood on his clothing. He stalked the victim and it doesn't look as though he intended to stop. And he left the hostel on the Tuesday, so he was free at the time of her death. He also seems to be an expert in survival and camouflage, which means he could have been hanging round the victim's home without anybody being aware of it. He might have been keeping an eye on the comings and goings, and as soon as he saw Margaret go out and realised Lexi was alone, he seized his opportunity. If Lexi screamed or said the wrong thing when she saw him, I can see him losing control and killing her. He's had plenty of time to brood and fantasise about her while he's been locked up. And if he found her alone and vulnerable in that swimsuit . . .'

'I agree. He's our most likely candidate so far. Anyone else?'

'The husband, Lord Pilton, is out of the frame because he was thousands of miles away at the time, although he hardly seems grief-stricken. We know he was aware of Lexi's affair with the gardener. And there's always the possibility that he hired a professional killer.'

'Wouldn't a firearm be a hitman's weapon of choice?'

'Possibly. We don't have much experience of that sort of thing here in Eborby, though, so who knows? The ex-husband, Connor Nuffield, has also got a cast-iron alibi, even though he probably had a motive if Lexi refused to come up with the cash to get him out of financial trouble. We've yet to talk to her former boyfriend, Pascal Allard. He'd been in touch via Artemis asking for money, and according to Merseyside, he's not at his address. He told his neighbours he was going away for a while because his restaurant is closed for refurbishment at the moment. Merseyside are trying to trace his whereabouts, and they'll let us know as soon as they find him. I'm not saying he's at the top of our suspect list, but he might be able to provide some more background on the victim.'

Emily thought for a few moments. 'We don't know much about Lexi's life before she became famous, do we? While we're going through possible suspects, should we consider Fleur Chandler from the museum? She had every reason to hate Lexi Verity.'

'We're still trying to confirm her movements on the day of the murder. She doesn't have a car, and Eaglethorpe's not easy to access by public transport, but taxi firms are being contacted. What about Silas Sellie? He and Lexi were lovers at one time, and it seems they didn't part on very good terms.'

Emily raised her eyebrows. 'Did I just catch a glimpse of the green-eyed monster, Joe? Looks as though Sellie and your ex, Maddy, are an item now, so do you think your judgement might be a bit . . . skewed?'

'There's nothing wrong with my judgement.' Joe was aware that he'd snapped out the words, and immediately regretted letting the thought of Silas Sellie get to him. He knew he needed to remain dispassionate and professional, even though he'd taken an immediate dislike to the good-looking, charismatic man and, after seeing the mannequins he kept in his flat, was quite willing to believe he had a dark side to his nature.

'Well, I didn't like him either, which means we can't rule him out. Although no vehicle registered to him was spotted on camera at the relevant time.' She grinned. 'Sorry about that.'

Joe felt the colour rising in his cheeks. 'It still looks as though Nathan Corde's our man.'

'Well, he's not going anywhere for the time being and I've asked the lab to pull out all the stops. Every contact leaves a trace, so they say. Who else should we be considering? What about Caradoc Karling?'

Joe shook his head. 'I can't see him as a likely candidate, can you?'

'Not really.'

'Then there's Harry York, the victim's gardener and bit on the side.'

It was Emily's turn to disagree. 'Why would he need to kill her? I know I could be wrong, but . . .' She stood up. 'On that note, let's call it a day and get home. With any luck, forensic will come up with something soon and we'll be able to charge Corde and get the whole case wrapped up.'

'Think he'll make a confession?'

'We can only hope.'

Joe returned to his empty flat and put some music on while he made tea. In his opinion, a Palestrina mass went well with omelette and beans. As soon as he'd finished eating, George Merryweather called. When Joe saw his name on the caller display, he answered immediately, keen to hear a friendly voice.

'I can hear beautiful music in the background,' George began. 'Are you at a loose end this evening, by any chance?'

'I've been at work all day. Labouring on the Sabbath, I'm afraid, but I'm free now.'

'I'm sure you'll be forgiven as it's in a good cause. How about a pint? I know you're up to your eyes in this terrible murder, but I've got something that might interest you. A distraction, if you will.'

'Not crime?'

'Not that I know of. We won't be talking shop, so you're quite safe.'

'In that case, I'll see you at the Star in half an hour.'

Joe hurried to the bedroom to get ready, straightening the bedclothes he'd left unmade that morning because he'd been in such a hurry to get out. As he changed his shirt, he was struck by the silence of the place. Some people were happy with their own company, but after Kaitlin's death, he'd soon realised that he wasn't one of them. He thought of Maddy with Silas Sellie and shuddered.

The Star on Boargate was a historic pub accessed down a narrow snickleway. Like so many ancient buildings in Eborby, it was reputed to be haunted by soldiers from the Civil War who'd been taken there after battle, and according to the stories, their screams and cries could still be heard. Not only that, but two ghostly black cats were said to appear from time to time in the dimly lit interior that had changed little over the centuries.

George was waiting for him in the lounge bar at the front of the pub, along with a pint of Black Sheep. He had ditched his cassock and dog collar for an open-necked checked shirt and looked every inch the retired academic – or maybe an off-duty solicitor or doctor of the old school. He smiled and stood up as soon as he spotted Joe.

'Joe, it's good to see you. How are you?'

'Good to see you too, George. I'm fine.' Lying to a clergyman wasn't something he often did, but the reply was automatic.

It was a few seconds before George spoke again. 'You're not fine, are you, Joe? I can tell.' He tapped the side of his nose. 'Canon's intuition.'

Joe took a sip from his pint glass. The beer tasted good. 'I've just been really busy, that's all. We're under a lot of pressure to get the Lexi Verity case wrapped up.'

'Well, like I said, I've got something that'll take your mind off it. That little ghost puzzle I mentioned; the one about the children's imaginary friends. A man called Ben Greengrass has recently moved into a new house. It dates back to the seventeenth century and had been derelict for years, but Ben and his wife have had it renovated. It's in Kirkgate, off Gallowgate, and it used to be a pub.'

'And this Ben Greengrass thinks it might be haunted?'

'He's been doing some research and discovered there was a fire in part of the premises some years ago that killed a little girl. The poor child's father was so eaten up with grief that he hanged himself shortly afterwards. It's probable that he'd started the fire himself for the insurance and failed to reach his daughter in time to save her. Poor man must have killed himself out of remorse. Guilt is a powerful emotion.'

Joe knew there was a lot of truth in George's words. He'd felt guilt about Kaitlin's death, even though it had been a tragic accident; a terrible clinging guilt that he'd never truly been able to shake off. 'And this Ben Greengrass thinks the people who died are still on the premises?'

'That's right. A little girl and a man. Ben's son calls him Jack and says he looks sad.'

'You've checked out the story yourself?'

'Oh yes, there are plenty of newspaper reports from the time. Unusual to be able to find such definite confirmation.'

'Could Ben Greengrass's kids have found out about it somehow? Maybe overheard him talking about it?'

'Unlikely. The family have come here from down south and have no connection with Eborby, so they weren't aware of the tragedy until Ben started delving into the newspaper archives at the central library. And the incidents began long before he found out what had happened.'

'You've visited the premises, said the usual prayers?'

'Ben's wife thinks it's all nonsense. He says she won't allow me in the house and he's reluctant to go behind her back. She's at work all day, so I told him I'd be willing to call while she's out. I said I'd be discreet and she wouldn't even know I'd been there, but he still wasn't happy with the idea.'

'So unless you can persuade him to go against his wife's wishes, the alleged ghosts won't be going anywhere.'

'That's about it. Look, Joe, I'd like to learn more about the case and I suspect the police must have been involved at some point, so I was wondering whether you could take a peep at the relevant files.'

Joe drained his pint, fearing he was about to disappoint his friend. 'Sorry, George, I really don't have time at the moment. I'm fully occupied with the Lexi Verity murder.'

'Any suspects?'

'We have someone in custody but there's still a lot of evidence to gather. If we get the case tied up within the next few days, I'll try and find some information about the pub fire for you. But I'm afraid I can't promise anything.'

George nodded. He understood. They passed the remainder of the evening in pleasant conversation and Joe felt a little more relaxed as he made his way back to his empty flat. Time spent in George's company always had that effect on him.

The following morning, Joe got up early. Although he'd told George he didn't have time to look up the details of the pub fire, their conversation the previous night had intrigued him, so before he had his shower, he took out his laptop and searched for some details about the case. There wasn't much; all he could find was an old piece from the local paper stating that the fire had only affected a couple of bedrooms. And that it had definitely been arson.

Eighteen

Jamilla had been assured by an officer from Merseyside Police that Pascal Allard was expected to report for work when the restaurant reopened on Tuesday, but when Emily was told about the delay she banged her fist on her desk in frustration. Joe told her in his best calming voice that they'd have to be patient. They'd speak to the chef as soon as he showed his face.

To distract her from her disappointment, he told her about his meeting with George the previous evening.

'He thinks it might be linked to an old arson case,' he said. 'I looked it up on my laptop at home this morning, but there wasn't much. Just a couple of news-paper reports.'

'Come on, Joe. We're under pressure here. We've no time to waste on distractions. The media's circling like vultures and the top brass want results.'

'We've got Nathan Corde in custody.' Joe tried to sound optimistic.

'But do we have enough to charge him? Sadly, thanks to TV crime shows, everyone knows to wear gloves, so no prints were left at the scene, and we're still waiting for the lab to get back to us with any DNA results. Let's just hope Corde's been careless and the lab can come up with something. Because if this case drags on much longer, it's going to bring all the conspiracy theorists crawling out of the woodwork.' Emily put her head in her hands.

'What time are we interviewing Corde this morning?'

'No time like the present,' she said, standing up. 'But with no new evidence to confront him with . . .' She gave a long sigh and glanced at her watch, jumping when her phone began to ring. It was one of the officers stationed at the crime scene, and Emily pressed the key so Joe could listen in to the conversation.

'Just wanted to tell you, ma'am. Lord Pilton's returned to the house and he's asking to speak to the detective in charge.'

'That'll be me,' she said, suddenly enlivened by the possibility of a fresh development.

'What about Corde?' said Joe.

'It'll do him good to wait. Let's get over to Eaglethorpe. We can ask Lord Pilton if he knew about Lexi's affair.'

Half an hour later, after battling through Eborby's traffic, they arrived in Eaglethorpe. The sun had decided to shine, showing the village at its best. They passed the Blue Boar, with its colourful window boxes and freshly painted signs. His lordship had been staying there until the police had finished in the rectory, but his call suggested that he'd decided to return home. Joe wasn't sure how he'd feel about moving back to the house if he was in his lordship's position, surrounded by reminders of what had happened. Since Kaitlin's death he'd had no desire to return to Devon. Beautiful as it was, it held too many painful memories.

There was a growing shrine of flowers at the entrance to the rectory drive, and a bevy of journalists had gathered. Camera shutters clicked as the electric gates opened painfully slowly, but Joe and Emily kept their eyes fixed ahead, trying to ignore the intrusion.

'All this attention. This must be what it's like being a celebrity,' Emily muttered. 'Don't envy them, do you?'

Joe didn't answer as the car tyres crunched along the gravel drive. He knew the noise was meant to provide a deterrent for intruders, a natural early-warning system. But as Lexi had been in the pool at the back of the house, she wouldn't have heard it. She'd have been swimming in her expensive white costume, oblivious to Margaret Cramp's failure to lock the French windows. She wouldn't have felt particularly vulnerable as death approached in the form of Nathan Corde. Although he hadn't dismissed the possibility that she'd been killed by someone else entirely; maybe someone she'd trusted.

He thought Emily looked uneasy as she pulled down the passenger mirror to touch up her lipstick and comb her hair.

They were surprised when Margaret Cramp opened the front door to them. She looked drawn and nervous. Her sneaky Botox didn't seem to have worked any magic.

Emily came straight to the point. 'You're still working for his lordship?'

'Yes, of course. Why wouldn't I be?' Margaret sounded jumpy.

'I wondered whether you'd still be here once his lordship found out what you did – or rather didn't do.'

The woman's eyes widened. 'What do you mean?'

'The CCTV cameras. And the French windows. What did you think I meant?'

Joe wondered whether he'd imagined the look of relief on Margaret's face; there for a split second then gone.

'I've promised him that nothing like that will ever happen again. I called the security company and they came first thing yesterday morning,' she said breathlessly. 'His lordship wanted the cameras fixed before he moved back in because of all the journalists who've been making a nuisance of themselves.'

'I know. We saw them hanging round the gate like wasps around a jam pot. Hopefully the fuss will die down once we charge someone. Always does,' added Emily. 'We believe his lordship wants to speak to us.'

'I'll tell him you're here,' said Margaret before she hurried off, leaving them standing in the hall.

'Did you notice how she reacted when you mentioned the CCTV and the French windows? She looked positively relieved, as though she'd been expecting you to say something else.'

'You mean she might have something else to hide?' said Emily.

'Maybe we should have another word.'

'I'll put it on my to-do list.' She sounded as though she was carrying the world's burdens on her narrow shoulders. 'It's growing longer by the minute, so one more thing can't hurt.'

Before Joe could reply, Margaret reappeared and showed them into the drawing room, where Milo Pilton was waiting for them, standing with his back to the empty fireplace, looking slightly awkward.

'Detective Chief Inspector Thwaite, Detective Inspector Plantagenet. Please sit down.'

It was more of an order than an invitation. But they did as they were told.

'You asked to see us,' said Emily.

'I wanted to know how the investigation into my wife's murder is progressing. You have her stalker in custody, I believe. When are you going to charge him?'

'We don't have enough evidence to charge him just yet, but we've obtained an extension to the time we're allowed to hold him. We're questioning him further later this morning,' Joe said formally.

'You are going to charge him, though, aren't you? He mustn't be allowed to wriggle out of this by using some legal loophole.'

'We're still waiting for some forensic results and we'll keep you updated of any further developments.'

Emily jumped in. 'We did actually have a few further

questions, Lord Pilton. We think there are things you haven't told us.'

'What sort of things?'

Joe could tell the man was on his guard.

'We believe Lexi was having an affair with a gardener you employ.'

The shock on Pilton's face was unmistakable. 'How did you find out?'

'We were about to ask you the same question,' said Emily. They already knew, but they wanted to hear him say it.

'If you must know, Maria told me. She seemed to take great delight in it.'

Joe caught Emily's eye. 'Have you been paying Maria to keep you informed of any goings-on while you were away?' he asked.

Pilton's face turned crimson. 'It's not something I'm proud of, but I was protective of my wife.'

'You mean jealous?'

'Not at all,' he said quickly.

'You must have wanted to punish her for betraying you like that,' said Joe.

'You don't understand.'

'Make us,' said Emily.

Joe recalled something Harry York had said during his interview. 'We've been told you paid someone to assault a man who was involved with your former wife.'

'Who told you that?'

'It doesn't matter. Is it true?'

Pilton bowed his head before nodding. 'I'm a man who loves beautiful things. It's my job to deal with works of art; precious jewels and antiques. My wives have both been beautiful, and when someone else steals them from me . . .'

Emily smiled sweetly. 'You react like some thug in a pub who lands a man a punch on the nose if he thinks he's looking at his girlfriend.'

Pilton flinched. This was hardly how he would have viewed himself, but Joe suspected Emily was absolutely right. His lordship looked as though he was about to challenge her accusing words. Then he seemed to change his mind.

'Your wives weren't your possessions. They were people, not things.'

Joe could tell the boss was angry. He put a surreptitious hand on her arm. 'Let's get back to Lexi,' he said, taking over. 'You found out about her relationship with the gardener and you were jealous. Did you pay somebody to attack her? Did you intend to teach her a lesson and it went too far. Presumably you knew about the lack of CCTV?'

'I only found out about that when I returned from the States, I swear. And I can assure you that I only discovered about the gardener the day before I left. I had suspected something was going on, but I only knew for certain when Maria confirmed it. Very well, I admit I was jealous, but I had no chance to do anything about it. By the time I returned, Lexi was dead.'

'You're a wealthy man. You could have arranged the attack from the States,' said Emily, resuming her professional detachment.

'I probably could have done if I'd wished – but I didn't. And if I wanted to teach anyone a lesson, it would have been the gardener. I employed him and he betrayed my trust. I've contacted the company he works for, and he no longer does my garden.'

'Did you challenge Lexi about the affair the day before you left?'

'Yes, but she denied it. She asked me where I'd heard it and I told her about Maria. She was furious. I think she was planning to say something to her. Maybe give them notice. But I told her that Andrei was a good worker and I wouldn't want to lose him and said we'd discuss the matter when I got back.'

There was something cold and calculating about the man's words, and Joe suspected Maria was only kept on because of her reliable husband. Maria and Andrei came as a pair.

'After that, I left. I had a plane to catch from Manchester and Andrei drove me there. I swear I had nothing to do with Lexi's death. She was precious to me and I'm sure we would have sorted things out eventually.' He bowed his head again.

'We'll have another word with Maria – see if she confirms your version of events.'

'Please do.'

'Have you moved back into the rectory permanently now?' Joe asked.

'Yes. Your people appear to have finished here, and to tell the truth, I became rather tired of staying at the Blue Boar. I felt everyone was staring at me whenever I ventured into the public areas, and the media were hanging about outside even though no journalists were actually staying there. That was something I particularly requested, and the landlord agreed.'

'You paid him extra for a bit of privacy?'

'Why not? I'm mourning my wife, and some people wouldn't respect that.'

If Joe had the financial resources, he'd probably have done the same in the circumstances. But he could see the disapproval on Emily's face and he guessed that she considered the arrangement positively feudal. He couldn't shake off the feeling that Pilton's grief didn't go too deep. But if he'd regarded Lexi as a trophy, a lovely possession, this explained a lot. He wondered how long the marriage would have lasted if she'd lived.

Emily stood up. 'We'll be in touch as soon as we have more news.'

Joe rose from his seat too. It was time to go. They needed to have another word with Maria before they left Eaglethorpe, and time was marching on.

Maria admitted to everything, and as they left, they saw Andrei put his head in his hands, a gesture of despair, as though he realised that his wife's greed had put their jobs at risk

As soon as they returned to the incident room, Jamilla rushed up to them, brimming with untold news.

'Remember that man who was reported missing by his wife? Douglas Page. A body's been found.'

Emily stood for a few seconds in stunned silence, and it was Joe who asked the first question.

'Does it look suspicious?'

'Yes, according to the patrol who called it in. The body was found in woodland not far from the university. His car was parked nearby, and ID on the body confirmed it is the missing man.' Jamilla paused as though she was saving the most important revelation for last. 'The cause of death appears to be a knife wound to the neck, and the wound looks similar to the one that killed Lexi Verity. But that was only the FME's preliminary observation. We'll need to wait for the post-mortem to know for sure.'

Joe looked at Emily. 'The weapon that killed Lexi was never found.'

Emily shook her head. 'It could be a coincidence. But we need to find out more about the latest victim.' She looked at her watch. 'Let's get to the scene. I want to see it for myself.'

They grabbed their coats. Nathan Corde would have to wait.

Half an hour later, they were standing in an area of woodland on the edge of the city, not far from the university campus. It was a place frequented by dog walkers, joggers and what used to be known in Joe's parents' day as courting couples. These days you had to add to the list the inevitable gangs of youths hanging around smoking cannabis away from the parental gaze. But it was a dog-walker who'd actually found the body. Or rather her cocker spaniel had sniffed it out.

Douglas Page lay on his front at the foot of a slope on a carpet of dying vegetation. He was surrounded by the whole panoply of crime-scene investigation; CSIs in white overalls, photographers and, kneeling beside the body, Sally Sharpe. When she spotted Joe and Emily, she waved them over.

'What's the verdict, Sally?' said Emily.

Sally looked down at the dead man on the ground. 'The wound looks remarkably similar to the one that killed Lexi Verity. You don't think there's a serial killer on the loose, do you?'

Joe caught Emily's eye. 'Can't see it myself. Glamorous TV star one day and middle-aged businessman the next.'

'How long's he been dead?' Emily asked.

'I'd say around twenty-four hours. But that's just a guess.'

'His wife reported him missing. He went off on Tuesday saying he'd be back by the end of the week, but he never turned up.'

'Maybe it should have been treated as more urgent,' Joe mumbled, remembering the cuttings about Lexi Verity they'd seen at his home.

'We're not clairvoyant,' Emily said sharply. 'From the information his wife gave us, we couldn't have known he was in any danger.'

'Does it look as though he died here, or was the body dumped?' Joe asked.

'There's dried blood around, so I'd hazard a guess that he was killed here,' Sally answered just as one of the CSIs approached Emily. She was holding a clear evidence bag containing a mobile phone. 'We found this in the dead man's pocket, ma'am. His wallet's there too, so we can probably rule out robbery as a motive.'

Emily thanked the young woman and passed the bag containing the phone to Joe. With any luck it would yield some clues. They needed to know how Douglas Page had come to be there. Had he arranged to meet his killer, or was it an unlucky chance encounter? Joe's money was on the former option.

'We need to speak to the wife,' said Emily. 'Or rather the widow. I hate this part of the job . . . breaking bad news. But we need to find out more about him.'

'We should get the tech people to examine his phone.'

'I'd like to have a quick peep first.' They walked back to the car, and as Emily was wearing crime-scene gloves, she slipped the phone out of its protective bag. She fiddled with it for a few moments, and Joe saw a triumphant smile spread across her face.

'It's not locked. Let's see who he's been in touch with.'

After a few moments, she frowned. 'There are texts here from someone called Izzy. "Can't wait to see you. Meet you at the hotel at three." That was on Wednesday morning. The day Lexi Verity was murdered. Three kisses.'

'Girlfriend?'

'Looks like it.'

'Killed by a jealous husband?'

'Or a jealous wife.'

She hadn't finished with the phone. She selected the photographs and scrolled through them. 'Well, well. If that's the girlfriend, she looks very young.'

She passed the phone to Joe. What she'd said was true. The girl in the photographs was blonde and bonny and she looked as though she was only in her teens.

'Could she be his daughter?' Emily wondered.

'According to the report on his disappearance, the couple had no children.'

She shrugged, and Joe suspected she was thinking the worst.

He scrolled down and found more pictures of the girl, including one of her in school uniform. Thankfully none of them were of a sexual nature. Then his heart began to beat a little faster. There were other pictures too, ones he hadn't expected to see: photographs of Lexi Verity. He passed the phone back to Emily.

'Right then,' she said, climbing into the car and fastening her seat belt. 'We'd better have a word with Mrs Page.'

Nineteen

The Page house was large and detached, built in the 1930s, with gleaming new windows and a new Mercedes in the drive. Joe could almost smell the quiet prosperity as Emily rang the video doorbell. This was a household that didn't take any chances with security.

Jackie Page was a thin woman with nervous, almost birdlike movements. When she invited them into a spacious front room filled with expensive-looking modern furniture, she kept glancing towards the door, as though she expected someone to burst in on them any moment. She invited them to sit on a large blue velvet sofa that looked brand new. As he sank down into it, Joe suspected that the act of getting up was bound to be undignified.

It had been a while since Emily had been obliged to break news of a death herself. The death knock was something every officer dreaded, and normally she would have left it to one of her underlings or an experienced family liaison officer. However, on this occasion she decided to come straight out with it, trying to sound as sympathetic as possible and glad that Joe was there with her. He was good at dealing with people at the nadir of their lives. Unlike her, he always seemed to find the right words.

As soon as she'd broken the news, she put a comforting hand on the woman's arm.

'I'm afraid someone needs to identify your husband's body,' Joe said gently. He felt the statement was tactless, clumsy, but he knew it was necessary. 'Unless there's a relative or . . .'

'I'll do it. I don't mind,' Mrs Page replied, as though she meant it. Joe saw Emily raise her eyebrows a fraction. It looked as though the couple hadn't been on the most loving of terms.

'Do you mind if we ask you some questions?' Joe asked. 'Only if you're feeling up to it.'

'OK,' the woman said with a sniff.

'You said your husband, Douglas, had been away since Tuesday and he didn't return at the weekend as expected?'

'That's right. My sister persuaded me to report him missing. She said he might have had an accident.'

'He didn't tell you where he was going?'

She shook her head. 'He's been sneaking off a lot recently.' She hesitated. 'I thought he was involved with another woman.'

'Any evidence of that?'

'Douglas led his life and I led mine, Inspector. He had the good manners not to flaunt his relationships.'

'You told us some material relating to Lexi Verity

was found in his study here, and your sister suggested he might have had something to do with her death. Do you still think there might be a connection?'

A look of uncertainty passed across her face, and Joe suspected that she might have gone along with her sister's suggestion out of pique. She'd felt abandoned, so why shouldn't she get her husband into trouble?

'I don't know. It was just a few pictures cut out of magazines and newspapers, that's all. I never thought he was a particular fan of hers. That's why I was surprised he'd kept them there in his desk drawer.'

Emily took out the phone they'd found and showed Mrs Page the photograph of the girl. 'Do you recognise her?'

'She looks a bit young for Douglas.' Mrs Page averted her eyes. 'My husband was many things, but I never thought he was a dirty old man.'

'I'm afraid we have to ask this,' said Joe. 'You said the two of you led separate lives.'

She looked away. 'We couldn't have children, you see. It never bothered me, but Douglas . . . Over the years, we drifted apart. I know he's had quite a few relationships and I've always turned a blind eye. I have my own career and friends and the arrangement suited us both. I suppose ours became a marriage of convenience.' A look of disgust passed across her face. 'But I must say I'm shocked if he did go with such a young girl. I never thought he was like that for one moment.'

'Did he ever mention Lexi Verity to you?'

She considered the question. 'Now that I think about it, he did say something about her a while ago. She happened to be on TV and he said he was sure he recognised her from years back – before she was famous, he said.'

'Did he say when this was . . . and where?'

Jackie shook her head.

'Tell us about Douglas,' Joe said softly as he leaned forward.

'I met him after he'd inherited the business from his father. He hadn't wanted to work there, but when he was in his late twenties, his father became ill and he stepped in.' She gave a bitter smile. 'He told me he used to be an idealist when he was younger; wanted to put the world to rights. He even joined the police at one time.'

Joe and Emily looked at each other. 'When was this?'

'It must have been in the late 1990s. He said he wanted to make a difference and help people, but that all changed when he took over his father's gambling empire.'

Joe caught Emily's eye and guessed what she was thinking. Who'd choose scraping along on a police officer's salary when you were offered untold riches from a company you didn't even have to go to the bother of setting up?

'Once he was responsible for the firm, he felt people's livelihoods depended on him, so he left the police and put his heart and soul into it. Maybe if he hadn't, we'd still be together. The business made us comfortably off financially, but there's something to be said for following your heart, even if it doesn't pay much.'

'Tell us about the business,' Emily said, genuinely curious.

'His father was a bookie – owned a string of betting shops – but nowadays it's online gambling. Hardly the most noble profession. I suppose his niece will take over now. She's a hard-nosed madam. I'm sure she'll make a success of it.'

'What's the company called?'

'Eborby Gaming.'

The name rang a bell in Joe's brain. Lexi Verity had received a call from the offices of Eborby Gaming a few weeks before her murder, but they'd assumed it was work-related.

'To get back to Lexi Verity – can you remember anything else he said about her?'

'Only that he thought he recognised her from years ago but she looked completely different then. I wasn't really paying attention.'

'So it might not have been her? Just someone who looked like her?'

Jackie shook her head. 'That's one thing you could rely on Douglas for. He never forgot a face. Even from his days in the police. He could walk down a street and pick out someone he'd met twenty or thirty years ago.'

'Could he have recognised Lexi from his time in the police?' Emily asked, unable to keep the excitement out of her voice.

'No idea. He could have come across her at any time over the years, I suppose.' Jackie frowned. 'Surely you can't think he had anything to do with her murder. He might have had his faults, but he wasn't a killer. I can promise you that.'

'But he wasn't at home last Wednesday, the day she died.'

She shook her head and took a tissue from the box on the coffee table, As she wiped her eyes, she looked annoyed with herself for yielding to emotion.

The silence was interrupted by the inappropriately cheerful chimes of the doorbell. Joe rose awkwardly from the meringue sofa and walked into the hall. The visitor turned out to be the family liaison officer Emily had called earlier.

'We'll leave you in peace now,' Emily said after she'd introduced the newcomer. 'But we'll have to keep your husband's phone, I'm afraid.'

Jackie made a dismissive gesture with her hand, that said, 'do what you like with it'.

As soon as Joe and Emily reached the station, they handed Douglas Page's phone to Sunny and Jamilla and asked them to have a closer look at the contents. If it contained any more clues, they needed to know. In the meantime, Emily wanted another go at interviewing Nathan Corde before their time ran out. The DNA results still hadn't come through, but she was pinning her hopes on Corde cracking in the meantime.

Once Joe and Emily had gone down to the interview room, Sunny brought up the photographs on the victim's phone.

'You can learn a lot from the photos people take,' he observed as Jamilla peered over his shoulder to see what he was looking at.

Then Jamilla saw his face suddenly turn pale, as though he'd had a shock.

'Sunny? What is it?' she asked. 'What's wrong?'

'Some of these pictures are of a girl called Isabel. She's a friend of my Leanne's.'

He handed the phone to Jamilla, who frowned as she scrolled through the photos. Then she checked the messages sent and received. 'There are texts here from someone called Izzy.'

'I'm going to call Leanne,' Sunny said, selecting his daughter's number.

After a terse conversation, he turned back to Jamilla. 'Leanne told Pauline that Isabel went missing for a few days but came back yesterday.'

'She didn't tell you her friend was missing?'

'I knew something was wrong, but the truth didn't come out till last night.' Sunny seemed stung by his daughter's failure to confide in him.

'How old is Isabel?'

'Eighteen. She's the year above Leanne – in the sixth form.'

'We need to speak to her.'

Sunny hesitated. 'OK. We'd better tell ma'am when she gets back.'

Jamilla thought he didn't look happy, and she suspected that after the Margaret Cramp connection, the case had trespassed just a little too close to home.

Nathan Corde was still being uncooperative, reciting 'no comment' like a mantra. The clock was ticking, but Emily was confident that she'd be able to obtain a further extension. The man wasn't a criminal mastermind, so if he'd been inside the rectory, he was bound to have left some forensic evidence.

But during the interview, the long-awaited news came through from the lab. No trace of Nathan Corde's DNA had been found anywhere inside the rectory and no trace of Lexi's DNA or blood had been discovered at Corde's makeshift shelter.

Emily reluctantly terminated the interview. 'I'm still applying for another extension,' she said as they made their way back to the office. 'He did it. I know he did.'

Joe couldn't share her confidence, but he said nothing.

As soon as they reached the office, Sunny rushed up to them.

'The photos on the victim's phone. I know who the girl is.'

'Well, Sunny,' said Emily, 'don't keep us in suspense. Who is she?'

He took a deep breath. 'She's a friend of Leanne's – my daughter. She's eighteen, a year older than Leanne, and her name's Isabel. She went missing last Wednesday, and Leanne and her friend Phoebe have been really worried about her. I knew Leanne was keeping something from me and Pauline. I've just spoken to her and she's finally come clean. The girls saw Izzy get into a car with an older man, but she swore them to secrecy. Could the man have been Douglas Page? Was he . . . taking advantage of her?'

'We need to speak to Isabel.'

'Want me to do it?' said Sunny.

Emily looked at him. He was Isabel's friend's dad, another generation. 'Perhaps she'd be more comfortable talking to Jamilla?'

Jamilla was young, lively and pretty. She was also good with people, a sympathetic and unthreatening presence. If Isabel was going to confide in anyone, it would probably be her. She might even regard Jamilla as a big sister figure, providing she didn't emphasise her connection with Sunny.

'Are you up for that, Jamilla?' Emily asked.

Jamilla nodded. 'Perhaps I should have a word with Leanne first, if that's OK. Then I'll speak to Isabel.'

'Good idea,' said Emily. 'But how could Page having pictures of an eighteen-year-old girl on his phone connect him to Lexi Verity?'

Joe didn't answer. He was thinking of the post-mortem they'd be attending the following day; the examination that might confirm whether Lexi Verity and Douglas Page's lives had been ended by the same killer.

Twenty

When Jamilla Dal spoke to Sunny's daughter, Leanne, the thing that struck her most was how worried the girl had been about her friend. Isabel had failed to tell her where she was going even though she'd made her swear to say nothing about her absence. Leanne seemed rather hurt by this apparent lack of trust. Friends should share their secrets, but Isabel had broken this unwritten rule.

Jamilla's next port of call was Isabel herself. At first her mother hovered about, and Jamilla wished she'd go and leave them alone. Her instincts told her that the girl wouldn't open up as long as she was there.

Isabel herself was tall and willowy, with sharp features and blonde hair tied back in a silky ponytail. She stayed standing, seeming reluctant to relax, and kept glancing at her mobile phone as though she was expecting an important message. Or perhaps looking at it had become an ingrained habit.

Isabel's mother offered tea and Jamilla accepted

gratefully. Once the woman had left the room, Jamilla took the opportunity to break the news.

'Isabel, maybe it would be best if you sat down. I've got something upsetting to tell you.'

The girl's eyes widened. 'What is it?'

'Do you know a man called Douglas Page?'

She appeared to freeze.

'You recognise the name? He had your photo on his phone.'

'What's happened to him?'

The next words stuck in Jamilla's throat. But she knew she had to get it over with. 'I'm afraid he was found dead this morning. I'm so sorry.' She paused. 'How did you know him? What was your . . . relationship?'

She was surprised to see a tear trickling down Izzy's cheek. She waited. Joe Plantagenet had once said that patience was an important weapon in a detective's armoury.

'Douglas was my dad. Him and my mum . . . It was before she married my dad – the man I'd always thought was my dad. Douglas got in touch and I got a hell of a shock when he told me who he was. We'd been meeting up for a while and we found we got on really well. We had a sort of . . . bond, if you know what I mean.'

Jamilla nodded. She understood the importance of family ties. 'Tell me where you've been since last Wednesday.

'Like I said, me and Douglas had been meeting for a few weeks, but I really wanted us to get to know each other better. I had a massive row with my mum. She said I was going out too much and not working hard enough for my A levels. She wants me to go to uni, you see, but . . .'

'You're not so keen?'

'I don't know. Anyway, I called Douglas and asked if I could stay with him. He said his wife didn't know about me, but a friend of his owned a cottage near Beverley where I could stay, and it would give us a chance to talk. We met at a hotel and he drove me there.'

'Why didn't you tell your mum where you were going?'

Jamilla saw a flash of anger in Izzy's eyes. 'Because she didn't deserve to know. Douglas told me he'd been paying her for my upkeep all these years but she never said one word about him. She kept the truth about my real dad from me.'

'And you didn't message your friends to tell them you were safe?'

'It went out of my head. I was busy getting to know my dad. They knew I had something planned – I made them swear not to tell my mum – so I never thought they'd be worried.' A sad smile played on the girl's lips. 'Me and Douglas spent a lot of time talking, and it was as though I'd known him all my life.' The tears began to flow down her cheeks. Jamilla passed her a tissue and waited for her to compose herself.

'When did you last see him?'

'He dropped me at the end of my road yesterday morning. Mum was furious when I arrived home, and I knew she'd go ballistic if I said I'd been with Douglas, so I told her I'd been with a boy.'

'Can you tell me what you and Douglas talked about?'

'Everything. What I wanted to do once I'd left school. Family. His job. He told me that him and my mum parted on bad terms. She never told him she was pregnant with me and she went away to have me, so he didn't find out I existed until someone told him a few years later. That's when he got in touch with her.' She rolled her eyes. 'She might not have wanted anything to do with him, but she didn't mind taking his money. She sent him her bank details and he made payments directly into her account. Since then, she's moved house a couple of times and he didn't know where we were living until six months ago, when he hired a private detective to find me.' She gave another sad smile. 'It was just like something from the movies. He said his wife couldn't have children, so I was his only chance of . . .' Another tear slid down her face and she dabbed it away with the crumpled tissue. 'How did he . . .? Was it an accident? A car crash?'

Jamilla hesitated. She couldn't help feeling for the girl, who'd just got to know her father and then almost immediately lost him in the most terrible way. She knew she needed to choose her next words carefully. 'We think someone killed him.'

Isabel shook her head in disbelief. 'No. He wasn't the kind of person anyone would . . . He was so nice.'

'Did he ever mention someone called Lexi Verity?'

Isabel had been fidgeting with the tissue, but all of a sudden her hands became still. 'Yes. He said he'd seen her before she became famous; when she was around my age. He spotted her a few months ago at the opening of one of his betting shops and spoke to her, but she said he was mistaken. Only my dad had this brilliant memory for faces, and he knew it was her. He knew she was lying.'

Jamilla said nothing, thinking that tales of Douglas Page's miraculous recognition skills had probably been exaggerated. On the other hand, any connection with Lexi Verity, however tenuous, had to be taken seriously.

After a few more gentle questions, she stood up to leave. The DCI would be impatient to hear what Isabel had had to say.

Shortly after Jamilla returned to the station and related her conversation with Isabel, Emily received news that made her furious. Nathan Corde's lawyer's application for bail had been successful, and in spite of Emily's strong objections, her superiors had yielded to pressure. Corde was now free, residing in a bail hostel after promising to attend the police station as required. But he'd broken that promise before, when he'd first been released from prison, so to Emily, his assurances just weren't good enough.

'He's bound to do a runner again, Joe. Sometimes I don't know why we bother.'

Joe couldn't help agreeing with her, but one thing was certain. Nathan Corde couldn't have killed Douglas Page, and if Sally Sharpe found evidence at the post-mortem the following morning that the two murders were identical, that would mean that Corde was off the hook.

He saw the DCI staring at the children's pictures that gave her grey office a splash of bright colour, deep in thought. 'If Page dropped Isabel off yesterday morning like she said, he must have been killed soon after that. We need to find out who he met.'

'Isabel said she didn't know. He didn't mention that he was meeting anyone.'

'So maybe the meeting was arranged after he dropped her off. Or he didn't think it was worth mentioning it to her.' Emily sighed. 'We should get home, Joe. We need to make an early start in the morning.'

'Agreed. Don't forget Sally's arranged the post-mortem for nine-thirty.'

A sly smile appeared on Emily's lips. 'You and Sally . . .'

'There is no me and Sally.'

'Just that I always thought you'd make a good couple. If you like women who cut up dead bodies for a living.'

The kiss he'd shared with Sally at the party a long time ago had gone down in station legend. And he knew Emily wasn't going to let him forget it.

As he left the station, he saw that there were still a number of determined journalists hanging around the entrance, hoping to pick up crumbs of fresh information. The powers-that-be had been on at Emily to do another press conference to keep the media up to date on their progress. Lexi Verity's murder had attracted a lot of public interest and Emily was under pressure to get a result. As senior investigating officer, she'd be held responsible if they failed to find the culprit, and the strain was starting to show. Joe hoped that an evening at home with Jeff and the kids would do her some good.

As he was heading for his flat, walking alongside the city walls, his phone rang. It was George Merryweather, so he answered at once.

'George. How are you?'

'I'm well, thank you, Joe. I was wondering whether you're free for another chat this evening.'

Joe's spirits rose. Meeting George the previous night had done him no end of good. He'd been anticipating a quiet evening at home slumped in front of the TV watching something mindless. But time spent in George's genial company was a far more appealing prospect.

'Let's grab something to eat at the Star again.'

'Sounds perfect. Eight o'clock suit you?' George hesitated. 'Are you still busy with that Lexi Verity case?

'Afraid so. And there's been another suspicious death.'

'Oh dear. I wanted to pick your brains, but if you have too much work on . . .'

'I'm still up for the Star. After the day I've had, I'm desperate for a change of scene and some time away from the case.'

'You're so right, Joe. Everyone deserves a break sometime.'

When the call was over, Joe walked on past the entrance to the Museum Gardens. It was busy with people returning home after the end of the working day, but among the crowd he spotted two familiar figures walking close together. Silas Sellie had his arm around Maddy's shoulders in a proprietorial manner. What was worse, in Joe's opinion, was that she didn't seem to mind. They were chatting, and he found their intimacy unexpectedly disturbing.

He couldn't forget what he'd seen in Sellie's flat; the dummy with the rope around its slender neck. Fleur Chandler had described Sellie as a pretentious creep, and a creep was the last kind of person he wanted to see Maddy involved with. But he walked on, telling himself it was no longer his business. Unless, of course, Silas Sellie had something to do with Lexi Verity's death.

Ben Greengrass was feeling overwhelmed by his new home, and this wasn't only due to the cost of the extensive renovations. He'd experienced a strange sense of unease ever since they'd moved into the property, but he'd tried to convince himself it was because he was stuck there alone during the day while the children were at school and Elspeth was out settling into her new job at the theatre. Increasingly she'd been working late, saying that she was still finding her feet and trying to establish herself as part of the new team. But Ben couldn't help wondering whether she kept delaying her return home because she felt the same about the house as he did.

There were still things he needed to sort out; ornaments, books and vases to unpack. Elspeth had wanted to get rid of anything she deemed unnecessary clutter, but some of the ornaments had belonged to his parents and he remembered them from his childhood. As he knelt beside the wooden crate and released the items from their bubble-wrap cocoons, he couldn't help smiling at the memories they evoked. His parents were dead, but the sight of their tawdry treasures brought them back to life for a moment.

He arranged the things round the room, on the empty mantelpiece and the sideboard, knowing that Elspeth was bound to move them when she got home, muttering about junk cluttering the place up. He put some vases away in the utility room, telling himself they'd come in useful for flowers, and soon the box was empty. Another job done.

He went to the cupboard underneath the stairs, knowing there was more to unpack. He was about to take out another of the boxes supplied by the removals firm when he spotted a package behind them; an unfamiliar cardboard box that had nothing to do with the movers. The printed logo on the side suggested it had once contained tins of soup, and he realised he'd never seen it before in his life.

Curious, he pulled it from its resting place and knelt beside it on the wooden floor. The top was sealed with gaffer tape, and he ripped it off. Inside were some children's picture books, old and stained, and a note that someone, probably the builders, had placed on top: *Found in the loft. Didn't like to put in skip.*

There was a doll, its plastic flesh yellowed as though it was suffering from some dire disease, and a few wooden toys, along with a small doll's pram and a miniature high chair. As he pulled the things out, he saw that his fingers were black with soot, and he realised that the items must be survivors of the fire. The sight of the doll made him shudder; there was no way he was going to allow the children to see it. The whole box was going straight into the wheelie bin by the back door. But then something caught his eye. An album covered in wallpaper, once brightly coloured but now stained with soot and grime.

When he took it out and opened it, what he saw made him catch his breath. On each page were faded colour photographs of a man and two children. In all of them, the face of the younger child had been obliterated, stabbed out with a sharp blade. The one child who remained was taller, possibly around eleven or twelve years old, but it was impossible to tell whether it was a boy or a girl. He or she was just a fuzzy image, half hidden at the back of the little group. One of the pictures showed an older teenage girl wearing a short skirt and standing slightly apart from the others, but her face had been damaged too.

Ben dropped the album as though it was contaminated. The hatred behind what he'd found almost knocked the breath out of him. He needed to get it out of the house. Now.

Twenty-One

Joe changed out of his working clothes before going out to meet George, glad to shed the reminders of the day, even though he couldn't forget the wounds he'd seen on Douglas Page's body, wounds that looked remarkably similar to Lexi Verity's. If Sally confirmed it the following morning, Nathan Corde might be out of the frame, and that would dash their hopes of a swift solution to the case.

He found himself looking forward to his meeting with George. The diocesan consultant on deliverance and the occult somehow always managed to help him banish any unwanted inner demons that might be lurking in his head. Being in the presence of goodness might be unnerving for some, but Joe recognised it for what it was.

When he arrived at the Star, he found it busy, mostly with tourists. As his eyes adjusted to the dim light, he spotted George sitting alone in a far corner, already furnished with a pint of beer. After Joe had been to the bar, he joined him, receiving a hearty handshake.

'This is getting to be a habit. Twice in as many days.'

'A good habit, I hope. You look tired, Joe. Hope you haven't been working too hard.'

'Someone's got to keep the good citizens of Eborby safe from evildoers,' Joe replied with a grin as he picked up the laminated menu on the table. He chose fish and chips and George told him to make that two. After they'd ordered and drunk half their pints, Joe spoke.

'Do you remember Maddy?'

'Of course. I did hope you and her . . .'

'So did I, but after Kaitlin . . .'

'You feared a second loss if you committed yourself. I might not agree with your misgivings, but I can understand them.' George took a drink. 'I'm guessing you're concerned about Maddy for some reason. Want to tell me about it?'

Joe hesitated for a moment. 'She's involved with a suspect in our murder inquiry. And I think he might be bad news. We interviewed him in connection with the Verity murder, and I've just seen her with him.'

'You think he did it?'

Joe hesitated. He felt he couldn't lie to George. 'He isn't our prime suspect.'

George looked at him as though he'd read his mind. 'But you still think she's making the wrong choice?'

'He's very charming on the surface, but . . . well, someone who once worked with him described him as a creep. I don't like to think of her with him. That's all.'

'You do realise that envy is one of the seven deadly sins?'

'I'm not jealous. Just concerned for a friend, that's all.'

'Of course you are,' George said with a sceptical smile. 'I think you still have feelings for her. Am I right?'

Joe didn't answer the question. He missed Maddy, and the visceral shock he'd felt when he saw her with Sellie had surprised him, so maybe George was right. However, at that moment he wasn't sure what he wanted to do about it.

George reached out and patted his arm. 'If I were you, I wouldn't worry about it. I've met Maddy and I think you can rely on her common sense.' He took a couple more sips from his glass.

'Too right. Any particular reason why you wanted to see me?'

George took a deep breath. 'I thought it was a long shot, but something's worrying me.'

Joe leaned forward, sensing this was a conversation George wouldn't want any of their neighbours in the pub to overhear. 'What is it?'

'That man I told you about. Ben, the one who asked for my help. He called me a couple of hours ago. I think things are escalating.'

'This is your territory rather than mine, George. In a free moment I did see if I could find anything, but all I can tell you is that the fire was started deliberately. I'm afraid I really haven't time to find out any more at the moment. Sorry.'

Joe took a swig of beer. It tasted good. Then, just as he was about to speak again, their food came. Fish and chips with mushy peas on the side. He tucked in. He'd had so much on his mind that he'd almost forgotten how hungry he was.

'Has Ben made any progress with his research?' he asked after he'd cleared his plate. Even though he'd no time to pursue the case, he couldn't help being curious.

'Not really. He seems to have hit a dead end. All he can find are old newspaper reports, and they only give the bare bones of the story. He's made enquiries among the neighbours, but it seems none of them were there when the fire happened, which is a shame. Honestly, Joe, you should see the poor man. He's worried sick about the children having these imaginary friends – if that's what they are.'

'If I was him, I'd ignore the wife's objections and invite you in. What harm can it do?'

George gave a shrug. 'I wouldn't want to encourage him to go behind her back. Dishonesty always comes to light in the end.' He looked Joe in the eye. 'If we could find out more about what actually happened . . .'

'You said things were escalating?'

'The workmen renovating the place found an old box and shoved it under the stairs. When Ben looked inside . . .'

'What?'

'There was a photograph album. Someone had damaged some of the pictures. A young girl's face had been obliterated with a sharp object. It upset him, as you can imagine. The child in question looked about the same age as his own daughter, Freya; around six.'

'I can see how that would upset him.'

'What if the child in the photographs is young Freya's imaginary friend, Anna?'

Before Joe could answer, George's phone rang. He mouthed an apology and answered it.

'Ben. What's the matter?'

In the silence that followed, Joe could just make out the tinny tones of someone talking fast on the other end of the line. He thought the voice sounded increasingly frantic.

When the call was finished, George looked up at him. The worry on his face was plain to see. 'That was Ben. He's at the end of his tether. Freya won't go to sleep. She says she's playing with Anna, and is laughing and throwing things around. His son's started wetting the bed – his parents' bed – and his wife's threatening to move into a hotel. She's out at the moment and he's asked me to go round because he says he can't cope any more. He says the smell of burning is growing stronger, and his daughter keeps saying Anna is crying and asking for someone called Tilly.'

'If I were you, I'd get over there now. It sounds like he needs help.'

'He's desperate, that's for sure.'

They left the pub together, and as Joe watched his friend hurry off in the direction of Kirkgate, hands in pockets and head bowed against the night-time chill, he felt suddenly worried for him. But he knew there was no room for distractions.

'Have you ever wondered what it would be like to kill someone? To feel that power over life and death? To play God?'

Maddy Owen hadn't invited Silas Sellie back to her flat after their drink, but he'd come anyway, ignoring her polite hints that she needed to be up early in the morning. He'd helped himself to wine and made himself comfortable on the sofa. And now she wished he'd go.

At first she had found Silas exciting and creative, with an attractive edge of unpredictability. And she'd been delighted when he finally asked her out on a date at an upmarket wine bar, after flirting with her at work for weeks. But over the course of the evening, she had started to wonder if he was actually just a pretentious poser and a little . . . strange. Some of the things he did and said had begun to make her uncomfortable.

'I must say it's never occurred to me to want to kill somebody,' she replied.

He swigged down his wine, and once his glass was empty, she grabbed it. It seemed that subtle hints weren't enough.

'You know that detective, don't you? The one with the strange name. Plantagenet.' He savoured the word. 'Now there's a family who thought nothing of disposing of their rivals. They say medieval monarchs were rather like Mafia dons. Pious and thuggish at the same time. Is your Plantagenet like that? Is murder in his DNA?'

'No. Besides, when the Plantagenets ruled England, centuries ago, life was very different.' She made a show of checking the time. 'Sorry, I'm going to have to ask you to leave. I've got an early start in the morning.'

Silas stared at her for a few moments, as though her request had hurt him deeply. Then he reached out and took her hand, squeezing it until she pulled it away.

'I'd think about that if I were you, Maddy. I'm an expert in murder, don't forget.'

'Are you threatening me?' she said, suddenly feeling vulnerable.

He began to laugh. 'Of course not. It was a joke. Have you lost your sense of humour?'

'You should go.'

He rose slowly from the sofa and kissed her cheek. 'See you tomorrow then.'

Once he'd left, her heart beat fast as she double-locked the flat door and utilised the chain. She selected Joe Plantagenet's number on her phone, but then put it down. It was far too late to call him. Besides, maybe Silas was right. Maybe she had imagined the threat behind his words. *I'm an expert in murder.*

Caradoc Karling left the White Swan after what he thought had been a successful psychic evening. Unlike last time, there had been no police presence, although he hadn't felt particularly intimidated by his brush with the forces of law and order. Years ago he'd been forced to come to terms with the fact that some people didn't believe in his powers. But he'd thought DI Plantagenet had kept an open mind during their interview, even though his superior, the motherly DCI Thwaite, had made it clear she was a sceptic.

Unlike the session attended by the two police officers, that evening he'd had no need of subterfuge. He'd seen things very clearly and had been able to reassure a man whose wife had left him a year ago that the woman he was so worried about was now living her best life in the Costa del Sol with a new partner, a statement that had needed all the tact he could muster. He'd been able to see other things too; a motorcycle accident and, more cheerfully, an exam success. But his gift, as some liked to think of it, was often more of a curse, and it could manifest itself at the most inconvenient times. This was one of them.

After leaving the pub, he found himself walking as though he was in a trance. He turned left off Gallowgate into a narrow winding street with old houses on one side and a small stone church surrounded by an overgrown graveyard on the other. He'd done the same thing the previous Thursday, drawn to the place by some force he didn't understand.

As he drew level with the largest house on the street, an ancient building with a protruding upper floor, detached from its cottage-like neighbours, he saw a glow at one of the upper windows. Fire. A man in uniform trying desperately to gain access to the building to extinguish the flames. A young woman with her arm around a traumatised child a few feet away from a man kneeling on the ground weeping bitterly while another woman tried to comfort him, stroking his hair with a secretive smile on her face. Then he felt a pain in his throat. And as he slumped to the ground, he saw it all. Fire and water. Death.

Twenty-Two

The next morning Joe and Emily walked to the hospital in the September sunshine. Sally Sharpe had
arranged the post-mortem for nine-thirty and she was
a stickler for punctuality, even though time no longer
mattered to her lifeless patients.

When proceedings were over, Sally delivered her
verdict. The wound on Douglas Page's neck was virtu-
ally identical to the one that had killed Lexi Verity. If
she were a betting woman, she said, she'd place good
money on the same weapon being used, which meant
that the same killer was probably responsible. Emily
wasn't sure whether this was good or bad news, but she
thanked her all the same.

'A couple more and we'll have a serial killer on our
hands,' Joe said as they left the mortuary.

'Serial killers usually target the same kind of victim.
Lexi Verity and Douglas Page couldn't be more different. One a familiar face on TV and the other a middle-
aged businessman.'

'They were both well off. Could it be someone who had it in for the rich?'

Emily shrugged. 'Who knows?'

'Do you think Leanne's friend Isabel being the victim's daughter is relevant?'

Emily stopped suddenly in the middle of the hospital corridor, causing a passing nurse to change course to avoid her. 'I can't see it myself, but do you realise there's one common denominator in both cases?'

'What's that?'

'Sunny.'

Joe snorted in disbelief. 'Surely you can't think . . .'

'Pauline's cousin was Lexi's housekeeper. And Sunny's daughter is friends with Douglas Page's daughter. In cases like this we always look for a link. And Sunny's a link. You can't deny that.'

Joe was lost for words. Sunny Porter might have been a bit old-school, a solid family man who nipped out for fag breaks and lacked ambition, but he was the last person Joe would suspect of being involved in any way. 'You're not saying we should take him off the case?'

For a brief moment Emily looked undecided. Then she spoke with certainty. 'Maybe for a while. Until Isabel and Margaret have been cleared of all suspicion.'

'I can't see Isabel as a killer. She's only a kid.'

'Kids sometimes kill, Joe. You should know that by now.'

His phone rang. It was the station. On Emily's instructions, officers had been interviewing people who'd known Douglas Page, but so far they'd learned very little. However, there was one piece of good news. Pascal Allard, Lexi Verity's former partner, was back in Liverpool and he wanted to speak to them.

Emily said little as they drove down the M62, past vast new warehouses on the site of a wartime airfield near Warrington that had sprung up like mushrooms since Joe's last visit.

He could tell Emily was thinking about what they were going to ask the chef when they got to Liverpool. Soon they'd be face to face with someone who'd known Lexi Verity before she became famous, so hopefully they'd get a picture of the true woman without the trappings of celebrity. Somehow the image they'd built up of her didn't seem altogether real. It was almost as though they were seeing her through a veil of her own publicity. They needed more.

Pascal lived in a flat on the first floor of a large Victorian house overlooking Sefton Park. It was an area Joe knew well from his childhood, and he recalled that those particular houses used to be rather shabby. Now they'd been gentrified into desirable apartments, and he concluded that the chef must be doing all right for himself.

Allard wasn't at all how Joe had imagined. He was a smallish man with receding hair and a waistline that suggested a love of his own creations. But he also had beautiful warm brown eyes. Joe imagined that in his younger years, when he and Lexi were together, he would have been an attractive man.

'Please. Come in. You would like coffee? Or maybe tea?' He had a pleasant French accent and he spoke quietly, almost without feeling, as though his mind was on something else.

'Tea would be lovely, thanks,' said Emily. Joe could tell by her grateful smile that she was rather taken with the man.

Once they'd settled down with their drinks, she came straight to the point. 'You'll have heard about Lexi's death.'

Pascal bowed his head. 'Yes. I've been back in France for the past few days visiting my brother, so I haven't kept track of the news in the UK. I didn't know until this morning, when someone at my restaurant mentioned it. It came as a massive shock and I called you as soon as I found out, but I'm not sure whether I can be of any help because I hadn't seen her in years.'

'According to her agent, you contacted her recently asking for money.'

The man's eyes widened as he went on the defensive, showing a spark of emotion for the first time. 'That is wrong. I wasn't asking for money, I was offering her an investment opportunity. That's all. My partners and I are planning to open another restaurant in Manchester. It would be an excellent investment and I thought I'd be doing her a favour. The Liverpool branch is thriving. I just wanted to expand and . . .' He took a deep breath. 'The truth is, I thought it would be good publicity to have her name connected to the new venture.'

'What did Lexi say to that?'

There was a long silence. 'Her agent, Artemis James, replied on her behalf and the response was . . . cool. She said Lexi was fully committed and couldn't consider it at the moment. I did wonder whether Lexi had actually seen my email. We parted on good terms. We just went our separate ways, that's all.'

'You never resented her success?' said Joe.

'Of course not. She lived in her world and I live in mine.'

'She could have used her influence to get you on TV cookery shows. If you parted on such good terms, why didn't she?'

Pascal looked awkward. 'I did ask her once, but she said I didn't have the personality.'

'That must have hurt.'

He shook his head. 'I knew she was right. I'm more at home behind the scenes in the kitchen than front of house. I wasn't blessed with . . . what do you English call it? The gift of the gab. I prefer to stay in the background, using my talents that way. But I guess it still hurt to hear her say it. Nobody wants to be reminded of their . . . inadequacies.'

'So you had good reason to resent her?' Emily's question was sharp.

'Not at all. I've learned to accept myself as I am. I'm a good chef with a good team around me and that's enough for me. My relationship with Lexi was in the past, and now I only concentrate on the future. I asked her to invest. She turned me down. It was her loss, as they say.'

'Are you in a relationship at the moment?'

He shook his head. 'I am in the middle of a divorce. My wife has had enough of coming second to the restaurant. It's – what is the phrase? – an occupational hazard. It's hard to find somebody who is willing to put up with the long hours you have to work.'

Joe understood. Police work was like that when they were in the middle of a major inquiry. He imagined restaurant life was equally relentless.

'Where were you last Wednesday?'

'In France. You can check if you like. I flew out from Manchester a week last Thursday and stayed with my brother in Nîmes. I will give you the details if you wish.'

'Thank you,' said Emily. Joe saw her glance in his direction. It was his turn to ask the questions.

'When did you last see Lexi?'

Pascal thought for a few moments, as though he was doing a calculation. 'It must have been over fifteen years ago – when she was still married to Connor Nuffield and before she met Lord Pilton.' His lips formed a sad smile. 'Amazing how time flies. It only seems like yesterday.'

'You've followed her life and career?'

He looked a little embarrassed. 'I've taken an inter-est. You do when you've known somebody, don't you? I read about that stalker who made her life a misery.

That was terrible. I'm glad he was caught and locked up.'

Joe didn't feel inclined to tell him that the stalker had been freed shortly before her murder. 'You must be one of the few people who knew Lexi before she became famous. What can you tell us about her?'

'When I met her, she was twenty-two and was about to start working in TV as a humble assistant, little more than a dogsbody who made the tea and fetched and carried. But she was very ambitious and she gradually got to know the right people and used her charm to get what she wanted. I could tell from the start that she was going to go far.'

'Why did you break up?'

'After a couple of years or so it became clear that a young chef wasn't going to play any part in her life plan. We parted amicably just before I took a job at a top hotel in London. Eventually I heard her career was going from strength to strength and she'd married Connor Nuffield – the star of *Holly and Ivy*.' He paused. 'I told you she was ambitious.'

'So you think that marriage was one of convenience?' said Joe, surprised at Pascal's candour.

'You're putting words into my mouth, Inspector. What I meant is that like attracts like. For a time they were what I believe is known as a power couple; seen at every party and premiere and never out of the media. Nuffield had his demons, I believe; even so, the marriage lasted a while. But in the end the inevitable happened and she moved on to someone with more . . . status.'

'You make her sound very calculating,' said Emily.

'She once told me she had a map for her life. She didn't want to be a nobody. A failure, she called it. That was when I knew it wouldn't take her long to outgrow me,' he added with a sad smile.

'Can you tell us about her background? We haven't been able to find out anything about her prior to her being in a relationship with you and starting her career in the media. Her publicity material says she was born and brought up in Hong Kong because her father was working there. Did she talk much about her childhood?'

'She never spoke about her upbringing. All she said was that her parents were dead and she found talking about them too upsetting. She was only seventeen when they died, you see.' He hesitated. 'I can tell you one thing, though. I suspect Lexi Verity wasn't the name she started off with.'

Joe caught Emily's eye. 'Do you know what her real name was?'

'Sorry, I don't. It's just that when we first met, she mentioned that she'd changed it because it sounded better than her real one. I asked her about her real name but she said it didn't matter. She'd decided to become a different person.'

Joe's heart sank. If Lexi Verity wasn't even the name she was born with, it was going to be harder than they'd feared to find out about her past.

'There was a file she kept hidden. I found it once, and when I asked her about it, she became angry and accused me of spying on her. I think that's when our relationship began to . . . The beginning of the end, as they say.'

'Did you see what was in the file?' This was the first intimation that Lexi Verity had had secrets she'd wanted to keep hidden, and Joe felt a sudden burst of optimism.

'No. She snatched it from me before I could open it.' He thought for a few moments. 'I've remembered something she did mention. She said that before we met, she'd been in hospital to have surgery.'

'Cosmetic surgery?'

'I'm not sure. I had to have my appendix removed soon after we met and she said she hated hospitals. When I asked her why, she said she'd had an operation once and it had taken a while to heal. And before you ask, she didn't say what the operation was or where she had it done.'

'And she never mentioned any siblings or extended family?' Emily asked.

Pascal shook his head. 'No. It was as though she'd arrived in the world like Venus in that painting by Botticelli. Fully formed, rising in beauty from the waves.'

Joe nodded. It was a good, if poetic, way of putting it. But it didn't solve the mystery.

'You must have been curious,' said Emily. 'If I'd met someone who was so mysterious about their background, I know I wouldn't have rested until I found out what they were hiding.'

Pascal smiled. 'That is why you became a detective, Chief Inspector. I am a humble chef, and she didn't encourage questions.'

'Did she say what she'd done before landing the TV job?'

He sat back in his armchair. Joe thought he looked relaxed, not like a man who had anything to hide.

'She said she'd done various things before we met.'

'What kind of things?'

'I don't know. She was very vague about it.'

'How did you meet?

'In a bar. I suppose you could say we met by chance. We got talking and I asked her out. On my night off we went to a little place I knew. Cheap and cheerful – I was only a junior chef back then and I hadn't much money. She didn't seem to mind.'

'When you met her, was she with friends?' Emily asked hopefully. If any friends could be traced, it might help them find out more.

'No. She was working behind the bar. Said it was her last week. It had been temporary until she began her new job with the TV company.'

'Which bar was this?'

'Somewhere near Covent Garden. I was in London a couple of years ago and I saw that it had closed. The restaurant where I worked was nearby. She was living in a rather sad bedsit at the time, but we moved in together after a couple of months.'

'Did you meet any of her friends or relatives then?'

Pascal shook his head. 'No. She always said she was completely alone in the world, and any friends we mixed with were mine rather than hers.'

'That sounds sad,' said Emily.

'Now that I think about it, you're right. But she seemed contented enough at the time. Our relationship lasted two years, during which we gradually grew apart as she devoted more and more time to her career.'

'Did you resent that?'

He shrugged. 'A little at first, I admit. But I knew she was the type of person who wanted more out of life. I saw her change. Blossom. Once we'd split up I think she had other relationships, but nothing serious until she got together with Connor Nuffield. I'd met someone else by then, so I had no regrets. My time with Lexi had run its course.'

They thanked him and rose, asking him to contact them if he remembered anything else. As they left his apartment, the sun came out, and Joe noticed that the trees around the park hadn't yet begun to change to their autumn brightness.

'Did you hear what Allard said about Lexi deciding to become a different person?'

'Lots of people reinvent themselves.'

'But didn't you notice that his words were similar to what Caradoc Karling said when we spoke to him? That at one time Lexi Verity might have been another person altogether.'

Twenty-Three

Joe felt optimistic as he headed to the station the following morning. He was a naturally brisk walker, and when he arrived at work he almost ran up the steps, eager to resume the investigation. Their talk with Pascal Allard the previous day had given them a lot to think about. Emily had been sceptical about any link with Caradoc Karling. Joe preferred to keep an open mind

As soon as he reached his desk, his phone rang. When he answered, it took him a few moments to recognise the panicked voice on the other end of the line. Then he asked Maddy to calm down and tell him what was wrong.

'It's Silas. I was expecting him to come into the museum today. The exhibition opens in a few days, but he hasn't turned up and he's not at his flat.' There was a short silence before she carried on speaking. 'I looked in the exhibition room first thing this morning and found . . .'

'What did you find?'

'Lexi Verity was discovered in a swimming pool with her throat cut. Is that right?'

'Something like that.' The circumstances of Lexi's death had been reported in the press, but Joe was reluctant to go into any extra detail. 'Why do you ask?'

'When I checked on the exhibits for the famous murders exhibition, there was one I hadn't seen before. Silas was working on it last night and it must have been a last-minute addition. It was a mannequin in a swimsuit lying in a pool with blood painted on her neck. The hair was just like Lexi Verity's. I think he's re-created her murder.'

Emily's reaction to the news was anger, and Joe stood and listened while she let off steam. 'That man thinks he's too bloody clever. Art?' She snorted. 'Sheer bad taste, that's what it is. And it's an ongoing inquiry, so he's in big trouble once I get my hands on him. Silas Sellie. Silly's a better name for him.'

'Do you want to get over to the museum?'

'You go, Joe. I'll stay here and hold the fort.' A sly smile formed on her lips. 'I'm sure you'll be able to comfort Maddy if you find she's in shock.'

Joe opened his mouth to object, but in view of what he'd just learned, he felt obliged to investigate.

Half an hour later, he was knocking on the door of Maddy's office. When she opened it, she looked pleased to see him. Pleased and relieved.

'I suppose I should take a look at what you found.'

Without a word she set off, leading the way through the dimly lit Victorian street, where visitors wandered round looking in shop windows, marvelling at how people managed to exist before the age of computers – and even before electricity.

In the flickering lamplight she pressed a keypad next to a hidden door. Immediately they were back in the present day. Joe blinked as his eyes adjusted to the harsh fluorescent light.

'It's through here,' said Maddy, her eyes fixed ahead as she walked on. When they came to a set of double doors, she stopped. 'We're just putting the finishing touches to the exhibition. I can promise you this particular exhibit wasn't part of the plan.'

She used another keypad to unlock the door and let Joe go on ahead, hanging back as though she was reluctant to see the thing again.

Joe stepped into a spacious room divided into sections by movable partitions adorned with pictures and information. Like the Victorian street, it was dimly lit, and most of its contents were shrouded in dust sheets. It struck him that it was the sort of place where anyone could hide undetected.

He turned to Maddy. 'Can you show me, please?'

She walked to the end of the room, where a display was shrouded beneath white sheets, and hesitated for a few moments before twitching the covers aside. Joe stepped forward and gasped. A life-size model of a blonde woman with a marked resemblance to Lexi Verity was lying on an expanse of some material convincingly painted to resemble the blue water of a swimming pool. There was a vicious gash on the model's neck, and mock blood trailed from the wound into the surrounding 'water'. He found it hard to tear his eyes away from the depiction of the violent death he'd been called in to investigate the previous week.

'Where is he?'

'If you mean Silas, I don't know. Like I said, he hasn't turned up, even though he's meant to be putting the finishing touches to the exhibition. He's not at his flat. I've checked. And he isn't answering his phone.' She paused. 'I know what you're thinking. If he made this display, he must have been at the murder scene. He must have actually seen it, don't you think?'

Joe put out a hand to touch her arm, an instinctive gesture of support. After a second, he withdrew it. He didn't want to be accused of taking advantage of her obvious confusion.

'If it's any comfort, he's got a few things wrong. The swimsuit's the wrong colour – it was white, not pink. And she was floating on her front rather than her back.'

'The mistakes could have been deliberate. He's devious.'

Joe's spirits suddenly rose. 'You and him . . .'

Maddy gave a bitter smile. 'Are nothing. We went on one date, but I soon realised he's far too weird for me. When I first met him, I thought he was so . . . gifted. He said he wanted to challenge the world and use his art to make people think. Later I came to realise that what he considered daring and exciting was just putting two fingers up to convention. Like an irritating kid trying to show off how clever he is by shocking the grown-ups.

'I told him I didn't want to carry on seeing him outside work. I said that from now on we should keep our relationship strictly professional.'

'How did he react to that?'

She didn't answer for a few moments. Then she spoke so quietly that Joe had to strain to hear her. 'He called me an unadventurous bitch. Said I was boring. Old beyond my years.' She gave a humourless laugh. 'Trouble is, he might be right.'

'You're not boring. You just have empathy with the victims.'

She looked round the room. 'Most of the murders in this exhibition are historic; the latest is from the 1950s.' She counted them off on her fingers. 'There's the trunk strangler; the highwayman in the 1780s who killed three people when he held up a mail coach just outside the city; the Victorian man who drowned his maid in the bath; the chimney sweep who killed his apprentice; the wife who poisoned five husbands in 1896. All notorious local cases from the past. That's why I was so shaken to find Lexi Verity among them. But then Silas says his aim is to shock.'

'He should do my job for a few weeks. See the reality of crime. That'd cure him. What are you going to do about that exhibit?'

'I'll have it removed, of course. Silas might consider that sort of thing cutting edge, but I don't and I have the final say. I'm going to have it dismantled so he can't sneak in here and put it back.'

Maddy led the way back into the corridor, switching off the lights, returning the shrouded killers and their victims to darkness, and they walked to the museum entrance in silence. As Joe was about to leave, she asked a question.

'Do you think Silas killed Lexi Verity?'

'Do you?'

'Let's just say it wouldn't surprise me.'

Twenty-Four

Maddy's words echoed through Joe's head as he made his way back to the station. She seemed to think the depiction of a recent murder was exactly the sort of thing that would appeal to Sellie's warped way of looking at the world; something he hoped would taunt the police and shock the public. Joe suspected she could be right. But she'd also refused to rule out the possibility of his guilt.

When he described what he'd seen at the museum, Emily wrinkled her nose in disgust. 'What a bastard,' she said. 'If any of Lexi's friends or her husband happened to hear about it . . .'

'You don't have to tell me that,' Joe replied. 'Maddy's going to have it removed and dismantled.'

'Good. Anyway, we need to speak to Silas Sellie; let's see if we can wipe the smug smile off his face.'

'There might be a problem. Maddy was expecting him at the museum this morning, but he seems to have disappeared.'

'I'll send someone round to his address. He might have turned up.' Emily paused, turning a pen over and over in her fingers, deep in thought. 'Do we know of any connection between Silas Sellie and Douglas Page?'

'Nothing so far. Any more progress with the Page angle?'

'His study at home has been searched, but we need to talk to his secretary and colleagues at Eborby Gaming.' She consulted some scribbled notes in front of her. 'Mrs Page said she'd no idea why her husband would be targeted and she doesn't know of any connection between him and Lexi Verity other than those press cuttings found in his desk and the fact that he said he recognised her from a long time ago. But perhaps we asked her the wrong questions. I'll ask Jamilla to pay her a visit.'

She stood up and began to pace around the room. Then she stopped abruptly and looked out into the main office. The atmosphere was tense as the team busied themselves looking for something, anything, in the lives of Lexi Verity and Douglas Page that might provide a clue to their deaths.

They had two cases to work on now and the media had been piling on the pressure. Emily was doing her best to keep morale up, but Joe suspected her energy levels were starting to flag.

'I forgot to make the kids' packed lunches this morning,' she said unexpectedly. 'Jeff says I'm becoming obsessed with this case.'

'We're all guilty of that.'

'Tell you what, Joe, let's get out into the fresh air.

Douglas Page's company office is in that new building in Hussgate, just outside the city walls.'

Joe knew the building. It was modern, glass and steel, and he was surprised it had been given planning permission as it was in such close proximity to a historic location. But the workings of the council planning office were a mystery to most people in the area.

He had only just returned from the museum, but he had no objection to another outing. When they arrived at Eborby Gaming's well-appointed offices, they were given visitors' lanyards and told to take a seat. Someone would be down to see them. The young woman on reception said how sorry they were to hear about Mr Page. He was a gentleman, she added meaningfully. Joe took it to mean that some who worked there couldn't be described as such. But that was a concern of the company's HR department, not the police.

He could tell that the ten-minute wait was making Emily tetchy. But just as she was approaching the reception desk to ask how long they were going to be kept waiting, a middle-aged woman appeared. She was dressed in a tweed skirt and sensible shoes and looked the capable, no-nonsense sort, a woman after Emily's own heart.

'Chief Inspector Thwaite and Inspector Plantagenet? I'm so sorry to keep you waiting,' she began as she shook the detectives' hands. 'Mrs Rita Catterick, Mr Page's PA. Pleased to meet you. I was on an important video call that went on longer than I anticipated. With

Mr Page's death ...' She didn't have to finish the sentence. Joe and Emily understood. The demise of the boss must have thrown the company into turmoil.

They were led up a sweeping staircase to a sumptuous office on the first floor. The room was filled with light and afforded a spectacular view over the city walls. It was lined with gleaming dark wood bookcases and dominated by a huge antique partner's desk. Their feet sank into the thick carpet as they crossed the room towards a smaller office behind a heavy oak door – Mrs Catterick's domain. This too would have been considered impressive in most commercial situations, and Joe saw Emily looking round admiringly.

'We'd like to ask you some questions about Mr Page,' she began.

'Of course. Anything I can do to help.' Mrs Catterick took a snowy white handkerchief from her pocket and clutched it in her hand as though she was anticipating tears.

'How long had you worked here?'

'Twenty years. I worked for Mr Page's father before him.'

'What was Mr Page like?' Joe asked.

There was a short silence before she answered. 'He was well liked and always generous to his staff. I haven't a bad word to say about him,' she added with a determined nod. 'His death has come as a shock to us all.'

Joe suspected she was giving them the edited version. He tried again. 'Was there anyone he didn't get on with?'

Mrs Catterick didn't answer straight away. It was as though she was choosing her words carefully. 'There were people – clients or punters, if you will – who found themselves in financial trouble, of course. It's the nature of the business. There was one woman whose son killed himself because of substantial debts. Blamed it on his addiction to gambling and led a media campaign against this company in particular.'

'How did Mr Page react to that?' Emily asked.

Mrs Catterick sighed. 'Douglas believed that everyone was responsible for their own actions. He made the right noises, of course. Said the company offered help to those who found themselves in trouble.'

'And do they?'

She didn't answer the question.

'Would Mr Page have dealt with the matter personally?'

'Of course not. That would have been the responsibility of the PR department. Mr Page would have had no direct contact with the people involved with the campaign.' A look of uncertainty passed across her face. 'Look, I don't like to speak ill of the dead . . .'

'This is a murder inquiry,' said Emily. 'We need a full picture if we're going to catch whoever killed him.'

'Mr Page was one for the ladies. Had a bit of a reputation, although he was always a perfect gentleman to me. I overheard him speaking on the phone a few weeks ago – by accident, of course; I wasn't listening in deliberately.'

'Of course not,' said Joe. He knew a half-truth when he heard one, but he didn't want to discourage this new fit of candour. 'What did he say?'

'He was talking to a woman. He said he wanted to meet her and he sounded quite sincere. As though he was genuinely affected by her. I think he called her something like Izzy or Isabel.'

'And you overheard this by accident?' Emily asked. She suspected the woman had been nosing into her boss's personal life. If she'd been in Mrs Catterick's position, she would have done exactly the same.

'That's right.'

'We've spoken to Isabel. And to Mrs Page, of course.' Joe looked at Emily and she gave him a small nod. 'Isabel is Mr Page's daughter from a previous relationship.'

Mrs Catterick nodded slowly. 'I see. Did Mrs Page know about the daughter?'

'We don't think so.'

'You don't think she found out and . . . I mean, she might have lost patience with him and . . .'

'We're not ruling anything out at this stage,' said Emily non-committally.

It had been Jackie Page who'd reported her husband missing and they hadn't regarded her as a serious suspect. But Mrs Catterick's words made Joe wonder if they'd been too swift to dismiss the possibility.

'Are there any other women you know about? Ones who became involved with Mr Page and who might bear a grudge against him?'

'I understand there were others, but I'm afraid I

don't know who they were. Apart from Fiona in Accounts. They had a brief fling about a year ago. His poor wife had a lot to put up with, if you ask me.'

Joe was pleased that the woman was beginning to open up to them. He'd feared that whatever loyalty she might have felt to her late boss would trump the temptations of scandal and gossip, but it seemed he was wrong. He saw that Emily was listening intently. There was nothing she loved so much as a touch of indiscretion. But it turned out that Mrs Catterick was long on supposition and short on hard facts. Apart from Isabel, the newly acknowledged daughter, and Fiona from Accounts, her knowledge was disappointingly vague.

'Has he ever mentioned Lexi Verity?'

'No. I heard about her murder. Terrible. You can't think Douglas had anything to do with it?'

Joe and Emily didn't answer the question.

'Lexi Verity received a call from these offices a month ago,' said Joe. 'Do you know anything about that?'

Mrs Catterick looked puzzled and shook her head. 'No. But Mr Page often made private calls.'

'What about Silas Sellie?'

'Sorry. I don't recognise that name.'

'Is there anything else you can tell us?' Joe asked, fearing they'd learned all they were going to. Fiona from Accounts would be spoken to in due course, but he suspected they'd draw a blank there.

'I'm sorry, I can't think of anything. But if I do . . .'

As they left Eborby Gaming, the sun went behind a cloud and Joe's phone began to ring. It took him a few moments to recognise the voice on the other end of the line.

'I need to speak to you,' said Caradoc Karling. 'I've remembered something. I think I might have seen Lexi Verity's killer.'

Twenty-Five

'Seen as in imagined? Or seen in real life?'

Joe could hear the scepticism in Emily's voice. 'Not sure. And we won't know unless we ask. He says he's at home if we want to speak to him. Coming with me?'

Emily shook her head. Her fair curls looked even more unruly than usual. With the hours she had to work and her domestic responsibilities, there was little time for personal grooming. 'No, you go. I'd better get back. I'm sending someone round to Silas Sellie's flat. I want him picked up. I'm dying to see what he's got to say for himself.'

When they parted, Joe headed down Gallowgate towards Caradoc Karling's flat, hoping he wasn't wasting his time. When he reached the narrow snickleway, he knocked at the familiar door and waited. After a while, Karling appeared. He looked anxious, and Joe wondered why.

'You said you have something to tell me.'

Karling didn't answer. He led Joe upstairs and invited him to sit, offering tea as though he was trying to put off the moment when he would make his revelation. Joe refused refreshment. He wanted to get on with it.

Karling sat down heavily. 'I hope you don't think I deliberately failed to tell you when we last spoke. The fact is, I'd forgotten all about it until now. And when you arrested that stalker, I thought I'd only be wasting your time if ... Do you still think the stalker was responsible?'

'There was insufficient evidence, so we've had to release him.' Joe hated saying the words. They sounded like an admission of failure.

'Somehow I knew it wasn't him.'

'Do you know who it was?'

Karling bowed his head and placed a finger on his forehead, a gesture of concentration. After a while he looked up. 'I'm sorry. The picture is still very faint, but I have a strong feeling that what I'm about to tell you could be important.'

Joe leaned forward, trying to curb his impatience. 'What is it?'

After a short silence, Karling spoke again. 'Three weeks before Lexi's death, I went to the rectory. It was my first visit; she'd contacted me through Harry, her gardener, and asked to see me because something was worrying her. Someone from her past who'd reappeared and she didn't know what to do.'

'Who?'

'I couldn't see clearly and she didn't tell me. I make a point of never asking, you see. If my clients give me too many details, I might be accused of cheating.'

'I can understand that,' said Joe.

'I could sense she was worried and that she was concerned about someone she'd once protected. A child. I felt that she was carrying a burden of guilt . . . and that this guilt would put her in danger. I warned her to take great care. On subsequent occasions when we met, I smelled burning and felt panic.'

'Connected with the child she wanted to protect?'

'These things aren't always clear.'

'You mentioned burning when we spoke a few days ago,' said Joe.

'I know, but there's something new I need to tell you. When I visited Lexi that first time, I passed someone on the drive. They were leaving just as I arrived.'

'Who was it? Can you describe them?'

'It was a man. Medium height. Well dressed and middle-aged. He looked like a prosperous businessman, although I wasn't taking much notice because my thoughts were focused on my meeting with Lexi. I needed to be in the right frame of mind, you understand.' He took a deep breath. 'I've been meditating, trying to recall any details that might help you, but I'm afraid that's all I remember.'

'So it could have been anyone?' Joe found it hard to hide his disappointment. 'I suppose so.'

'Did Harry York mention seeing this person?'

'I don't think he was working there that day.'

'Did you see this man's face?'

'Briefly, but he was hurrying away.' He took a deep breath. 'I never gave him much thought because he didn't look like a crook. He looked very respectable. I thought he might have been her accountant or . . .'

Joe's mind was working overtime. The description was frustratingly vague, but it didn't sound as though the stranger was up to no good, although you could never tell. Con men could look very plausible.

'Have you ever come across a man called Douglas Page?'

Karling shook his head. 'Why?'

'His name hasn't been released to the media yet, but he was found murdered. And there are similarities to the death of Lexi Verity.'

The colour seemed to drain from Karling's face. 'Oh dear. I sensed that it wouldn't finish with Lexi's death.'

'And you didn't think to mention this?'

He sniffed. 'I suspect your chief inspector would have scoffed. Just as I know she wouldn't have taken my feelings about Lexi protecting a child seriously.'

'That might be true. I prefer to keep an open mind,' said Joe.

He produced the photograph of Page that his wife, Jackie, had provided and passed it to Karling. The man stared at it for a few seconds, then his eyes lit up with recognition. 'I only caught a brief glimpse, but I'm sure this is the man I saw at the rectory. Either him or someone very like him. You say he was murdered?'

'That's right. Did Lexi say anything about him?'

'No. I'm sure of that.'

Joe felt a frisson of excitement. If Karling was right about Page visiting the rectory, this confirmed that the two victims had been in recent contact. He couldn't wait to share his new discovery with Emily, but first he decided to ask the question that had been at the back of his mind since his first encounter with the psychic.

'You said when we last met that Lexi had once been someone different.'

'I had a strong sense of that, yes. Mind you, it could have meant that she led a different life before she became famous. I don't want you to read too much into it.'

'Could this other life be connected with the child she wanted to protect?'

Karling hesitated, and a distant look appeared in his eyes, a look Joe had seen before. 'Possibly. But I sensed a lot of guilt, maybe about an affair or something like that. And I'm not sure whether the danger was threatening the child . . . or if it was actually coming *from* the child.'

Then something seemed to snap him back to the present. 'I'm afraid it's all very hazy.' He looked Joe in the eye. 'I'm sorry, but my mind has been rather confused lately. Violent death, you see. It's not something I encounter very often.'

Joe took his leave and walked back to the station, so preoccupied with his own thoughts that he almost bumped into a Japanese tourist as he walked beneath the medieval edifice of Boothgate Bar, one of the ancient city gates still intact and standing proud, guarding the city and its inhabitants over the centuries. After profuse apologies, he continued walking, certain that Karling had been telling the truth about Douglas Page visiting the rectory in the weeks before Lexi Verity's murder. And he was intrigued by the psychic's claim that a child Lexi had been protecting might have been a source of danger. But he knew what Emily's reaction to that would be. She'd tell him to stick to the facts.

Sunny was busy at his desk, but he looked up and greeted Joe with a wave. Joe was glad that the sergeant seemed to be back to his usual self now that Leanne's worries about Isabel had been sorted out. Also, according to Sunny, Margaret Cramp had settled back into life at the rectory. It appeared that Lord Pilton had chosen to forget about her recent lapses, and she was busy making herself indispensable to her employer. It was still at the back of Joe's mind that Lexi could have threatened Margaret's cosy domestic arrangement if she'd made an issue of her mistakes. But the housekeeper's alibi for the time of Douglas Page's death had been checked and put her in the clear. She'd been with his lordship at the time and hadn't left the rectory all day, not even to visit Hilary, who was now at home in the care of her disapproving mother.

'No sign of Silas Sellie,' Emily said as he walked into her office. 'How did you get on with our psychic? Don't tell me. You're going to meet a dark, beautiful stranger and go on a long journey.'

'Very funny,' Joe said as he flopped down into the chair by the desk. 'He told me something far more interesting than that.'

When he went on to reveal that Douglas Page had been spotted visiting the rectory, Emily's eyes shone with excitement.

'It's not another of his visions, is it? You're sure he's not pulling your leg?'

'No. It was about three weeks before the murder, so he didn't think it was relevant. He said he'd been giving it a lot of thought and had decided to tell us just in case it turned out to be important.'

'If he's telling the truth and he wasn't imagining things.'

'I don't think he was. We know Page kept those cuttings about Lexi in his office at home, and she also received a call from his office.'

Emily's phone rang, and after a short conversation, she looked up.

'That was Isabel. Page told her he knew Lexi Verity and she's remembered more about it. She's coming to the station to add to the statement she gave to Jamilla.'

Twenty-Six

Isabel seemed nervous when Joe met her in reception. It was clear she'd been crying, and the mascara she had probably applied so carefully that morning had begun to run. He introduced himself, then led her into the comfortable interview room on the ground floor where Emily was waiting.

Emily stood to greet the girl with a welcoming smile before inviting her to sit and handing her a tissue.

'Thanks for coming in, Isabel. Are you sure you feel up to talking to us?'

Isabel nodded, sniffed and dabbed her eyes.

Emily opened her handbag and passed her a tiny mirror. 'Don't worry, love. You take your time,' she said.

Once Isabel had cleaned herself up, Emily continued. 'Tell us about Douglas Page. I believe you went off with him without telling your mum where you were going?'

Her voice was gentle. But the girl hesitated before replying and blushed.

'I already told that officer who came to see me.'

'Jamilla?'

'That's right.'

'We've seen the statement you gave, but we'd like to hear it in your own words.'

Isabel sniffed again and straightened her back, ready to begin. 'When Douglas got in touch, I was a bit scared of meeting him at first, but he turned out to be really nice. Better than I could have hoped. That's why I wanted to spend some time with him; so we could get to know each other.' Her eyes filled with tears again. 'I'd only just found my real dad and then someone went and killed him. It's not fair.'

'I agree,' Joe said softly. 'It's not fair. That's why we need to find out who killed him.'

Isabel nodded vigorously. 'When you catch whoever did it, you should hang him.'

Joe was surprised to hear such vehement words coming from the mouth of someone so young, but he guessed that her emotions were running high. He saw Emily reach over and put a comforting hand on the girl's arm.

'Is there anything you can tell us that might help us catch your dad's killer? Did he mention that anyone had been bothering him – or that he was worried about something?'

Isabel didn't answer for a few moments. At last she spoke. 'He never mentioned anything like that, but . . . When we were staying in the cottage, we were watching telly one evening and Lexi Verity's murder was on the news. My dad said he'd met her once a long time ago, before she became famous.'

'You mentioned that in the statement you gave to Jamilla.'

'I know, but I was still in shock then and everything went out of my head. Now that I've had time to think, I've remembered something else he said. He told me she had a different name back then.'

'Did he say what that name was?' Joe sat forward, Caradoc Karling's words echoing in his head. Lexi Verity had once been a different person.

Isabel shook her head. 'I think it was something beginning with T. Terry or Tilly, something like that.'

Joe leaned forward, suddenly alert. 'Tilly?'

Isabel suddenly looked unsure of herself. 'I think so but I can't be sure. It might have been Tammy. Sorry, I was only half listening.'

'Is there anything else you can tell us?'

She looked up. 'You know my dad used to be a policeman when my mum met him; when he was young?'

'Yes,' said Joe. 'We've been trying to find details of cases he worked on. Just in case one of them might be connected to his death.'

'Well he said he met Lexi Verity while he was working in the police. I think she might have been a witness in one of his cases. He told me he'd recognised her when he saw her on telly a few years ago, and he'd been following her career. He could recognise people

258

even after years had passed and they'd changed their hair and all that. Said it was his superpower.'

She gave a sad smile, and Joe felt for her.

Emily leaned forward. 'Did your father say anything about the case Lexi was involved in?'

'Sorry. We had eighteen years to catch up on and he only mentioned it the once. But I thought I'd tell you about it, seeing as she was murdered as well.'

Joe took a deep breath. 'A witness has come forward who saw your father calling at Lexi Verity's house in Eaglethorpe. Did he mention that to you at all?'

They weren't expecting a positive reply, but as soon as the words had left Joe's lips, Isabel looked up, her eyes shining. 'He did say something about going there because he wanted to tell her something.'

'What did he want to tell her?' Joe could tell Emily was holding her breath, waiting for the reply.

Isabel thought for a while before answering. 'I think he said he needed to tell her he'd seen someone he recognised.' She shook her head, and her silky blonde hair fell around her face. 'I thought he was trying to impress me by saying he knew Lexi Verity. But . . . well, she's not really on my horizon, let's put it like that. It's mainly old people who like her shows, isn't it.'

Joe got the message. To Isabel and her contemporaries the likes of Lexi Verity were decidedly uncool.

'When did he say he'd visited her?'

'I think it was about three weeks ago – maybe a bit longer.'

'And he went there because he thought he'd recognised someone?'

She suddenly looked unsure of herself. 'I don't know.' A worried expression appeared on her face. 'Lexi Verity was murdered. Do you think Dad was killed because he knew something about it?'

Joe looked at Emily, wondering how much to tell the girl. She gave a little nod. It was time for the truth.

'We think it's possible.'

There was a long silence before Isabel took a deep, shuddering breath. 'My dad asked me if I'd like to take over his company after he retired. He said it would be years yet, but if I wanted to start working there instead of going to uni, I could learn all about it. He said I was his only child and he'd like me to inherit it one day.' The tears began to flow again. 'He said he owed it to me. He said blood was thicker than water and he promised to put things right. He said he'd already set things in motion to make everything official.'

Emily passed her a handful of tissues, wondering whether Douglas Page's best intentions would come to nothing.

They saw Isabel off the premises, having arranged for a patrol car to give her a lift home. Emily thought it was the least they could do for her in the circumstances.

There was something Joe couldn't keep to himself any longer. As they were climbing the stairs to the CID office, he told Emily about his meeting with George Merryweather a couple of nights before.

'Is your mate still doing his exorcisms?'

Joe chose to ignore the mockery behind her question. 'Someone called him in to deal with a situation.'

He told her about Ben and the problem of his daughter's imaginary friend, Anna. And her brother's terror of somebody called Jack. He could see the scepticism on the DCI's face.

'Sounds like a case of overimaginative kids to me. If my kids moved into a creepy old place opposite a graveyard in a strange town, I think they might react the same – if I didn't nip it in the bud.'

'The little girl says her imaginary friend keeps asking for someone called Tilly. Isabel said—'

'Isabel wasn't sure. She thought it might have been Terry. Or Tammy. Besides, Tilly's a popular name, and there are lots of Annas and Jacks about. Maybe they knew kids with those names in their old school and they're making it all up. And kids at the new school might have heard about the house from their parents or grandparents.' Emily huffed. 'I can just imagine their classmates teasing them about living in a haunted house. Kids can be cruel. And they love things like ghosts and haunted houses. Believe me. Mine love Halloween.'

'George thinks there's something in it.'

'That's his job, isn't it? If he didn't believe it, it would be like us saying there's no such thing as crime. He'd be making himself redundant.'

Joe was about to point out that George didn't work like that; that he approached every problem with a degree of scepticism. But he knew he'd be wasting his breath. Emily was the type of person who wanted proof. And this wasn't something he could give her just at that moment.

When they reached the CID office, they were greeted by Sunny. Because of his relationship to Margaret Cramp and his daughter's friendship with Isabel, Emily had taken him off the case temporarily to deal with a series of burglaries in the Pickby area of the city. She'd told him she wanted them cleared up because some of her neighbours had been targeted and she needed one of her best officers on it. But Sunny hadn't been pleased about being sidelined from the main investigation, and he wasn't taken in by the DCI's attempt at flattery.

'I understand you've been talking to Isabel,' he said to Joe once Emily had retreated to her office. 'How is she?'

'Upset. You've heard Douglas Page was her biological father?'

'Leanne told me. He must have been the older man she was seen with. Just shows how you can leap to the worst conclusions, doesn't it. This job does that to you; makes you see the darker side of human nature. Did she tell you anything useful?'

Joe felt it would be unkind to point out that Sunny was no longer on the case. Besides, the information wasn't particularly confidential. 'Page used to be in the job, and he told Isabel that he recognised Lexi Verity from a case he worked on years ago.'

Sunny's eyes lit up. 'Which case?'

'We're not sure yet, but according to Isabel, he said Lexi used to be known by another name, possibly beginning with T. Tilly, or something similar.'

'The burglaries are almost wrapped up. Uniform made an arrest this morning, so if ma'am thinks it's OK, I could go through the files – look for cases featuring someone with the name Tilly, or any similar name beginning with T.'

'That might be quite a job, Sunny. We don't know when this was, but it must have been sometime before she met Pascal Allard down in London.'

'Leave it with me.' Sunny looked so eager that Joe took pity on him. The sergeant wasn't the sort of person who was happy watching from the sidelines.

He returned to his desk and started to scribble notes, hoping to get things clear in his mind. Douglas Page had recognised Lexi from a case he'd dealt with during his days serving in the police. George had told him about a little girl who talked about someone called Tilly. But could George's investigation into a possible haunting on Kirkgate have anything to do with their case?

He picked up his phone. There was somebody who might be able to throw some light on the matter, and that was Artemis James. She was Lexi's agent and claimed to be a close friend. If anyone would know, surely it would be her.

Artemis sounded wary as she began to answer the question. Then her tone changed. 'Funny, I spend so much time defending my clients' image, it becomes a habit. But poor Lexi's dead now, so nothing can harm her career any more, can it?'

'I'm afraid not. If you tell us everything you know, it might help us catch whoever killed her.'

There was a short silence while Artemis took this in. Then she spoke. 'I honestly don't know much about her background because it was something she never talked about. It was almost as though she only appeared on this earth when she began working as a production assistant. I do know that her full name was Alexandra – Lexi for short. As for her surname, she once told me Verity was her mother's maiden name and she changed it by deed poll from something quite ordinary because she thought it sounded better.'

'Can you remember that name?'

'Afraid not.'

'Did you ever hear her being called Tilly?'

'No. Why?'

'You don't know anything about her being involved in a police case when she was young?'

'What?' Artemis seemed genuinely surprised. 'No. I wasn't aware of anything like that.' There was a long silence. 'Did she commit a crime? Is that why she changed her name? I honestly had no idea, and I thought I knew her well.' She sounded upset, as though she felt she'd been betrayed somehow.

'We haven't found any evidence that she ever did anything wrong,' Joe said quickly. 'But the investigation's ongoing. You mentioned a new true-crime series she was due to start working on.'

'*The Killers Among Us.* Yes.'

'You said one of the cases was personal.'

'That's right.'

'You assumed it was about the stalking. But what if it was about something else? Something in her distant past? Are you sure she didn't drop any hints?'

'Quite sure.' She paused. 'But she was a bit . . . reticent, and she insisted on writing the script herself, which puzzled me a little. After all, the Nathan Corde case is in the public domain, isn't it?'

'Have you ever heard the name Douglas Page?'

'It's not familiar. Is he in the TV industry? Or the theatre?'

'Neither. Thanks for your time,' Joe said before ending the call.

Twenty-Seven

Isabel's statement was intriguing, but the connection to Lexi's murder was tenuous to say the least. However, Joe wanted to speak to George again about the 1997 pub fire and find out whether he had any further information. Until now, it had merely been an intriguing distraction. But in his quest for any promising cases featuring a Tilly, he nursed a hope that he would find a solid link that would lead to a breakthrough.

He approached Sunny's desk and asked him to look for any incident attended by a PC Douglas Page involving the death of a child.

'You realise this is like looking for a needle in the proverbial haystack?' Sunny grumbled. 'And I'm already looking for Tillys, not that I've had any luck yet.'

'I know, but if anyone can find something, you can. And it could be linked to the Lexi Verity case.' He didn't mention George because he suspected Sunny would share Emily's opinion about George's work.

He was about to return to his desk when his phone

rang. He saw Maddy's name on the caller display and answered at once.

'He's come back,' she began breathlessly.

'Silas Sellie?'

'That's right. He was furious that I'd ordered his display to be removed.'

'Where is he now?'

'He said he was going home. But not before he smashed up other parts of the display. We're going to have to postpone the opening.' She sounded as though she was on the brink of tears.

'We've been trying to get hold of him. I'll send someone down to the museum straight away and we'll get him picked up.'

'He was shouting at me. Ranting. It was scary.' She hesitated. 'And he said something about Lexi Verity. Said he knew things about her and it was time to tell the world what she really was. Said she'd deserved everything she got. He completely lost it, Joe. I've never seen him like that before. I think he killed her. I really do. Are you going to arrest him?'

'We certainly need to ask him some questions. And if you want to make a formal complaint about the damage at the museum . . .' A charge of criminal damage would make it easier for the police to hold him if necessary. And Joe had a feeling that Sellie might prove to be slippery.

'I'll assess the damage and think about it.'

As soon as he ended the call, he asked one of the DCs to attend the scene, resisting the temptation to go to the museum himself and offer Maddy his support. Emily had also sent a couple of officers to Sellie's flat to bring him in for questioning. The man had claimed to know something about Lexi Verity, so they needed to speak to him as a matter of urgency. And they needed to find out whether he was linked in any way to Douglas Page. Sellie's artistic *enfant terrible* mask had slipped, and he'd just proved that he was in possession of a violent and uncontrolled temper. He was rapidly moving up Joe's list of possible suspects.

He had a sudden idea, and called Sally Sharpe at the mortuary. She sounded pleased to hear his voice, but Joe told himself that she was probably just glad of the distraction from cutting up corpses.

He felt elated when she gave him the answer he was looking for. When he asked whether the weapon used to kill Lexi Verity and Douglas Page could have been an instrument used in model-making – the sort of blade Silas Sellie might use to create his works of art – the answer was a non-committal 'It's possible.'

Joe called the officers who'd gone round to Sellie's flat and asked them to search the premises for a similar weapon.

While he was waiting for the officers to report back to him, Joe wandered into Emily's office to tell her about the new development.

She raised her eyebrows. 'When Sellie's brought in,

I want to sit in on the interview. We need to see what he has to say for himself.'

Before she could continue, her phone rang, and after a terse conversation she ended the call and turned to Joe.

'That was Maria from the rectory. She's found something she thinks we should see.'

'What?'

'She says she'll meet us in the tea shop in Eaglethorpe in an hour. It all sounds very mysterious, but I think we should go. If Sellie arrives in the meantime, it'll do him no harm to be kept waiting.'

They picked up their vehicle in the station car park, where they were forced to run the gauntlet of media people who were still hanging round the entrance in the hope of fresh morsels of information. The pack had increased in number since they got wind of the second death, and they shouted questions to Emily, who told them there'd be another statement in due course. Joe couldn't help admiring her cool approach. He found the shouts slightly intimidating.

They arrived in Eaglethorpe earlier than the appointed time, and as they drove past the rectory gates, Joe noticed that the shrine to Lexi had increased in size since their last visit; a hill of flowers in cellophane shrouds that the victim would never get to see. They parked in the village, and as they entered the old-fashioned tea shop, the bell above the door announced their arrival. They were about to order coffee when the bell jangled again. Maria had turned up five minutes early.

'I believe you've got something to show us,' Joe began, looking around to make sure they couldn't be overheard. The nearest table was some way away, so if they kept their voices down, he was confident they could speak in private.

Maria opened the large basket she was carrying and took out a carrier bag bearing the name of a well-known Eborby department store.

'I find this in the bin. I look inside and . . . See for yourself.'

The bag contained scraps of paper, torn into small shreds. It would take some time and effort to put them back together.

'I see her put it in bin. She look round but she not see me. She look . . . secretive. Like she is ashamed.'

'Who are you talking about?' Emily asked. Joe could hear the impatience in her voice. If Maria was playing games, the DCI had no wish to indulge her.

'Margaret. The one who never called the man to mend the cameras so killer could get in. It was her. She was hiding something.' Maria gestured towards the carrier bag. 'You put together. Yes? You see what she hides from police.'

Emily seized the carrier bag and stood up without a word, but Joe thanked the woman. 'If you think of anything else . . .'

'You talk to that ex-husband of madam's? The famous actor?' She seemed concerned that they might not have followed up the lead she'd given them.

'Connor Nuffield. We've already spoken to him.'

'I no like him. He not nice man like he is in *Holly and Ivy*.'

Joe wondered if her disappointment at the actor not being like the amiable Chief Inspector Holly had clouded her judgement.

As they climbed into the car, Emily asked him what he thought.

'Margaret might just have been getting rid of old documents like everyone does from time to time. Maybe we should ask her.'

Emily shook her head. 'If there is something in Maria's suspicions, I don't want to put her on her guard. Let's get the stuff pieced together first. Find out what we're dealing with.'

The reconstruction of the bag's contents would be a tedious job for some unfortunate DC. Joe didn't envy whoever drew the short straw.

When they returned to the station, Joe was pleased to find that Sellie had already been brought in and taken to the interview room. They'd feared he might be hard to find, but as it was, officers had been waiting for him when he'd returned to his flat at the sign of the red devil. When they'd told him he was being taken in for questioning, he'd behaved as though nothing unusual had happened that morning, announcing calmly that he'd come to the station with them, but he couldn't be long as he needed to work.

When the two detectives entered the interview room, the suspect stood up, his body language signalling that he was angry about being kept waiting.

'Our apologies for the delay,' Joe began, oozing calm as he switched on the recording machine after reciting the words of the caution. 'We had urgent business to attend to. You've had a cup of tea?' He smiled disarmingly while Emily looked on, her face impassive. Good cop, bad cop sometimes worked.

'I've had something that tasted like bilge water if that's what you mean. Why am I here? I have things to do.'

'For the exhibition?' said Joe.

'That and other projects.'

'I understand you've refused the services of a solicitor?'

'I don't need one. I can speak for myself.'

'That's up to you. We've been told that you lost your temper with Maddy Owen this morning. She was very upset.'

'The woman has no understanding of what I'm aiming to do.'

'And what's that?' Emily asked.

'I want to challenge the public's perception of violence, and by including a recent violent death among all those Victorian horrors, my intention was to bring home the reality of murder.'

'That's as maybe, but it's an ongoing case.' Emily's

voice was sharp, as though she was already losing patience with the man. 'What you did was unacceptable to the police – and to anyone else with a modicum of sensitivity. Lexi Verity is a victim, with friends and family.'

Sellie folded his arms and looked away, defiant.

'You and Lexi once had an affair, I believe,' said Joe, watching the man's face carefully. 'I would have thought you'd feel some emotion about her murder. Instead you make a model of it. That's not how I'd react to the death of someone I'd once been close to.'

Sellie sniffed. 'Who said we were close? Our affair, as you call it, was purely physical and temporary.'

'When we spoke to you before, you told us she ended it. Did you part on bad terms?' Emily asked.

The answer was a shrug. 'I told her she was a narcissistic bitch. I suppose you could call that bad terms.'

'You told Maddy Owen you knew something about Lexi,' said Joe. 'Can you share it with us?'

Suddenly Sellie looked awkward. 'I don't know if . . .'

'You were lying to Ms Owen then,' Emily said. 'Trying to impress her, were you?'

He didn't answer.

'Do you know a man called Douglas Page? He's the head of Eborby Gaming.'

'I've heard of Eborby Gaming; they own all those bookies, don't they? And you can't miss the adverts for their online bingo. But I'm afraid gambling's never been one of my many vices, Inspector. And I've never heard of this Donald Page. Why would I?'

Joe suspected he'd got Douglas's name wrong deliberately, unable to resist another opportunity to provoke. 'He was murdered. And we're linking his death to Lexi Verity's.'

'Sorry. Can't help you. Can I go now?'

Joe caught Emily's eye. She opened her mouth to speak, but was interrupted by her phone ringing. She left the room to take the call, returning after a few moments, a solemn expression on her face.

'That call was from the officers who've been searching your flat.'

'You had no right—'

'You've been arrested on suspicion of murder. We had every right. Especially as they found a bladed weapon matching the description of the one that killed Lexi Verity and Douglas Page. Have you anything to say about that?'

Silas Sellie sat stunned into silence for a few moments. Then he spoke in a feeble squeak. 'I want a solicitor.'

Twenty-Eight

Silas Sellie had been charged with criminal damage and taken down to the cells. If he had been involved in the recent murders, at least they had him where they could find him.

Joe walked home that evening thinking that he'd never seen such a dramatic change in a suspect. The cocky, establishment-baiting artist had turned into a subdued, rather pathetic figure. As for him being guilty of two murders, Joe wasn't entirely convinced. The knives found at his flat had been taken away for examination, and Emily seemed confident that the forensic results would settle the matter once and for all. Joe hoped she was right. He too wanted the case wrapped up as soon as possible.

As soon as he arrived home, he called Maddy to bring her up to date with the latest developments. She sounded relieved that Sellie was safely in custody. Before he ended the call, he asked her if she fancied going out for a drink.

'Sorry, Joe. I don't feel up to it. Today's been ... stressful.'

He told her he understood, and when she rang off, he sat there staring at the phone in disappointment. Then his mind turned to Emily. She'd worked late as well, but she had Jeff and the kids to go home to. At times like this he could never help thinking of Kaitlin, and what might have been if it wasn't for that fateful day in Devon all those years ago. The argument over some trivial matter that Joe could barely recall; his frantic search for her when she stormed off. Then the discovery of her body at the foot of a treacherous flight of steps. The later accusations against him by her sister, Kirsten. At dark times he relived it all.

He hadn't deleted the message Kirsten had left on his answering machine a few days before, and he pressed the key to listen to it again. Could he call her? It would be typical of Kirsten to make mischief, to pick at the scab of grief just to cause him more pain. In the end he decided to try her number, but there was no answer.

Being on his own, brooding in his silent flat, was doing him no good, so he made the decision to go to the pub. Just for one pint. He was contemplating calling George Merryweather to see whether he wanted to join him when his phone rang. The number was unfamiliar, but when he answered, he heard a voice he recognised. Caradoc Karling.

'I hope you don't mind me calling you out of office hours, as it were.'

'Not at all. What can I do for you?'

'Can we meet?'

'When and where?' Joe hadn't wanted to drink alone. However, his feelings about meeting Karling were ambiguous. The psychic was involved in the case so the meeting would seem more like work than leisure. Even so, he agreed to meet at the Black Horse on Boargate. It was another historic pub, often full of tourists. But the booths there would give them some degree of privacy.

Half an hour later, he was sitting with a pint of Black Sheep in front of him when he spotted Karling looking round, full glass in hand, as though he was lost. Joe called to him, and a look of relief passed across the psychic's face.

Once the man had taken a seat, Joe came straight to the point. 'You wanted to see me?'

'That's right. I believe you've arrested somebody for the murders?'

'We're questioning a suspect,' said Joe, wondering what was coming.

'You've got the wrong person.'

He was beginning to suspect that Karling was wasting his time. He took a long swig of beer. It tasted good. He drained his glass and was about to stand up when the psychic spoke again.

'The man you're questioning has nothing to do with it.' Karling put his head in his hands for a few moments Then he looked up, his face haggard. 'You need to find the child. When I saw Lexi, I felt her guilt. Lexi Verity had a very dark secret, Inspector. Once you find out what that secret was, you'll find her killer.'

'What about the man who died? Douglas Page?'

'He was an innocent. In the wrong place at the wrong time. It was his gift that killed him.'

'Gift?' Joe felt puzzled.

When Karling didn't elaborate, Joe picked up his empty glass, undecided whether to get another drink or leave. 'Is that all you have to tell me?'

Karling looked sheepish. 'While I was at home today, I experienced a sort of trance. It happens unexpectedly like that. That's why it's so hard to perform to order. It's the reason I have to use certain ... techniques until the real messages come through. You witnessed that when you attended my evening at the White Swan with DCI Thwaite.'

'DCI Thwaite didn't believe a word of it.'

'But Lexi believed. That's why she consulted me.'

Joe looked at the empty glass again. He was tempted to go to the bar for a refill. He felt he'd learned all he needed to from Caradoc Karling, so he told the man he had to go because he had somewhere else to be. He wondered whether Karling's 'powers' would pick up on the lie.

'Someone blames you for something terrible that happened years ago, a bitter woman who wants to do you harm,' said the psychic as he stood up. 'This woman said you were responsible, but somebody else was there. Someone who ended the life of a person who was close to you.' He looked Joe in the eye. 'You have nothing to feel guilty about.'

Joe flinched and felt a sudden urge to rush away; to

be on his own. It was as though Karling had seen everything – Kaitlin's death, Kirsten's misplaced desire for revenge. And the mention of someone else being present when Kaitlin died had shaken him.

He walked back through the narrow streets, hardly aware of his surroundings as he trod the grey pavements shiny with moisture even though it hadn't rained that evening. And that night he found it hard to sleep as Karling's words echoed through his mind. His late wife might not have died in a tragic accident as he'd always believed. She might have been murdered.

Nobody quite knew how the smoke-stained doll from the box under the stairs had found its way into Freya's bedroom, but now it sat on the shelf at the end of her bed. The glass eyes fringed by lush black eyelashes snapped shut whenever the doll was put on its back to sleep, but now they were wide open, watching. Anna said the doll was called Betty and that it was her favourite. She'd lost it once, but Tilly had found it. She knew that Bobby had hidden it out of spite. Bobby did things like that.

Freya could hear her brother crying, which meant Jack must have appeared in his room again. She'd told him that Jack wouldn't hurt him because he was just sad. And worried too, because according to Anna, Bobby was still around somewhere. Anna told her a lot of things. Freya knew she was trying to warn her that something was wrong.

Freya had insisted that her dad leave the night light on, because Anna had told her there was someone else nearby; someone dangerous. Maybe someone who was still in the land of the living.

She'd seen her dad talking to that vicar with the kind face while her mother was out at work. The vicar was called George and her dad had said he'd come there to help them. Anna said it would take a lot to set things right – and that they needed to make Bobby pay for what had happened. Freya was glad she'd never seen Bobby. She thought she'd probably be scared of him.

She propped herself up on her elbows and watched the doll, Betty, hoping she'd do it again. And when the doll blinked her bright glass eyes and turned her head, Freya smiled. Anna had come to play again.

Twenty-Nine

Emily arrived in the office late the next morning look-ing harassed. Jeff had forgotten some books he needed urgently for that day's lessons, and when he'd returned home just as she was about to go out, she'd had to help him look for them.

'But you don't want to hear about my domestic prob-lems,' she said with a sigh as Joe entered her office to bring her up to date with developments. 'Anything new?'

He told her about his meeting with Caradoc Karling the previous night.

'You don't think he was trying to get some inside info on the investigation?'

'Why would he do that? You can't think he's a seri-ous suspect.'

Emily considered the question for a moment. 'He has solid alibis for both murders.' She sounded disap-pointed.

'He said Lexi had a secret.'

'Well her life before she met Pascal Allard is a bit of a mystery, don't you think?'

'What about the change of surname that's been mentioned?'

'People often change their names when they're in showbiz, don't they. Anything else?'

'Karling said something odd. He told me that Douglas Page died because of his gift.'

Emily rolled her eyes. 'Gift? What gift?'

'I don't know, but Lexi obviously consulted Karling because she was worried about something.'

'Probably the thought of Nathan Corde getting out of jail and stalking her again – and who can blame her?'

'Or Silas Sellie might have been bothering her.'

'Well, he's been causing a lot of trouble in the cells. On my way in just now, Sunny told me that when the custody sergeant took him his breakfast, he threw it on the floor and demanded that we release him because he had important work to do.'

'What about Corde?'

'Reporting to his local station daily, meek as a lamb, I've heard. He was in custody when Douglas Page died, so if Lexi and Page were killed by the same person, we have to rule him out. Pity, he seemed like the ideal candidate.' Emily checked the time. 'I'd better give my morning briefing,' she said with a sigh.

Joe shared her frustration. Nathan Corde seemed like the perfect suspect; a deluded stalker whose twisted version of love could so easily have changed to a bitter desire for revenge when the object of his affection rejected him.

'Unless you want to do the briefing for me?' She sounded hopeful.

'I wouldn't rob you of the pleasure,' was Joe's swift reply.

After gathering the team together, Emily asked if anything new had come in overnight. A young DC, new to the department and still finding his feet, put up a nervous hand. 'I've been reconstructing those documents; the ones from the rectory. I've made good progress, but there are still quite a few to do."

It took Joe a few seconds to remember what he was talking about. He thanked the officer, and once the briefing was over, he carried the documents, now reassembled with clear tape, into Emily's office and laid them on a clear area of her desk.

'Piecing these together was a rotten job,' said Emily appreciatively. 'I'll buy DC Jenkins a cake at break time.'

'Quite right. He deserves it,' said Joe, looking at the young officer's handiwork.

'According to Maria, Margaret Cramp put the pieces in the bin,' Emily said before she began to scan the documents, a puzzled frown on her face. 'But these don't appear to belong to Margaret. They're about someone called Matilda Smith.'

Joe experienced a moment of excitement. 'Matilda. Tilly,' he whispered under his breath, his gut telling him that they'd just found an important link.

Emily flicked through them. 'There's all sorts here. Birth certificate; an out-of-date passport; letters; diaries.' She studied the birth certificate. 'Matilda Alexandra.

Mother's maiden name, Susan Verity. Didn't Artemis say Lexi had taken her mother's surname? I think these belonged to Lexi Verity. We need to know how Margaret came to have them.'

'There's only one way to do that and that's to ask her.'

Twenty minutes later, Joe and Emily were driving out of the city towards Eaglethorpe.

They went straight to the rectory, crunching slowly up the gravel drive and coming to a halt by the front door. There was no sign of Harry York. Instead, a young man Joe didn't recognise was mowing the lawn in the expansive front garden. Lord Pilton had kept his promise about not allowing Harry to set foot on the premises again.

It was Margaret herself who opened the door. She said it would be best if they spoke in the kitchen, because Lord Pilton was at home. As they followed her, Joe noticed that she walked stiffly, as though she was terrified of what was to come. He was suddenly impatient to watch her reaction to the questions he needed to ask her.

She didn't bother offering them tea. Instead she sat down at the kitchen table, the fear in her eyes unmistakable.

'You disposed of some torn-up documents in a bin?' Emily began.

There was a long silence, and they could almost hear her brain working, thinking up the best excuse for her behaviour. 'I found them.'

'Where did you find them?'

Another long pause followed. 'In Lady Pilton's room.'

'Our officers made a thorough search of Lady Pilton's room. Nothing like that was discovered.'

'Er . . . I found them before the room was searched. I was tidying her ladyship's things one day and discovered a loose board at the bottom of her wardrobe. After she died, I took the papers out and hid them in my room.'

'That was interfering with evidence. Nothing should have been touched.' Emily sounded indignant.

Margaret bowed her head. 'I was guarding her privacy. Everyone has a right to privacy, even when they're dead.'

'The documents wouldn't have been made public, unless they were directly linked to her murder. Was it you who tore them up?'

She hesitated before nodding, avoiding their eyes.

'Why?'

'Because of . . . If she'd hidden them so well, they must have been things she wanted to keep secret, even from his lordship. Though at first I didn't even think they belonged to her ladyship.'

'Why was that?'

'The name on the birth certificate is Matilda Alexandra Smith. Then I saw the mother's maiden name was Verity, and I worked it out. Alexandra can be shortened to Lexi. I guessed that her ladyship had changed her identity.' There was a long pause. 'And I recognised the name. Matilda Smith.'

'Where from?'

There was a long silence before Margaret answered.

'I was brought up in Eborby and it was in all the papers years ago.'

'What was?'

'The fire that killed a child. Matilda Smith was the name of the tart who was in bed with a man while his little girl burned to death. She was supposed to be the child's nanny, but . . . I remember my mother talking to her friends about it.' She sniffed. 'Why should a woman who's capable of something like that be ordering me about?'

'Where did this fire happen?' Joe asked. He thought he already knew the answer, but he wanted to hear her say it.

'It was in Eborby, but I'm not sure exactly where. No wonder she never went into town.'

'And when?'

'Must have been the late 1990s. I was in my twenties, working at Brown's at the time. Ladies' fashions. I liked that job,' she added with a note of sadness, maybe for her lost youth.

'You say you found the papers after Lexi died?'

Margaret's face turned red.

'We need the truth,' said Emily firmly.

There was another long silence before the woman spoke again. 'I hoped she wouldn't miss them.' She lowered her voice almost to a whisper. 'I needed something to use as . . . insurance.'

'Insurance?'

'I need this job. The flat here is my home, and I thought . . . One day when she was telling me off about not getting the security cameras repaired, I told her I'd found the papers. Otherwise she would have dismissed me on the spot, you see. She said I'd got it all wrong, of course. Said she had them because of some research she was doing for a new documentary. But I knew she was lying. She was Matilda Smith all right.'

'So you knew your employer's secret?' Emily said, unable to keep the disapproval out of her voice. 'And if she dismissed you, you'd go to the tabloids. That's what we call blackmail. And it's a serious offence.'

There was no reply. Margaret gazed out of the kitchen window, her lips pressed together in a stubborn line.

'You don't deny it?' said Emily, watching her closely.

After a few seconds, Margaret turned her head to face them, her eyes defiant. 'She had everything. I had to skivvy for her while she lived in luxury. She used to drop her clothes on the floor and expect me to pick them up and put them away. Used to complain if they weren't on the hangers properly. She was even unfaithful to his lordship, who's a real gentleman. I once saw her going into the bedroom with that gardener lad. Shameless, she was. A tart. Everyone thought she was wonderful, but I knew what she was. I never killed her, though.'

Suddenly she seemed to grow in confidence, and a satisfied look crossed her face. 'Anyway, you can't prove a thing. There's nothing in writing. Unless I confess to doing something illegal, you can't charge me with anything, can you?'

The trouble was, she was speaking the truth. Her demands had been verbal and her victim was dead, so they had no evidence they could take to court.

Emily moved to go. 'We'll be in touch,' she said ominously before she walked out of the room.

Joe could sense her frustration. The woman they'd once felt sorry for had been a blackmailer. But unless she made a confession or they had solid evidence, there was nothing they could do about it.

Emily and Joe were impatient to reach the station and take another look at the reconstructed papers. Joe called Jamilla and asked her to find out all she could about the pub fire and Matilda Smith's involvement. George's case was no longer merely an interesting distraction. It had just moved to the centre of the investigation. Now the fire and the child with the imaginary friend who asked for Tilly was something even the sceptical Emily couldn't ignore.

He checked the time before starting the car. Almost two o'clock. They'd be working late again, tracking down everyone connected with the fire and trying to confirm that Lexi Verity had indeed been the same Matilda Smith who'd been involved in the tragedy, because there were bound to be a number of people with the same name. It would be another night when Jeff would have to cook for Emily's children; another night when Joe would grab a takeaway or have something to eat at the pub.

As soon as they arrived back at the station, they were greeted by Jamilla.

'I've found something about Matilda Smith – an old press cutting with a photograph of her coming out of the inquest. "Pub Fire Nanny gives Evidence". I must say it doesn't look at all like Lexi Verity.'

'Let's have a look,' said Emily as she took off her coat. Jamilla followed her into her office, with Joe bringing up the rear. She had placed the file full of reconstructed paperwork in the centre of Emily's desk along with printouts from crime records. Emily picked up the cutting and handed it to Joe.

The picture showed a miserable-looking girl in her late teens or early twenties with mousy shoulder-length hair that looked as though it needed washing. She was nondescript, the kind of girl you'd pass in the street without a second glance. Joe was struck by how young and ordinary she looked. Hardly the scheming Jezebel Margaret had described. The most remarkable thing about her was the scarring on the right side of her face, a legacy of the fire, perhaps.

'You're right, Jamilla. It looks nothing like Lexi,' said Emily. 'We might have got it wrong. Or rather Margaret did.'

But Joe wasn't inclined to give up. 'Lexi was only ever seen with immaculate make-up and expensive clothes, and she must have had access to numerous beauticians and a good hairdresser. The newspaper report says Tilly Smith was nineteen, and according to Pascal Allard, Lexi had undergone surgery before he met her three years later. Could that have been to deal with the scarring?'

They all pored over the photograph and Joe fetched the picture of Lexi from the noticeboard in the main office for comparison. He covered up the bottom of both photographs so that only the top half of the faces was visible.

After several minutes, he gave his verdict. 'The eyes are the same. I'm sure it's her.' He paused, anticipating Emily's reaction to his next statement. 'Caradoc Karling said that Lexi used to be someone else altogether.'

Unexpectedly, Emily nodded in agreement.

She looked at Jamilla. 'We need to find out about the child who died in the fire. According to Margaret, Matilda or Tilly was a nanny and she was in bed with the child's father when the fire broke out. Could someone have blamed her for what happened and wanted revenge after all these years? We need to go through the case with a fine-toothed comb, though that will have to wait until tomorrow.' She checked the time. 'We'll have another word with Artemis and Connor Nuffield. Lexi must have told someone about her true identity.'

'Or someone found out and that's why she was killed,' said Joe.

'Is Nathan Corde out of the frame then?' Jamilla asked.

'Sally Sharpe was pretty sure the murders were identical,' said Joe. 'Same MO. Same weapon.'

'And Sally's never wrong.' Emily gave him a knowing grin.

Joe didn't answer. He'd been resisting Emily's attempts at matchmaking ever since he'd broken up with Maddy, and he wasn't going to respond.

'If Lexi's murder is connected with this fire, what on earth could Douglas Page have to do with it?' Emily said as though she was thinking aloud. 'Even if someone was seeking revenge on Matilda Smith, why kill Page? It doesn't make sense.'

'Page was a police constable around the time of the fire. We need to find out as a matter of urgency whether he was one of the officers who attended the scene. It was a long time ago and the records might not have been digitised, so the details might take some digging out.' Emily smiled at Jamilla, who'd started to look overwhelmed.

'I'll get the ball rolling, ma'am.'

Emily sighed. 'You can do that tomorrow. Why don't you get home? Early start in the morning.'

Jamilla looked grateful as she fetched her coat and hurried from the office. Sunny had been told he could stop looking for past cases featuring a Tilly, but he was still at his desk and Joe wondered whether to bring him up to date with the development regarding Margaret Cramp. But he decided that breaking the news that his cousin-in-law was a blackmailer could wait until another time. And as no charges were likely to be brought, perhaps there was no point in telling him at all. It might only upset Pauline.

But he did have something to ask him. 'Sunny, has your Leanne mentioned how her friend Isabel is doing?'

'She went to see her and the poor lass is in pieces. A family liaison officer is looking after her as well as Jackie Page, who doesn't seem particularly devastated. According to the FLO, she's more interested in sorting out the business side.'

'Thanks. I'll have a word with the FLO tomorrow and ask her to speak to Jackie. We need to find out what she knows about her husband's time in the police. And if he ever mentioned a fire – or the name Matilda Smith.'

Thirty

The following morning, Silas Sellie appeared before the magistrates and was let off with a fine and a caution. Emily could barely conceal her annoyance that he'd been allowed to slip through her fingers. But Joe knew that a charge of criminal damage had been unlikely to land him in custody.

'The report's come back on those knives found at Sellie's flat,' said Joe as he took a seat in the DCI's office. 'No trace of blood, and the only DNA belonged to Sellie himself.'

Emily looked at him and frowned. 'He might have disposed of the knife he used before his premises were searched.'

'What reason could he possibly have for killing Douglas Page?'

'I don't know yet, but no doubt we'll find one in due course if we ask some more questions. Gambling debts?'

It seemed to Joe that Emily was clutching at shadows. 'Eborby Gaming's a big company. Douglas Page wasn't a small casino owner who'd threatened to send the heavies round if Sellie didn't pay up. Even if he did have debts, killing Page wouldn't do him any good.'

Emily stood up and stared out of the window as though she was seeking inspiration.

'You know that man who called George Merry-weather to deal with a possible haunting?'

'One thing's for sure, Joe. Lexi and Page weren't murdered by a ghost.'

Joe ignored her remark. 'The house he's just bought, Church Cottage on Kirkgate, used to be a pub called the Smithy. The owner's been doing some research in the newspaper archives, and he found out that a little girl died in a fire there and her father hanged himself. Sound familiar to you?'

Emily nodded. 'That's the case Matilda Smith was involved in.'

'According to Margaret, Matilda – or Tilly – was the nanny who was in bed with the father when the child's room was filling with the smoke that killed her.'

Emily slumped down in her chair again. 'And your friend George thinks the dead child is still on the premises?'

'Along with the father who hanged himself. George is used to sorting hoaxes from real phenomena and he says the new owner is desperate because his children are talking about the people who died there. And the little girl talks about someone called Tilly. Matilda.

The young woman Lexi Verity used to be before she changed her name and identity.'

Emily sat silently for a few moments before she spoke again. 'OK. Tell me your thoughts.'

'The newspaper reports of the inquest said it was a straightforward case of arson to get the insurance money, with the poor child as collateral damage. But what if someone else was involved; someone who doesn't want the truth to come out now? Jamilla's trying to find out more about the case, and I'll be interested to see what she comes up with.'

Emily looked sceptical. 'On the other hand, Lexi's murder could stem from something much more recent. People in the public eye make enemies – or attract obsessed stalkers like Nathan Corde.'

'What about Douglas Page?'

'He was seen visiting Lexi, so maybe he spotted the killer. Are we a hundred per cent sure they were killed by the same weapon?'

'Sally says they were. And she never commits herself unless she's certain.'

Emily knew Joe was right. Pathologists always erred on the side of caution when they were giving their verdict, and Sally was no exception.

Joe was about to leave Emily's office when there was a knock on her door. It was Jamilla, and by the eager look on her face, it seemed she had news.

'I've found details of the inquest on the child who died in the fire at the Smithy,' she began. 'It took a while to dig them out. I don't think it made me very popular.' She deposited a couple of large box files on the desk. They'd been stored in a warehouse facility and they smelled musty.

'Well, don't keep us in suspense,' said Emily. She sounded impatient.

Jamilla opened one of the files, wrinkling her nose against the dust.

'The story begins with a tragedy. In 1996, Diane Halliday was killed in a car crash on the bypass, leaving her husband, Jack, who'd been divorced from his first wife, with a pub to run and a little girl to bring up. Jack had no family nearby; his parents were both dead and his only brother lived abroad, so he needed help. He couldn't afford to pay for an experienced nanny, so he found a young woman who'd been brought up abroad and had come back to England to live with an elderly relative when her parents were killed. The girl, Matilda Smith, was nineteen and wanted to earn a bit of money, so she answered the advert Jack Halliday placed in the local paper.'

Emily winced. 'Bit risky to employ an inexperienced teenager like that. Poor man must have been desperate.'

'I think he was. Anyway, Matilda Smith turned up on his doorstep with a reference from her grandmother, who said she was sensible and responsible. Jack Halliday employed her and she lived above the pub with him and the child.'

'How long was she living there before the incident?'

'About five months. At first the arrangement went well. She became particularly close to the daughter,

Anna, who was six. Jack Halliday said at the inquest that she got on well with the kid and became like a big sister to her. There's a transcript of Matilda Smith's evidence. She was questioned about how the fire started and her answers seem rather evasive.'

Emily thought for a few moments. 'Covering up for Jack Halliday. After all, according to the newspaper reports, she was sleeping with him.'

'It's possible,' said Jamilla. She hesitated. 'It says here that the fire broke out at ten p.m. Halliday had closed the pub early because there were no customers. He and Matilda attempted to rescue the little girl before the firefighters arrived, but they were driven back by the flames and smoke. Halliday was badly burned and had to be taken to hospital, and Matilda also suffered some burning to her face. The pub wasn't doing well, so it was concluded later that Halliday started the fire for the insurance money and things got out of hand.'

'Could the kid have been messing about with matches?' Joe asked.

'Apparently accelerant was used. And the little girl was asleep. It didn't take long to put the fire out and the professionals managed to limit the damage to a few upstairs rooms. However, the pub closed, never to open again.'

Jamilla turned a page, frowning. 'It says here that there was a second child staying on the premises. Bobby, aged eleven, child of Halliday's first marriage and little Anna's half-sibling. But according to Matilda's statement, he wasn't there when the fire broke out because he was out at the cinema with a kid from down the street he'd become friendly with. He didn't attend the inquest and nobody bothered to check the cinema story at the time. He was whisked off somewhere down south by his mother, Halliday's first wife. He'd only been staying with his father for a few days when the incident happened – part of the divorce agreement.'

'Poor kid,' said Emily.

'The report produced by the fire investigator is in the file too. It concluded that the fire started in an empty bedroom on the top floor next to Anna's. It was started deliberately using some sort of accelerant, possibly nail polish remover; the remains of a bottle were found near the seat of the fire. It had been sprinkled on spare bedding stored in the room, and when the fire took hold, smoke and fumes had seeped into Anna's room, overcoming and eventually killing the sleeping child.

'Jack Halliday was suspected of killing his daughter by accident, but before he could be arrested for the crime, he ended his own life. He returned to the damaged premises and hanged himself. The coroner concluded that he'd been unable to live with the dreadful consequences of his reckless actions.'

'Is there anything to say what happened to Matilda the nanny?'

'She vanished after the inquest. No further trace of her.'

'So if Lexi was Matilda in a former existence, which is looking increasingly likely, she knew both the kids.' Emily pondered the implications for a while.

'I want to know what happened to Bobby,' said Joe. 'Where is he now?'

Emily frowned. 'Are you thinking what I'm thinking?'

'We need to trace Bobby and talk to him about what happened.'

'Robert Halliday,' said Jamilla. 'I'll start the search.'

Freya Greengrass walked home from school with her dad and big brother, Tom. She'd had a good day; come top in her class spelling test. But as she left her new friends in the playground and neared the home that had become hers over the past few weeks, she developed a strange feeling in her stomach. She was far too young and sheltered to have experienced fear, so she didn't recognise it for what it was. All she knew was that she was reluctant to go through that front door, newly painted in heritage green and flanked by a pair of tasteful bay trees.

When she walked into the kitchen, a room that still smelled new and strange, she was surprised to find her mother there. Usually she was at work until it was time for Freya and Tom to go to bed, and it was her dad who made the dinner and supervised bath time. It was also her dad who read them stories while her mum stayed downstairs eating a late dinner washed down by a glass of wine. Sometimes Freya crept out of bed and stood at the top of the stairs, listening to her mum and dad arguing.

'Hi, Mum,' she heard Tom saying. Her mum looked up and flashed a smile. But Freya thought she looked sad.

'You're home early,' she heard her dad say.

'There was a burst pipe at the theatre, so tonight's performance had to be cancelled. You've got me for the evening.' Her mum lowered her voice. 'I hope that exorcist hasn't been round again. When I walked in on you, it felt like something out of a horror film.'

Her dad laughed. 'Horror film? He's a nice harmless clergyman and we were drinking tea.'

'You know what I mean.' Freya's mum sounded cross as she turned away. 'You've been putting ideas into the kids' heads with all that nonsense.'

Freya didn't hang around to hear any more. Mummy didn't believe in Anna. But she was wrong. Anna was real. And Anna told her things.

She caught her brother's eye and they ran upstairs. Tom followed her into her bedroom and Freya knew why. He was scared of seeing Jack again. Since Jack had started coming into his room, Tom had been sleeping in Mummy and Daddy's bed. Mummy wasn't happy with the situation and she always ordered him to go back to his own room. But Tom had started sleeping on Freya's floor instead. Freya welcomed her brother's company – but Anna didn't, because she wanted Freya to herself. Her special friend.

Anna said Freya would help her stay safe if Bobby ever came back again.

Thirty-One

The team had contacted all the Robert Hallidays they could find. Some were too young; some were too old; and those of approximately the right age claimed to know nothing about a fire in Eborby in 1997. Neither did any admit to having links with Lexi Verity other than watching her on TV. As for Douglas Page, nobody claimed to know anything about him, even though a good few had heard of Eborby Gaming and its slogan – *Join in Yorkshire's finest fun with Eborby Bingo.*

All the feasible candidates had provided details of their whereabouts on the relevant dates, and these were being followed up. Although Emily wasn't holding out much hope of success in this Herculean task.

'He could be anywhere. He could have emigrated to Australia.'

'Well if he's down under, he's not our man.'

'I realise that, Joe, but it would mean we'd be wasting a lot of time trying to find him.' Emily sounded despondent.

But Joe felt more optimistic. At least they now had a name to follow up. Tilly the nanny had provided an alibi of sorts for Jack Halliday, and if Lexi Verity and Tilly were one and the same person, Joe wondered whether she'd changed her name and appearance to distance herself from what had happened. For her to go to those lengths to hide that part of her background suggested that she had something to be ashamed of. And there was something else he had to consider: what if that shame was caused because she herself started the fire that fateful night for some reason he couldn't yet fathom? If this was the case, they had to look for a person who would want revenge. And Bobby fitted the bill.

As they could probably eliminate Margaret Cramp from any association with the fire, Emily reckoned they should give Sunny the job of tracing any living relatives of the tragic child, Anna. Joe watched her break the news and saw Sunny's normally morose face light up. His association with Margaret Cramp had left him an outsider in the investigation. Now he was being brought in out of the wilderness, into the centre of things again.

It was four-thirty. The time when many office workers were glancing at the clock on the wall as they anticipated the journey home to the bosom of their families – or to a lonely house or flat depending on their circumstances. The CID office was still buzzing with activity as officers spoke on phones or tapped computer keyboards. Then at ten to five exactly, Emily emerged from her office and called Joe over.

'I've just had a message to say that Silas Sellie wants to speak to us. He says he knows something that might be to our advantage and he'll be at home till six if we want to call round. Makes it sound like a flaming social invitation.'

Her words took Joe by surprise. 'I thought he'd want to avoid us in the circumstances.'

'So did I. I want to know what he's up to.'

'There's only one way to find out. Let's pay him a visit.'

Emily hesitated. 'We don't want to let him think he only has to whistle and we come running.'

'But can we risk ignoring him if he really does have something useful to tell us?'

Emily reached for her coat. Twenty minutes later, they were weaving their way down Boargate, looking for the sign of the devil. Soon they spotted it leering down at them, as though it was amused by their failure. Joe looked up at it and shuddered.

Silas Sellie opened the door immediately, as though he'd been waiting to surprise them. 'Welcome again to my humble abode. They let me go with a slap on the wrist, as you see. Said I'd been a very naughty boy and made me promise not to do it again.'

'If it had been up to me, they would have thrown the book at you,' said Emily.

'Let me guess – the Ladybird book of crime investigation?' Sellie smirked at his own joke.

'You said you had some information for us,' said Joe, seeing Emily was in danger of losing her patience.

'You wanted to know about Lexi. Well, there's something I've remembered.'

'What's that?'

There was a long, teasing silence as though the man was playing with their hopes. Emily opened her mouth to speak, but Joe touched her arm gently. If they rose to the bait, Sellie would delight in keeping his secrets – if he had any.

His tactic was rewarded when Sellie finally spoke. 'Me and Lexi were drunk one night and we were having a game of truth or dare. You know the sort of thing.'

'Not really,' said Emily. 'Enlighten us.'

'Well, she said that when she was young, long before she was famous, she slept with her employer and bad things happened.'

'What bad things?' Joe suspected he already knew, but he wanted to hear the man say it.

There was another long silence before Sellie continued. 'Someone died and she lied to protect the person who was really responsible.'

'Who did she lie to protect?'

'She said it was a kid. But don't ask me who, 'cause I don't know. She just said someone died and she was involved in a cover-up. She told me to forget she'd ever said anything, then she called a taxi and left.' His lips formed a secretive smile. 'It had been a good night up till then, but it rather put a damper on the evening. After that . . . well, she kept her distance. We didn't get together again and she ignored me at work.'

Joe felt a frisson of satisfaction. The part about Lexi lying to protect a child opened up fresh possibilities.

'Why didn't you tell us this before?'

For the first time Sellie looked embarrassed. But he didn't answer the question. 'If you don't mind, I have things to do . . .'

'Ever heard the name Bobby?'

'No. Who is he?'

Joe didn't answer, and they'd turned away before Sellie spoke again. 'I'll tell you something for nothing. Lexi Verity had her demons. She wasn't a happy woman.'

The following morning, Joe and Emily agreed that Sellie's claim that Lexi had lied to protect someone vulnerable – a child who might have been guilty of murder – could be a vital lead.

As far as they could see, the only child in the case, apart from the little girl who'd died, had been her older half-sibling, eleven-year-old Bobby. It was an uncomfortable thought, but it was one they had to face. Bobby might be a killer and they needed to find him sooner rather than later.

'What if he's changed his name?' Emily put her head in her hands.

'The words needle and haystack spring to mind. But if we're going to treat Bobby as a suspect, that means he must have been around here at the times of both our murders.'

Emily lifted her head. She hadn't bothered with the concealer she normally used to camouflage the dark rings under her eyes, and Joe was struck by how exhausted she looked. Every time they seemed to be making progress, the solution appeared to move further out of their reach.

They sat in silence for a while, until the despondent atmosphere was shattered by a knock on Emily's office door. It was Jamilla, and she was looking remarkably cheerful, considering the state of the investigation.

'DC Jenkins has been putting together the rest of those torn-up documents from Lexi Verity's room – the ones Margaret Cramp was throwing out.'

'I thought they'd all been done,' said Emily.

'Most of them had, but it wasn't a quick job – bit like doing a thousand-piece jigsaw.' Jamilla sounded keen to defend her colleague, and Joe sympathised. When he'd been a junior officer in Liverpool, he'd been given some pretty awful jobs himself.

'Has he found anything interesting?'

'There was a fan letter addressed to Lexi care of her agent, Artemis James. It had obviously been forwarded unopened, and it wasn't the usual kind of fan mail.'

Emily sat up straight, and Joe noticed that she suddenly looked brighter.

Jamilla had a clear plastic folder in her hand. It contained a letter, stuck together with clear tape. She cleared her throat and began to read.

Dear Lexi,

    I hope I haven't made a mistake, but I think you used to be our nanny, Tilly. If you are, can you call me on this number? I really need to speak to you.

I know you think I did that terrible thing, but I promise you I didn't. I've had a lot of time to think about what happened and I've come to real- ise that you might have thought it was me and lied to protect me. If that's the case, there was no need because I swear I didn't do anything wrong. I don't know whether it's important, but I've remembered that somebody else had access to my dad's pub around that time. Do you know who I mean?

I live in Leeds now, but I can meet you in Eborby any time that's convenient to you. I know you must be really busy with filming and all that.

If I've got this completely wrong, please ignore this letter and accept my apologies.

Yours sincerely,

Roberta Harris (née Halliday)

'It's dated five weeks before Lexi's murder. And the phone number's given at the bottom. I've called it and left a message asking her to ring me.'

Joe and Emily sat in silence for a while, taking in the new development, while Jamilla looked at them expectantly.

'Roberta. Bobby. How could we have got it so wrong, Joe?'

Joe said nothing. He too had made assumptions. But he was beginning to think it didn't really matter.

Mrs Harris clearly had a lot to tell them, and they needed to speak to her urgently.

'I'm wondering why she didn't get in touch with us when the news of Lexi's murder broke,' said Emily quietly.

'I agree.'

Emily tried calling the number herself, but again there was no reply. She made no effort to hide her frustration as she thanked Jamilla and asked her to contact Artemis to see whether she knew anything about the letter. And whether Lexi had got in touch with Mrs Harris.

'There's no address. That means we're going to have to get Leeds police to track down everyone of that name. We need to find this Roberta.'

'Bobby. We should call her Bobby. Sunny's looking restless. He's had no luck yet with the search for Anna's relatives, so I'll get one of the DCs to take that over and give him the job of tracing Bobby.'

Emily frowned. 'Yes, I reckon that's more urgent. Bobby clearly knows of someone else who might have been responsible for that fire, and that means she could be in danger. Either that or she's dead already.'

There was a new atmosphere in the CID office. Frantic activity blended with fresh hope. It was discovered that the phone number Roberta Harris had given in her letter matched the mystery pay-as-you-go number Lexi Verity had called in the period leading up to her death.

Officers had been trying it at regular intervals but had had no luck.

Joe paced up and down Emily's office impatiently. The news from Leeds seemed to be a long time coming. He thought about George's haunting. Everything was starting to fit. The little girl called Anna who cried for Tilly, the nanny. The sad man called Jack. But before he could say anything, the door burst open, revealing a breathless Sunny.

'You're not going to believe this, ma'am. Roberta Harris has only been staying at a retreat for the past two weeks. She's planning to become a nun.'

Thirty-Two

Emily swore under her breath. The news was surprising, to say the least.

'I've spoken to her sister-in-law. She says Bobby's husband died two years ago, and since then Bobby's been going to mass every day.'

Joe understood the new widow's quest for spiritual comfort, but Emily saw it as an irritation.

'She must only be forty and she's locked herself away from the world,' she said, shaking her head in disbelief. 'There must be a way we can speak to her.'

Sunny looked smug, as though he'd just solved a problem that had been nagging at them for a while. 'There is, ma'am. She hasn't taken her phone with her, but the nun I spoke to, Sister Veronica, said Roberta's happy to talk to you any time. She's at the Benedictine convent near Ripon, with a view to becoming a . . .'

'Postulant?' Joe was familiar with the term from his time at the seminary.

'That's it. Sister Veronica was very helpful.'

Joe smiled. 'You were expecting obstruction from a dragon-like mother superior, were you?'

'Something like that. Mind you, everything I know about convents comes from watching *The Sound of Music* every Christmas.'

'You're an expert, then,' said Emily, teasing. Her mood had certainly brightened since the discovery of Roberta's whereabouts and the fact that she was safe. She turned to Joe. 'Let's get over there and speak to her.'

An hour later, they arrived at the convent, a modern building filled with light from tall windows set in the white facade. Joe saw the surprise on Emily's face.

'I expected something a lot older.'

'Old Henry the Eighth got rid of all the ancient stuff back in the sixteenth century,' he said. 'I have a feeling these sisters have moved with the times.'

They were greeted by a smiling Sister Veronica herself, dressed just as Emily had anticipated in the long black habit of a Benedictine nun.

'Bobby's expecting you. She's in our guest house. I'll show you the way.'

'Thank you, Sister,' said Joe as they started to follow the nun. He glanced at Emily, feeling suddenly excited at the prospect of coming face to face with someone who might finally be able to throw light on the mystery of Lexi Verity's background.

When Sister Veronica knocked at the door of the guest house and it was answered by an ordinary-looking woman wearing a loose floral dress, he felt a little disappointed. She had a pleasant face devoid of make-up and framed by bobbed brown hair, and looked the down-to-earth sort. An unlikely murderer. Although he had been wrong about these things before.

Sister Veronica left them to it, and after the introductions were made, Bobby invited them to sit. The room was plain but pleasant, with weak September sunlight streaming in through the south-facing window.

They took their seats on a new-looking sofa while Bobby made tea in the small kitchen area at the far end of the room. Once the mugs were on the coffee table in front of them, Emily began to speak.

'We're here about the letter you sent to Lexi Verity.'

Bobby nodded. 'I've only just heard about her death. It's terrible. I believe you're treating it as murder?'

'I'm afraid so.'

She shook her head sadly. 'Poor woman.'

'Your younger sister was killed in a fire in 1997, I believe.'

'That's right. Anna was my half-sister. The daughter of the woman my dad married after he split up from my mum. I lived with my mother most of the time, so I don't feel that I knew Anna well. Even so, it was a terrible thing to happen and I was in shock afterwards. Then I heard that my father had . . .'

'Taken his own life,' said Joe gently.

'Yes. He must have been stricken with grief. And guilt.'

'Guilt?' Emily seized on the word.

'I was eleven at the time and my bedroom was next to his. There were noises, but I was an innocent child so I didn't really know what was going on. I figured it out later, though.' Bobby gave a knowing nod. 'And I admit I hated him for it. Tilly, the nanny he employed, was only young, and she was supposed to be looking after Anna. Anyway, I called my mum and asked if I could come home, but she was going on some sort of course.'

'So you had to stick it out.'

'That's right. I was bored and I was at that age when young kids like Anna seem like a nuisance. Then I had to watch my father fawning all over Tilly and I hated seeing that.' She paused and took a sip of coffee. 'I used to do spiteful things. I remember getting a photo album and stabbing pictures of poor Anna's face with a pair of scissors. I confess I took out my resentment on her, although it wasn't her fault. I think in the end she was a bit scared of me. It isn't a time of my life I like to think about, and I'm ashamed of the way I behaved.'

'You wrote to Lexi to ask her if she was Tilly.'

'I wrote to her via her agent, hoping she'd pass my letter on. I'm not very good with emails and all that.' She smiled. 'I like letters. I suppose you could call me old-school.'

'What made you think Lexi Verity was Tilly?'

'I didn't watch much TV when my late husband, Brian, was alive. He died of a heart attack. He was only forty-three,' she added sadly. 'I'd heard of Lexi but I hadn't really paid her much attention. But when Brian died . . .'

'You succumbed to the temptation of spending the evening in front of the box,' said Emily. 'Don't worry. I do the same myself at the end of the working day.'

'It was company, you see. The feeling that when the TV was on, I wasn't quite alone. It took a while for me to realise who Lexi Verity really was, and once I did, I asked my sister-in-law to look on the internet and find out everything she could about her background. I'm sure she thought I'd become a crazed fan, but I never told her the real reason. In the end, I discovered a gap in Lexi's life story and that's when I decided to contact her. If I was wrong, the worst thing that could happen was that I'd make a fool of myself, and she probably got a lot of crazy fan mail.'

'What did you hope to achieve by getting in touch with her?'

It was a few moments before Bobby answered the question. 'I've done a lot of thinking since Brian passed away, and I came to realise that Tilly lied for me. She told the police I wasn't there on the evening of the fire – she said I was out at the cinema and that I only got back when the fire engines arrived. But that wasn't true. I was there all the time, but as soon as I smelled the smoke, I managed to get out through the back door without anyone seeing me. I thought Anna would escape too, but she didn't.' She bowed her head. 'I didn't understand then about how smoke inhalation can render you unconscious. You don't have to be burned to die in a fire; poisonous fumes can kill you just as effectively. I thought she would just walk out of the place like I had. If I'd known, I would have tried to rescue her, I swear.'

'Of course.'

'I know Tilly tried to save her and got burned in the process.' She paused. 'And as I said, she lied for me. She said I wasn't there when the fire broke out.'

'You never contradicted her story?'

'I was only eleven at the time, and I was confused.' She looked away. 'I'm ashamed of the way I treated Anna. I was really unkind. I used to ignore her – and tell her things to scare her, like that there were monsters in the wardrobe. Looking back, I must have been a bitter, twisted child, still aching from my parents' break-up and resentful of my dad's new family. I never really understood why Tilly lied to the police about where I was, and why my dad backed her up, but now I realise she must have known how I felt, and my dad felt guilty about it too.' She took a deep breath. 'I can only conclude that they both thought I'd started the fire out of spite and they didn't want me to get into trouble because I was so young and the consequences would ruin my life.'

'*Did* you start the fire?' Emily's question was sharp.

Bobby shook her head. 'No, of course I didn't. I might have hated my father's behaviour and I had no love for my half-sister, but even in those days I knew right from wrong. I treated Anna appallingly, something I've bitterly regretted ever since, but I'd never have harmed her deliberately. She was my own flesh and blood.'

Her words were spoken with such sincerity that Joe believed her.

'When I finally plucked up the courage to send the letter to Lexi via her agent, I was really surprised to get a call from her. We arranged for me to visit her house in Eaglethorpe when her husband was away. Looking back, I can only think that he didn't know about her past and she didn't want him to ask any awkward questions. It was fine weather and we met in a summer house outside because she mentioned that she had a nosy housekeeper. I'd never been anywhere like that before and I was probably a bit overawed. But she was very nice. Not at all like I expected. I'd hardly known her when I was a child, and my resentment of her relationship with my father coloured the way I remembered her. But when I met her all those years later, I found her quite ...' she searched for the word, 'approachable, even though she was a TV star.'

'So you had a good talk?' Emily prompted.

'Yes. I asked her why she'd lied for me and she said she'd been convinced that I'd started the fire because I was angry about her sleeping with my father and jealous of Anna. She said she'd kept quiet because she felt guilty that she'd triggered the chain of events that led to the death of an innocent child and my father's suicide. She said she'd felt sorry for me and she'd known that if she told the truth it would ruin the rest of my life. She didn't think I should be put away in some institution for a stupid mistake I'd made when I was only a child. She seemed surprised when I told her that I'd always believed what the authorities said – that my father had started the fire for the insurance money. Or that maybe Tilly had done it herself because she wanted to get rid of Anna and marry my father. It turns out that we'd both been very wrong. My dad was with her at the time so she knew he had nothing to do with it. Neither did she. And neither did I.'

'You said in your letter to her that someone else had access to the pub around that time.'

'I've had years to think about it, and there was someone who worked behind the bar part-time who was always hanging round my dad. She'd been given her own key, just in case nobody else was around at opening time. I think she had a serious crush on my father, more like an obsession actually. I didn't particularly like her. She used to trail after him like a lovesick calf, and I saw the way she looked at Tilly; if looks could kill . . . Dad seemed flattered by the attention, but . . . If I didn't start that fire, and neither did Tilly or my dad, there's only one person who could have done it.'

'Who are you talking about?'

Joe found himself holding his breath while he waited for the answer.

Thirty-Three

Before leaving the convent, Joe asked Bobby how much she'd told Lexi when she'd spoken to her. Bobby answered without hesitation; she'd told Lexi everything she knew, both facts and speculation. Lexi had listened carefully, taking it all in. And she'd seemed anxious to find out more. She'd believed in Bobby's guilt for years, but after their meeting, she'd come to realise that only one person could have been responsible for the fire.

When they arrived back at the police station, Emily gathered the team together to tell them about their meeting. The elusive Bobby had seemed like a potential suspect, but as it turned out, she had managed to convince both Emily and Joe that she'd had nothing to do with the fire at the Smithy all those years ago. The woman had been honest about her feelings concerning her father and the teenage nanny. And they believed she'd told them everything she knew.

Once Emily had finished speaking, Joe heard a murmur of disappointment.

'This Bobby might have been an extremely good actress,' said Sunny.

'Sorry, Sunny. She has the perfect alibi for both murders – with a convent full of nuns as witnesses. But she gave us a name, and that's something we need to follow up urgently. We have to find this person sooner rather than later.'

It was like a complex and frustrating jigsaw. Joe felt they only needed another piece to get the whole picture.

When Emily had finished addressing the team, Joe asked Sunny whether anything new had come in while they'd been out of the office, but was told that the only notable thing to report was that Nathan Corde had reported to the station as arranged.

'And if it is all about the fire at the Smithy, where does Douglas Page come into it?' Sunny asked, puzzled.

'Good question,' Joe said. But it was one he couldn't answer.

He called over to Jamilla. 'Have you managed to find out whether Douglas Page was one of the officers who attended the fire in 1997?'

Jamilla shook her head. 'Sorry. Digital records don't go back that far. I asked somebody to look through the files for me.' She grinned. 'Didn't make me very popular, and I'm still waiting for an answer.'

Joe told her to keep on nagging. But he knew these things took time.

Realising there was nothing more he could do that evening, he reached for his coat and trudged back to his flat, hands in pockets, going over the case in his mind. When he was walking beneath Monk's Bar, his phone rang. It was Jamilla, and he felt a sudden rush of hope.

'You know you were asking about Douglas Page? Well you must be psychic, because a message has just landed in my inbox. PC Douglas Page was one of the officers attending the scene of that fire in Kirkgate. The pub called the Smithy.'

Another piece in the complex jigsaw had fallen into place and Joe couldn't resist smiling to himself. Douglas Page, a callow young constable faced with a tragedy, possibly for the first time, had just provided the vital link.

'Thanks, Jamilla. I'll read the report tomorrow. In the meantime, why don't you get off home?'

'Ma'am's already ordered me to,' said Jamilla. 'But I wanted to get a few things cleared up first.'

She rang off just as he reached his flat, and as he unlocked his front door, he suddenly remembered something. It was something someone had said; something he'd dismissed as irrelevant at the time. But now he suspected it had been vitally important.

Freya Greengrass didn't eat her dinner. Instead she took it to her bedroom, because she wanted to share it with Anna.

Ben could tell that Elspeth was simmering with rage. 'We need to put a stop to this once and for all. It's not natural.'

'She's got an imaginary friend,' Ben replied, trying to stay calm. 'She's bound to grow out of it when she gets more settled at her new school.'

'Imaginary friend? You said it was a bloody ghost. Make up your mind.' Elspeth's voice had risen an octave. 'You even got that vicar in.'

'Bad things happened here, Elspeth. I'd never have bought the place if I'd known.' Ben couldn't help raising his voice. The house was getting to him. And he knew it was getting to his wife too. 'If things don't settle down, we can always think of moving somewhere else. You like your job at the theatre, don't you?' The question was hopeful.

'I don't know. It's more ... provincial than I expected. They're in the middle of an Agatha Christie at the moment and they're about to start rehearsing the Christmas pantomime. Hardly the cutting-edge productions I envisaged.'

'People love pantomimes ... and Agatha Christie gets bums on seats,' he said feebly. 'Anyway, you deal with the admin, so you're in the office all day. You don't have to watch every performance.'

'I know, but I feel I need to be there. I'm the new girl. I have to make my mark.'

She turned away so he couldn't see her face. He was starting to think the move to Eborby might have been a mistake.

He saw Elspeth's fists clench. She was on the brink of tears. 'This house is destroying us, Ben. I can't stay here much longer.'

Ben stood helpless as his wife disappeared upstairs, and a few moments later, Freya appeared at the top of the stairs.

'Daddy, can you read me and Anna a story.'

Ben forced a smile. 'Of course, darling.'

As soon as he reached the landing, Tom emerged from his room. 'What were you and Mum arguing about?' The child's voice was strained with worry, and Ben knew he needed to calm the situation.

'Nothing important.' The lie slid easily from his lips as both children followed him to Freya's room.

Tom was old enough to read by himself at bedtime, but he lay on the bed next to his sister and waited for the story to begin. Ben chose a book, Freya's favourite, and was relieved when Anna wasn't mentioned.

But as he began to read, he glanced up. The old doll was sitting on the shelf above the bed, and he saw it turn its head, slowly. At first he thought he'd imagined it. Then he realised it was real. He hesitated before carrying on, trying to keep the panic he felt out of his voice.

He'd just finished the first page when he heard a knock on the front door. He put the book down, promising the children he wouldn't be long, and rushed downstairs.

When he opened the door, he found Penny from next door standing there.

'Is everything all right, Ben? I was out in my back yard and I heard raised voices, so I wondered . . .'

'Everything's fine, thanks, Penny.'

She hesitated, as though she didn't quite know how to phrase what she was going to say next. 'I just thought . . . if you and Elspeth need some time to yourselves, I'm happy to look after the children for a couple of hours.'

To Ben the offer seemed irresistible. If he and Elspeth could just talk the matter over without interruptions, maybe over lunch one day, they might be able to resolve their problems.

'That's really kind of you, Penny. Thanks.'

He shut the door and ran back upstairs. Freya would be waiting for her story. And he needed to remove that terrifying doll from her room.

On Sunday morning, Joe woke up with a headache. He'd had three bottles of Black Sheep the previous evening in an attempt to relax and banish all thoughts of work. But his efforts had failed badly, and he'd lain awake going over all the possibilities. But as he climbed out of his rumpled bed at six-thirty, the fog in his mind began to clear. There was somebody they needed to trace as a matter of urgency; the only other person who'd had access to the Smithy on the night of that fatal fire.

He arrived at the office to find that Emily was already at her desk. She looked up as he walked in. 'I've been thinking,' he began.

'So have I. It sounds as though Halliday's love life was interesting, to say the least. In bed with the nanny and pursued by the barmaid. I've had another look at that report Jamilla found, and there's a photo of him. I must admit he was an attractive man.'

Joe laughed. 'You're supposed to be a happily married woman.'

'I was only making an observation. Jamilla's managed to dig out the police file.' She pushed a folder across the desk to Joe. It smelled musty and the pages had begun to turn brown at the edges.

Joe flicked through it. PC Douglas Page had indeed been the first officer at the scene. He'd taken statements from a Matilda Smith and the father of the dead girl, Jack Halliday, before they'd been taken off in an ambulance for treatment for their burns. Anna Halliday had been alone in the part of the building affected by the fire, and the firefighters had brought her body out. Page's report was unemotional. But who knew what his actual feelings had been when he'd witnessed the tragedy?

One of his colleagues had also spoken to eleven-year-old Roberta Halliday, but Matilda Smith had insisted that the girl hadn't been there when the fire started. She'd claimed that Bobby was visiting a friend that evening and had only returned to the premises as the fire engines arrived. In the confusion, the story hadn't been challenged, so it was assumed that Bobby had nothing to do with the incident. But now they knew that Matilda had been lying.

The case had been closed. Bobby had returned down south to her mother the day after the fire, and the young nanny, Matilda Smith, had left the area, destination unknown. Later she'd undergone surgery to hide the scarring she'd suffered during her attempt to rescue Anna. She'd dyed her hair blonde, changed her name and her appearance and moved to London, where she'd concealed the truth about her past with remarkable success. She'd reinvented herself and begun a whole new existence as Lexi Verity – but of course none of this featured in PC Page's report.

Once Joe had finished reading, he passed the file back to Emily.

'Now that we've eliminated Bobby, there's only one person left.'

'The barmaid who had the keys to the premises and an unhealthy infatuation with Jack Halliday.'

'Got it in one, Joe. If she did kill Lexi Verity and Douglas Page – and it's still a huge if – she must still be around here somewhere. We need to find her. We could do an appeal, but it would put her on her guard, and if she's guilty, that's the last thing we want.'

Joe didn't answer. He had someone to call in the hope of learning the answer to the question that had been on his mind since the previous night.

Isabel's mother put her on the line. The girl sounded nervous, and Joe asked his questions gently. The last thing he wanted to do was upset her.

'Isabel, you talked about your father's superpower. What was it?'

'He could recognise faces; even people he'd only seen once many years ago. He said it came in really useful.'

Joe's heart began to beat a little faster. Caradoc Karling had spoken of Douglas's 'gift', and he'd wondered what this meant. Now he suspected he'd just found out.'

'Isabel, did Douglas, your dad, tell you he'd recognised somebody recently?'

'No. I don't think so.'

'Did he go anywhere during the few days you spent with him? Did he mention that he'd arranged to meet anyone?'

'I don't think so.' There was a short pause, then Isabel spoke again. 'Well, he did go out one morning when we were first staying at the cottage. He said he needed to sign some documents. Something legal. A process he'd set in motion a few weeks ago, he said.'

'Do you know what it was?'

'Yes. When he got back, he told me he'd been to a solicitor's to draw up a new will and he'd just been to sign it. He said that I was his only child, so he wanted to leave me his money. I said I didn't want it, but he said I should have it. He insisted. Said it was only right.'

'Which solicitor did he use?'

'I don't know.'

'And the day you last saw him – the day he dropped you off. Did he say anything?'

'I can't remember.'

'Please, Izzy. Think. This could be important.'

There was a long silence. Then she spoke quietly. 'He said someone had asked to meet him but he didn't say who it was. I was thinking about what I was going to tell my mum, so I was only half listening.'

'Are you sure he didn't say who this person was?'

'I'm sorry, that's all I remember.'

She sounded close to tears, so Joe decided not to question her further. Instead he called Douglas's PA, Mrs Catterick, at home and asked her which solicitor he usually used. Then he called the solicitor's mobile number, but the answer was no help because they'd had no direct dealings with Mr Page for the past couple of months. And they certainly knew nothing about a new will.

Joe felt disappointed, but he knew he was on the right track. The search needed to be widened to other law firms, but that would be a job for one of the DCs assigned to the case. That meant Joe would have to be patient.

He strolled out into the main office and looked round. 'Has anyone had any luck with that name Roberta came up with yesterday?'

A young civilian investigator raised her hand. 'I've been looking through the electoral register and I've found someone of that name living at this address.'

Joe hurried over to her desk and she handed him a piece of paper. The address he saw written on it left him shocked for a moment. 'Are you sure about this?'

The answer was a nod. 'Absolutely sure.'

'Thanks,' he said before hurrying to Emily's office and thrusting the address in front of her.

'You realise where this is, don't you?'

She reached for her coat. 'Let's get over there.'

They left the station and headed over Wendover Bridge to the heart of the medieval city. The great towers of the cathedral were in view as they reached the narrow streets clustered around it. Soon they were passing the shops on Gallowgate, and after a while they turned onto Kirkgate. Opposite the little medieval church with its tiny overgrown graveyard, they saw the Smithy, now renamed Church Cottage, with its freshly whitewashed walls. Nobody would have imagined the building had ever been damaged by fire, but in 1997 the place had looked very different; a dilapidated, failing pub run by Jack Halliday with the help of a teenage nanny and a barmaid who allegedly was infatuated with him.

Joe's phone rang. It was Jamilla. It was Sunday, so all the solicitors' offices were shut, but the team had been trawling websites listing the staff at various firms. One name and address had stood out; the person they were looking for was a partner in a city-centre law firm not far from the offices of Eborby Gaming. He thanked her and relayed the information to Emily, who was staring at the house as though she was willing it to give up its secrets.

'She works at a solicitor's near Douglas Page's office. Now all we need to do is find out whether it's the same firm he used to make the will naming Isabel as beneficiary. My gut tells me it is. And if he could recognise faces from decades back, he must have been surprised to see her in that role.'

'If you're right, that's an understatement. We'd better have a word,' she said quietly before making her way over the road to the small cottage next door to Church Cottage and banging on the door three times.

When there was no answer, she tried again, but there was still no response. Joe left her side and tried Church Cottage, which now boasted a spanking-new video doorbell. He pushed the button and held his warrant card in front of the camera. This had the desired result. After a while, the door opened to reveal a man in his late thirties with short, neat hair and intelligent eyes, wearing a checked shirt. George Merryweather had spoken of Ben, who'd called on his services, and Joe guessed this was him.

'We're trying to contact your neighbour, Ms Harding.'

Ben looked surprised. 'Why? What's she done?'

'We'd like to speak to her, that's all.'

'She's out with Tom and Freya, my kids. She kindly offered to take them out for a couple of hours to give me and Elspeth a break.'

'Where have they gone?' asked Emily. Joe heard the anxiety in her voice.

'She mentioned the museum. We took the kids there when we first moved here and they loved that street. You know, with all the Victorian shops.' He seemed to pick up on Emily's concern and a worried look appeared on his face. 'There's nothing wrong, is there?'

'No, of course not,' said Joe quickly, not wanting the man to panic. 'Thanks for your time.'

Ben didn't shut the door, and when Joe looked round, he saw that he was watching them. When they were halfway down the street, he called after them.

'Can I come with you?'

Emily turned round and retraced her steps. Joe followed.

'It would be best if you left it to us, sir.'

'But the children . . .'

'No need to worry. We'll make sure they're OK.'

Ben shook his head. 'No. I'm coming with you. Hang on.'

He shouted to his wife, but she didn't come to the door to see what was going on and Ben didn't wait. He slammed the door behind him. He was going with them whether they wanted him to or not. And Joe couldn't blame him.

Thirty-Four

Emily called for a patrol car, emphasising the urgency, and insisted that the blue lights were switched on to clear the way. It didn't take long to reach the museum. When they swept up to the building, they leapt out of the car and made for the entrance with Ben following close behind.

When they arrived at the reception, Emily turned to him. 'Wait here, Mr Greengrass,' she said firmly. 'We'll bring the kids out to you.'

Ben hesitated before agreeing reluctantly. Emily and Joe flashed their ID at the girl on the desk and asked her if a woman with two children had entered the museum in the past hour or so. The girl nodded. Several people answering that description were in the museum at that moment. Joe thanked her, and as he glanced back, he saw Ben pacing to and fro. He hoped they'd be able to keep Emily's promise and return the children to his care sooner rather than later.

He marched through, making straight for Maddy's office.

'Shouldn't we be looking for the children?'

'There might be a quicker way of locating them. Trust me.'

When he burst into Maddy's office, she looked up, startled. He spoke before she had a chance to utter a word. 'Can we see your CCTV? We need to locate someone.'

Maddy picked up on the urgency in his voice. She stood up and took a key from a cabinet on the wall before leading them into a room down the corridor. It contained a bank of screens showing different parts of the museum. As Joe and Emily watched the images flickering on the screens, they realised that they didn't know what their quarry looked like. Joe turned to Maddy.

'There's a man called Ben Greengrass waiting in reception. Can you fetch him in here?'

Maddy hesitated for a couple of seconds, then left the room, returning a couple of minutes later with a puzzled Ben Greengrass. Emily summoned him over to the bank of screens.

'Can you see them anywhere?'

It only took Ben a few seconds to indicate the screen that covered the dimly lit Victorian street. Their quarry was with the children, pointing out the contents of the shop windows, stooping to speak to them. To Joe's relief, the children looked quite happy. They had no idea of the danger they might be in.

A number of other visitors were wandering around the cobbles, peering into windows and the little alleyways that branched off the main thoroughfare. The street was dotted with carriages pulled by realistic horses, and as they watched, their quarry vanished behind a large stagecoach. They waited a few moments for the group to reappear, but soon realised they must have entered either one of the alleys or a shop doorway.

'I can't see them.' There was a note of panic in Ben's voice.

'The street's a bit of a maze,' said Maddy. 'That's what makes it so popular.'

Joe looked at Emily. 'We should get down there.'

Emily nodded and looked to Maddy for guidance. 'Which is the best way?'

Without another word, Maddy led them out of the office and marched quickly up a ramp towards the main museum.

Emily turned to Ben. 'Best if you wait here, Mr Greengrass. Let us deal with this.'

Ben wavered before nodding. Emily was a mother herself, and he probably realised that his children would be in capable hands if she was in charge of the situation.

'How the hell am I going to explain this to Elspeth?' he said unexpectedly as they reached the doors.

'Hopefully you won't have to,' said Emily, turning round with a reassuring smile. 'Unless the kids spill the beans. Knowing kids, they'll want to tell everyone about their big adventure.' She touched his arm gently, a gesture of support.

Joe let Maddy lead the way through the museum, past reconstructed rooms from different centuries; from gloomy panelled Tudor to bright 1950s. As they entered a room lined with glass cases displaying historical costumes, he saw that the double doors to the special exhibition space that should by now have been displaying tableaux of famous Eborby murders were shut. And there was no sign of Silas Sellie. But there was no time for idle curiosity.

Finally they arrived at an archway leading to the Victorian street. The first thing that hit Joe was the smell. Horses and urine, he guessed. The authentic odours of the period. It took his eyes a few moments to adjust to the dim light of the flickering gas lamps illuminating the scene. He could see figures wandering about, but their voices were masked by the sounds coming from hidden speakers – horses' hooves on cobbles, conversation from the shops and music from the barrel organ outside a pub with etched windows hiding the polished wood interior.

The group they were looking for were nowhere to be seen. Emily suggested they split up to explore the alleyways branching off from either side of the main thoroughfare. She entered another archway leading to a mail coach depot, complete with horse and carriage, while Maddy automatically followed Joe into a side alley where he was surprised to see a taxidermist's shop window filled with the corpses of various dead animals displayed as they'd been in life. He hurried on until the sight of a lidless coffin propped up outside a carpenter's shop made him stop in his tracks. He could smell freshly sawn wood from the workshop, but there was no sign of Ben's children or the woman with them.

As he emerged from the alley, Maddy was still walking silently behind him, but he was so intent on his quest that he almost forgot she was there. When he met Emily back in the main street, she shook her head. No sign of them. They carried on together, dodging in and out of shops – the confectioner's, the draper's, the pharmacist with its gleaming mahogany counter and shelves filled with colourful bottles; down another alley and into a humbly furnished parlour, the little table set for tea. The re-creation was so realistic that Joe almost felt they were intruding on a family's mealtime.

They carried on, weaving in and out of the side alleys, on the lookout for a woman and two children.

'Think they could have gone out somehow?' Emily whispered.

'I'll run back and have a word with reception to make sure they haven't left the building. They might have gone into the café or gift shop,' said Maddy. She turned and dashed away.

As soon as she'd gone, Emily called for backup. If they'd got this right, they could be dealing with someone who'd already killed twice, three times if you counted little Anna all those decades ago. And the fact that two children might be in danger meant that they couldn't take chances. She touched Joe's arm. 'Is that them?'

Joe looked towards where the DCI was pointing. He saw a woman with two children of around the correct age. But his hopes faded when a tall man emerged from the pub, laughing, to join them. The family carried on down the street, oblivious to the fact that a couple of police officers were observing their every move. Joe looked at Emily and shook his head.

They carried on until they reached a bend, where another arch with a clock at its centre marked the next section of the street. Here they could see a toyshop displaying an array of colourful building bricks, a row of sinister-looking dolls with watchful porcelain faces, and a large Noah's ark in pride of place at the centre of the window. Emily darted inside but came out disappointed, shaking her head. They passed a milliner's and a dressmaker's; a jeweller's window filled with watches and sparkling rings; a grocer's with a large wooden figure of a soldier stationed outside; a printer's workshop and a clockmaker.

Emily spotted the open door of a schoolroom. Where better to take a couple of children to show them how things had once been done? There was a family in there, the father sitting on one of the old school benches scrolling through the messages on his phone. But again there was no sign of the people they were looking for.

Once they were back out in the street, Emily spotted the familiar sign of the blue lamp. The police station bore no resemblance to their own, with its tall sergeant's desk complete with quill pens, inkwell and a ledger open to record the felonies of the day. To the left of the desk was a cell behind a black iron grille – somewhere prisoners could be held until they appeared before the magistrates.

'Life was a lot simpler back then,' she muttered regretfully as she led the way towards a room painted in institutional green and furnished with a desk and bookshelves; presumably the station inspector's office.

But before she entered, she put up her hand to force Joe to stop and turned to mouth the words 'I think they're in there.'

Joe froze. The last thing they wanted to do was alarm the children, but they needed to separate their quarry from the little ones as a matter of urgency.

Emily ushered him forward and he fixed on his most reassuring smile as he took his ID out of his pocket.

'Penny Harding?'

The woman didn't answer.

'Can we have a word, please?'

To his dismay, she backed away and placed her hands on the children's shoulders. He could see her grip tightening, and Tom began to wriggle, although his younger sister, Freya, stood frozen in puzzled shock.

'You're hurting me,' Tom complained as he struggled to free himself.

Joe saw the woman's hand move down to seize the boy's arm, but Tom took the chance to shake her off. Emily beckoned to him and Tom got the message quickly. Emily pushed him behind her, shielding him from danger. Now they had to get Freya to do the same.

But the look of panic that had appeared on Penny Harding's face told them that she wasn't going to release her little hostage without a fight.

'Come on, Penny, don't make things worse for yourself,' Emily said, her voice calm and soothing. 'Let Freya go and we can talk about this.'

Freya's little body was shaking with desperate, terrified sobs and Joe was aware of her brother sheltering behind Emily's back. He wished he could get him out of there, but Ben and Maddy were in reception and he couldn't leave Emily to deal with the situation alone.

All of a sudden Penny disappeared through a door at the rear of the Victorian office, dragging a struggling Freya with her. Joe looked round and spotted the family from the schoolroom. He rushed over to them, showing his warrant card, and asked them to look after Tom, instructing them to take the boy to his father, who was waiting in reception. The startled couple hesitated before agreeing, and after some initial objections, Tom went along with them. That was one dilemma solved. Now they had to ensure that Freya was safe.

They darted towards the door Penny had disappeared through and saw a staircase in front of them. It was an area out of bounds to the public, but Joe guessed that the stairs led to the building's upper storey, to the illuminated lace-curtained windows looking down on the street. It had the temporary feel of a stage set.

Sure enough, he was right. And when they arrived at the top of the small staircase, they saw Penny Harding silhouetted against the light that shone in the window. They saw her swing round and heard the shattering of glass. She'd broken the thin window pane with her elbow and something was glinting in her hand. A pointed shard of glass, vicious as a knife.

Freya was sobbing, but she'd given up trying to wriggle from her captor's grasp. Joe glanced at Emily, whose eyes were fixed on the glass being held against the girl's neck.

'Hello, Freya. My name's Emily and this is Joe. We've come to help you. Your daddy's waiting for you downstairs with Tom.' She looked straight at Penny. 'Let her go and we can talk about this.'

But the woman's hold on Freya tightened and the little girl let out a pitiful sob.

Joe knew they ought to call in a trained hostage negotiator, but there wasn't time. They needed to get Freya away from danger as soon as possible.

They saw Penny turn to look out of the window. There hadn't been an opportunity to clear the street below, but craning over the woman's shoulder, he could see that it was empty, and he wondered whether Maddy had used her initiative and braved the objections of the visitors to make sure nobody else was placed in danger.

They needed to keep Penny talking. But she was backing towards the window, still holding on to Freya with an iron grip.

'As soon as you let Freya go, we can talk.'

'You don't understand.'

'Make us,' said Joe.

All of a sudden they heard voices down in the street. Police identifying themselves. Their backup had arrived. Penny automatically released her grip and Freya toppled forward. Emily grabbed her roughly and helped her to her feet before telling her to run downstairs and tell any police officers she saw that her dad and brother were in reception, and that DCI Thwaite was upstairs above the police station. The child froze for a moment before scurrying off like a frightened animal. Now all they had to do was deal with Penny Harding and disarm her if possible.

Emily stepped forward, but as soon as she moved, they heard a smashing of glass and the woman in front of them vanished from sight. Penny Harding had jumped through the window, which still had jagged glass protruding from the frame, and when Joe rushed forward to look down, he saw her lying perfectly still on the cobbles. For a moment he thought she was dead. Then she began to move, attempting to sit up, even though she was clearly stunned by her fall.

Emily hurried down the stairs to the street, where she spotted Freya being led away by a female officer, while her male colleague headed for Penny, who'd managed to struggle to her feet and was limping back towards the police station. Joe hurtled down the staircase to join Emily and suddenly found himself face to face with a breathless, bleeding Penny Harding. Even in the dim light, he could see terror in her eyes. Like a cornered animal.

'It's over, Penny. You might as well—' Before he could finish the sentence, she darted to her left, still limping badly. But the only place left for her to go was inside the cell. Joe thought quickly. He slammed the iron-barred door shut, and when he saw no way to secure it, he took his handcuffs out of his pocket and snapped them around the bars.'

'Very old-school,' said Emily as she came up behind him. 'Nice one, Joe.'

Thirty-Five

Penny Harding was a solicitor. Perhaps that was why she declined the legal representation she'd been offered. Either that or she thought it would be useless to deny what she had done. They'd witnessed her holding a shard of glass at the throat of a young child. And in Joe's opinion, there was no excuse for that.

When they switched on the recording machine at the start of the interview, she began speaking without being prompted. 'I'm sorry for what happened. I panicked. I would never have hurt the children. I swear.'

'Let's talk about Lexi Verity,' said Joe. 'You knew her many years ago when she was using a different name. Tilly Smith.'

'No comment.'

'You were brought up next door to the Smithy. In the same house you live in now.'

'No comment.'

'You stayed in Eborby when you studied at university. At a guess you lived at home on Kirkgate to save money.'

The suspect nodded.

'After you'd finished at university, what happened then?'

'I left home and worked in Birmingham for most of my career.'

'When did you come back to Eborby?'

'Five years ago, when my mother passed away. I inherited the house and moved back in.'

Emily took over. 'There was a fire at the Smithy while you were living next door in 1997. You were twenty-one at the time and you used to work behind the bar there. Very handy.'

'I was a student. I needed the money.'

'But money wasn't your only motivation, was it?'

She shifted a little in her seat. 'I don't know what you mean.'

'Jack Halliwell. The landlord. He was a widower twelve years older than you and you fell in love with him. More than love. You became infatuated. Obsessed.'

Penny was looking increasingly uncomfortable as she pressed her lips together in a stubborn line.

'But he was far more interested in Tilly Smith, the young nanny he'd employed to look after his little girl, Anna,' Emily continued. 'That must have made you jealous.'

Penny looked away. 'No comment.'

'Jack had another daughter from his previous marriage. Roberta, known as Bobby. She was eleven and she was staying with her father at the time of the fire.'

'Was she? I don't remember.'

'According to the fire investigation report, the blaze was started with nail varnish remover. A bottle was found in the debris. There were two young women around who wore nail varnish – you and Tilly. But I think that bottle belonged to you. I think you started the fire. You had keys to the premises and you crept into the spare bedroom and set it alight. What were you trying to do? Were you trying to get revenge on Jack because he rejected you?'

The answer was a vigorous shake of her head. 'I didn't want to hurt Jack. I thought it was Tilly's room. I thought she'd be sleeping next door to Anna, but . . .'

'But you got it wrong,' said Joe. 'Tilly was with Jack at the time, and the only person you killed was Anna. She was six years old.' He paused to let the words sink in. 'Then soon afterwards Jack killed himself. He'd been accused of starting the fire himself for the insurance money, and as far as the authorities were concerned, his suicide confirmed it. The pub wasn't doing well. Did you know that?'

'No. And I never wanted to harm that little girl.'

Joe could see panic in her eyes. 'Only Tilly. Did she need to be punished for the way she hurt you? I don't suppose it ever occurred to you that an innocent child might be collateral damage in your plan. Two innocent children. It was only by good luck that Bobby survived.'

Penny bowed her head and Joe knew his words had touched a nerve.

344

'Once Jack Halliday killed himself, the police didn't look any further for a culprit. Tilly thought Bobby had started the fire because she resented her father's second family. Bobby was young and vulnerable, so Tilly lied to protect her. In fact Tilly believed in Bobby's guilt for years, although she never said anything because of the child's age. Jack was dead; he'd taken the blame and Tilly was anxious to put the whole situation behind her and start a new life. And she did that with great success, going to enormous lengths to cover up her past. Maybe she blamed herself for being in bed with Jack. She was making love to the man you were obsessed with while she should have been looking after Anna.' He saw Penny wince. 'Maybe she thought that if she hadn't been . . . distracted, Anna wouldn't have died.'

It was Emily's turn to take over again. 'Bobby got in touch with Tilly recently – or should I call her Lexi, because that's the name she assumed when she began her TV career. Bobby recognised her from all those years ago. She'd lost her father and her half-sister in that fire, so she wanted to know the truth. They met and talked, and gradually the true picture began to emerge and Lexi realised what must have happened that night, although at that stage she had no idea where you were. Then she received a visit from Douglas Page, who'd been the first police officer on the scene of the fire. That man had a special talent. He had a miraculous memory for faces and he remembered yours. You were there that night outside the Smithy, watching. Did you talk to him? Did you ask him who was in the building? Who'd been hurt?'

Penny looked up. 'I don't know what you mean.'

'Did Douglas Page visit your law firm to make a new will? We'll easily find out as soon as the office opens tomorrow morning, so you might as well tell us now,' said Emily.

Penny took a deep breath, as though she knew that lying would be futile. 'OK. He'd recently discovered that he had a daughter, and he wanted to leave her a substantial inheritance and a major stake in his company. I presume he didn't want to use his usual solicitor because of the delicate nature of the business.'

'And when he arrived at your offices and recognised you, he thought Lexi Verity ought to know so he contacted her. After her meeting with Bobby, she realised that the only person who could have killed little Anna was you. You'd had keys to the premises and you could come and go as you pleased.'

The woman said nothing.

'He said he was going to tell Lexi where to find you, and you were afraid that, given her high profile, she might reveal your involvement on some chat show or magazine article. Then your world would come tumbling down.'

Joe could tell by the suspect's expression that Emily had hit a nerve.

'Did you hear somewhere that Lexi was making a series of programmes called *The Killers Among Us*, about old cases; ones that had been thought to be accidents but were really murders?' he said. 'Were you afraid that you were going to feature in it?'

Penny nodded slowly.

'Lexi went to great lengths to erase her past, so she probably wouldn't have included that case in the series. But you didn't know that, did you? You thought that what you'd done was going to be exposed on TV. You imagined the disgrace when the police came to arrest you, so you decided to take action. I think you went to Lexi's home to silence her,' Emily continued. 'Just like you later silenced Douglas Page.'

Penny lowered her head. But she made no attempt to deny her guilt.

'What has it been like living next door to the house where little Anna died because of your actions?' Joe was genuinely puzzled. 'I would have thought you'd want to get as far away as possible.'

The suspect looked up, her eyes brimming with tears. 'It's the house where I grew up. It's my inheritance. I was entitled to it. It's my home.'

'You're aware that Church Cottage is reputed to be haunted by the ghosts of Anna and Jack?'

Emily shot Joe an admonishing look. As far as she was concerned, ghosts weren't on the agenda.

But Joe carried on. 'Did Ben Greengrass mention it to you?'

Penny's lips formed a small smile. 'He asked me if I knew anything.'

'How did that make you feel?'

She gave a snort of derision. 'There's no such thing as ghosts.'

'You're being charged with threatening Ben Greengrass's children and your home will be searched for a weapon and other forensic evidence. Do you wish to make a statement?'

Penny considered the question for a while before answering.

'When Tilly Smith worked as Jack's nanny, she was a mousy little thing. But Jack still preferred her to me. I came in early one morning to clean the bar and I caught them in bed. I was so angry, I wasn't thinking. Honestly, I never intended Anna to get hurt.' Her eyes brimmed with tears of self-pity. 'Jack could have had me. I made it pretty obvious I fancied him, but he was obsessed with her. When I saw her on TV, I knew who she was, even though she'd changed so much. I recognised that voice of hers – deep and sexy. Jack used to say he loved her voice.'

'And you were still jealous of her.'

Penny looked Emily in the eye. 'I followed her career. The marriage to that actor from *Holly and Ivy*. The prime-time TV shows.' Her voice was starting to shake with emotion. 'Then she married that lord and moved back up here to Yorkshire.' She gave a bitter smile. 'You should have seen the house. And that pool.'

'Where you killed her.'

'Why should she have all that? Why should she have Jack when I loved him so much? I wasn't going to let her share my secret with millions of people and ruin my life. She was just a jumped-up little tart.'

After her outburst, the suspect shrank back into her chair and sat breathless for a few moments before straightening her back, staring ahead like a condemned prisoner resigned to her fate.

'I want to make a statement,' she said, almost in a whisper.

That was it. A full confession. Douglas Page had recognised Penny when he visited her office to make a new will, and during their meeting he'd mentioned that Tilly Smith was now the famous Lexi Verity and he'd met her at the opening of one of his betting shops. After brooding for a few weeks, Penny had called on Lexi, letting herself in through the French windows when she found them unlocked. She'd made her way to the pool room, where she'd taken Lexi by surprise. Lexi hadn't recognised her at first, not until she told her who she was. Then she'd nodded with understanding and said she'd been told by Douglas Page that Penny was back in the area.

That was when Lexi announced that she'd never believed that Jack had been responsible for little Anna's death because she'd been with him at the time the fire broke out. Besides, he'd never mentioned any plans to stage an accident for the insurance money. And they'd been close, so she was sure she would have known. She'd convinced herself that Bobby had done it and had stayed silent because of the child's age. But she'd spoken to Bobby recently and found out that she'd got it completely wrong. Bobby had had nothing to do with it. And as far as she could see, there was only one other possibility.

When Penny asked what she was planning to do about it, Lexi hadn't answered. She'd told Penny to see herself out before shedding the towel she'd wrapped herself in, preparing to get back into the pool. She'd turned her back on her visitor, unaware of the danger she was in. That was when Penny had struck her in the neck with the knife she'd brought with her, hitting the artery, and shoved her into the water before fleeing.

When Joe asked her why she'd taken the knife with her to the meeting, Penny said it was for self-defence, but Emily and Joe suspected that the attack had been planned. Lexi Verity had had the power to destroy the comfortable and respectable life Penny had made for herself. Her upcoming programme, *The Killers Among Us*, had been all over the media, and Penny couldn't risk her revealing the truth. She couldn't risk the disgrace – or the prospect of spending years in prison.

Douglas Page's knowledge of her past had sealed his fate. She'd asked to meet him again to discuss a technicality concerning the new will he'd just made, and suggested they do so in private, away from the office, because the matter was so delicate. She said she'd be walking her dog in the woods, and she could meet him there and talk while they walked. Douglas had expressed some surprise when they met, especially when he saw no sign of a dog, but he hadn't anticipated that he would actually be in danger. Not until Penny launched her attack.

Having disposed of the two people who could betray her secret, Penny stated coldly that she would have tried to find Bobby next. Emily shuddered at the lack of emotion in her words.

A couple of hours later, after Penny had been charged, Joe called Sister Veronica at the convent to tell her the news. She promised to pass it on to Bobby at once, and before she ended the call, she added that Bobby had made the decision to join the order. Joe told Sister Veronica he was pleased for her. Bobby had experienced a troubled childhood and she'd recently lost her husband; hopefully now she'd find peace.

At six-thirty, Emily called for the team's attention.

'We've got our killer in the cells and I think that calls for a celebration. Half an hour in the White Swan. First drink's on me.'

There was a murmur of general approval, even though Joe could tell everyone was tired after the long hours they'd been working. He saw Jamilla pick up her phone, probably to call her family to tell them that she was going to be late again. Sunny, stationed at the adjoining desk, sat back, hands behind his head, with a satisfied look on his face, like a man who'd just enjoyed a good meal.

'Everything OK?' Joe asked him.

The answer was a nod. 'Our Leanne's been spending a lot of time with Isabel. And Margaret's troubles seem to be over. According to Pauline, she's got her feet well and truly under his lordship's table. Funny, if Lexi had still been alive . . .'

He didn't have to finish his sentence. Lexi's death had benefited someone else apart from her killer.

'Coming to the pub?'

'Sorry. It's our wedding anniversary and I promised Pauline I'd take her out for a steak and a bottle of red. More than my life's worth to let her down.'

Joe understood. After the pub, he himself would be returning to an empty flat. He was tempted to call Maddy to ask her if she wanted to join the celebrations, but decided against it. After their experience earlier that day, he told himself it was too soon.

Elspeth Greengrass was angry. Ben had put the children in danger by placing them in the care of a murderer. His only defence was that he'd had no idea that Penny Harding *was* a murderer. As far as he'd been concerned, she was a kind neighbour doing them a favour. Just showed you how wrong you could be.

But his argument didn't impress Elspeth. It was the press preview of the production at the theatre that night and she needed to be there. As she left the house, her parting shot was to look over her shoulder and announce that she wanted to put Church Cottage up for sale. The place gave her the creeps. Ben said nothing. In his opinion she needed time to calm down and think things over.

With Elspeth at the theatre, it was Ben's job to put the children to bed. They seemed subdued after their shocking experience at the museum, and they changed into their pyjamas meekly and went to their respective rooms.

Ben looked in on Tom first, and to his surprise, the boy appeared more relaxed than usual, propped up against his pillows with a Harry Potter book open in his hands. Recently bedtime had been fraught with anxiety, and Tom had taken to crawling into his parents' bed, complaining that Jack was in his room. But that night he looked up at his dad and smiled as though the strain of the past weeks had melted away.

Ben left his son to his book, feeling that the atmosphere in the room seemed different, lighter. But he told himself that he was probably imagining things. He hurried to Freya, who would be waiting for her story, but instead of her usual happy greeting, he found the little girl curled up on her bed, sobbing her heart out.

'What's the matter, love?' he asked gently as he took her in his arms, assuming she must have been disturbed by the events of the day.

'Anna's not here. She's gone.'

He held his daughter for a while, lost for words. Then he selected a story he knew was her favourite and began to read, wondering if their problem had been solved.

That evening he called George Merryweather. He thought he ought to know.

Thirty-Six

As the team were about to leave for the pub, Joe took a call from George Merryweather. 'Just thought you'd like to know that Ben Greengrass thinks his ghost problem may have resolved itself.'

Joe smiled to himself. 'Ghost problem' sounded rather as though George was reporting on an infestation of mice.

'Well, we've just arrested the person responsible for our two murders. She also started that fire in 1997.'

'I wonder if that's significant, or just a coincidence.'

'We'll probably never know.'

After goodbyes were said, Joe went out to meet the rest of the team. However, one person he hadn't expected to see when they reached the White Swan was Caradoc Karling. It seemed the officers had unknowingly walked in on another psychic evening.

Emily marched her troops into another room. This was their victory celebration – if it could be called victory. Joe thought justice would be a better word; not only for Anna and Jack Halliday, but for Lexi Verity and Douglas Page, who had died to stop Penny Harding's darkest secret coming out.

As they were walking into the other bar, he turned his head and saw Caradoc Karling looking in his direction. He gave the psychic a brief nod of acknowledgement and assumed that would be the limit of their contact. Until a couple of hours later, when the team began to drift off to their respective homes.

As he left the pub, he saw a dark figure waiting in the doorway. Emily and the rest of them were saying their goodbyes, but Joe hung back, curious to hear what the man had to say.

'You and your friends look as though you're celebrating,' Karling began.

Joe resisted the temptation to make a comment about the man's psychic abilities. Before he could think of a suitable reply, Karling continued.

'The problem that's been troubling you for years. You'll hear something soon. News that will surprise you.'

'Good,' was the only thing Joe could think of to say. He said goodbye, and as he walked away, he glanced back over his shoulder and saw that Karling was watching him. He quickened his pace, suddenly uncomfortable.

When he reached his flat, the silence seemed heavy, like a pall of sadness had descended on the place. As he made his way to the kitchen, he noticed that the light on his answering machine was flashing. He hesitated. The last person to leave a message on the machine had been his sister-in-law, Kirsten. When he pressed the button, he heard her voice again.

'Joe, you never called me back. I need to speak to you. I've found a witness. The police won't do anything, but you can make them.'

He took a deep breath. His curiosity had got the better of him, and he punched out the number she'd given. She answered after three rings.

'Why haven't you called me?'

'I've been busy. I'm calling you now.'

'You need to speak to the police down here. I've found someone who saw Kaitlin the night she died.'

'Who's this witness?'

There was a short silence. 'An elderly man who lives near the hotel where you were staying. He was on his way back from the pub when he saw someone who fitted Kaitlin's description. She was talking to a short fair-haired man.'

'He doesn't fit my description then. That's a surprise.'

'You don't believe me?'

'Look, Kirsten, I've had a hard day and it all happened a long time ago. Why didn't this person say anything at the time?'

'I don't know. But he seems keen to help.'

'Keen to say what he thought you wanted him to say. As far as I know, Kaitlin didn't know anyone short and fair-haired who was in Devon at the time. I think you should leave it. Her death was an accident.'

'What if it wasn't?'

'Goodbye, Kirsten.'

He ended the call before she could say any more. Every time she brought up Kaitlin's death, it caused him pain. But he knew she'd never stop picking at the scab. It had become an obsession. And obsession could lead to tragedy, as he'd witnessed that very day when he'd arrested Penny Harding.

But Kirsten's words echoed in his head as he crossed the room to switch on the TV. What if there was something in it? What if he'd been wrong about his late wife's death? He told himself not to be so gullible. He was a police officer, a detective, and he knew for sure that all the evidence at the time had pointed to a tragic accident. Then he recalled Caradoc Karling's parting words. He'd hear surprising news about a problem that had been on his mind for years. For a brief moment he wondered whether Kirsten's message fitted the bill. But he dismissed the thought. Karling tended to deal with the general. It was his audience who fitted his words to their own lives.

He'd just picked up the remote control when the doorbell rang.

And when he spoke into the intercom and discovered the identity of his visitor, his spirits rose.

As Maddy entered the flat, he greeted her with a hug.

'Just thought you'd like to know, Silas Sellie's gone,' she said as she took off her coat. 'The exhibition opens tomorrow, so there's nothing to keep him here.'

'Where's he gone?'

'London. He had a hissy fit and said people aren't narrow-minded and provincial down there.' She grinned. 'Best place for him, in my humble opinion. How are you after all the excitement?'

'Our killer's been charged and I've just been celebrating with the team. Think I drank too much.'

'Does that mean you won't want to come out for another drink?' She looked at him hopefully.

'I might be able to manage another. I'll force myself.'

'That woman – the one you arrested. She looked so . . . ordinary.'

'I learned years ago never to judge by appearances,' he said.

She turned to face him and stood on tiptoe to kiss him on the cheek. Joe felt his breath catch.

'Thanks,' she said unexpectedly.

'What for?' He tried to regain his composure.

'For not saying "I told you so" about Silas.'

'No problem. Happy to oblige.'

They paused and looked at each other. Then Maddy stepped forward and kissed him again. A proper kiss this time. Joe felt all the reserve he'd been holding on to crumble.

'We don't have to go out, do we?' she said once they pulled apart.

'I thought you and me . . .'

'I know. But I'm happy to take a risk and give it another go if you are?'

Joe laughed and put his arms around her. 'That suits me fine. I've missed you.'

'The feeling's mutual.'

'A new start, then?'

Maddy nodded. 'A new start.'

Caradoc Karling had said it would be a day of surprises.

Acknowledgements

Many thanks to my editor, Hannah Wann, my copy-editor, Jane Selley, my agent Euan Thorneycroft and everyone at Constable. Thanks also to all the booksellers and library staff who help to bring my books to the reading public. And a very special thank you to all my readers. You make it all worthwhile.